PRAISE FOR

"Snarky, pacy and hellishly f̲ f
hero, with just the sort of life, to make you feel good about
yourself. Dark and delightful, like a naughty treat, this is a
rollicking story."
    Francis Knight, author of Fade to Black

"Peter McLean's debut novel is an absolute gem that hits the
ground running, a gritty, grungy, funny, sweary noir thriller
with added demons. Don Drake is a wonderful creation. You
wouldn't trust him with your life – he can't even be trusted
with his own life. It's a wonderful, headlong read and I
enjoyed it immensely. Very near the top of the half dozen
best books I've read this year."
    Dave Hutchinson, author of Europe in Autumn
    and Europe at Midnight

"Who wouldn't want to read a book narrated by a foul-
mouthed demon-botherer called Don? From dark streets to
sticky sewers, *Dominion* is a belting urban fantasy that takes
you on a breakneck tour of London's under-underworld,
with plenty of evil laughs (and F-bombs) along the way."
    Matt Hill, author of Graft

"What connects Chandler, Guy Ritchie, Harry Potter and
Buffy the Vampire Slayer? 'Not much' is probably *the answer,
until now. A punchy debut novel."*
    SFX Magazine

"*Dominion* is one of those books that I just didn't want to
end but couldn't stop turning the pages. Another fantastic
Burned Man novel by Pete McLean."
    Sue Tingey, author of Marked *and* Cursed

"The plot is intriguing and the pace is fast. There is plenty of
actio₁
    Tₕ

PETER McLEAN

DAMNATION

A BURNED MAN NOVEL

ANGRY
ROBOT

ANGRY ROBOT
An imprint of Watkins Media Ltd

20 Fletcher Gate,
Nottingham,
NG1 2FZ
UK

angryrobotbooks.com
twitter.com/angryrobotbooks
Damned if you do

An Angry Robot paperback original 2017
1

A catalogue record for this book is available from the British Library.

ISBN 978 0 85766 663 5
EBook ISBN 978 0 85766 665 9

Set in Meridien and Futur Rough by Epub Services.
Printed and bound in the UK by 4edge Limited.

For Diane, who caught me when I slipped.

CHAPTER 1

I never meant to start using again. I dare say no one ever does.

I woke up on the floor of the squat and managed to roll over and throw up on the rancid carpet before I choked on my own puke. God only knew who this place had originally belonged to, but they had shit-awful taste in carpets. I wiped a streamer of snot and vomit from my mouth with the back of my hand, and groaned. The rubber tube was still loosely knotted around my upper arm, dangling there like a flaccid worm. I dragged it off with a shudder of disgust and sat up, my amulet swinging against my sweaty chest on its rotting leather thong. My works were lying beside me on a dirty plate. I looked at the lighter and the burned spoon, the discarded cotton wool and disposable plastic syringe.

I sighed.

No, I never meant to start using again, but it helped. Smack might not affect the Burned Man but it sure as hell affected me, enough to shut the little fucker out of my head. For a while, anyway.

"Fucking hell, Don," I muttered to myself.

I put my head in my hands and pulled air in through

cracked lips, wincing at the sour vinegar aftertaste of heroin in the back of my throat. My stomach turned over and I shuddered, sure I was going to be sick again. It passed eventually and I dragged myself to my feet. I leant my arms on the windowsill and stared out through the filthy pane of glass at rows of grim, grey flats, the crumbling high-rise across the waste ground and the distant railway tracks. It looked like it might snow again later.

Edinburgh is a beautiful city, with its ancient Royal Mile and the castle and the stately Georgian New Town. I didn't live in that part of Edinburgh, though. This was the Muirhouse estate and it was an utter shithole.

I stooped and picked up the whisky bottle from beside my greasy sleeping bag. I took a swig and swished it around my mouth before I forced myself to swallow. Christ but it was hideous. You'd think you could get good whisky in Scotland, wouldn't you? Well you can, but not on my budget you couldn't. This stuff could have taken the paint off a car at ten paces.

Oi, tosser, the Burned Man thought in my head. *Are you off the fucking nod yet?*

I groaned. As soon as the heroin wore off, the fucking thing came straight back again. Every fucking time.

"Fuck off," I muttered, and took another gulp of whisky.

Put that down and go check the traps.

"Fuck the traps," I said.

Are you falling over money all of a sudden? it sneered at me. *You've got a fucking job tonight, and you need that money. You want to go without your fix? You're good and fucking hooked now, you stupid cunt. You need the money.*

I groaned again, and looked down at my works. It was right, of course. I had maybe half a gram of gear left in the grubby little plastic bag. I *did* need the money – I needed to score, and soon. I pulled on a stained T-shirt, scrubbed my hands over my straggly beard, and picked my coat up off the floor. That had been a good coat once, a full length wool and cashmere blend. It wasn't looking too good now, I had to admit.

Tell me again why we aren't just taking what we fucking want? the Burned Man said. *This is fucking pathetic, cocking about like this. Is this what I made you powerful for, so you could live in this shithole and catch fucking rats? You need drug money? Go and take it, then. Rob a fucking bank! I can burn any cunt who tries to stop us.*

It wasn't really that fucking simple, was it?

I could hardly explain that to the Burned Man, though. The thing was a sodding archdemon for fucksake, and it had absolutely no conscience and no morals whatsoever. Now I'm no one's idea of a white knight, don't get me wrong. I was a recently reformed hitman, for one thing, but back when I was working I had killed gangsters and terrorists and black magicians, for other gangsters and terrorists and black magicians. I had never killed an innocent – right up until the day that I did.

I was racked with guilt about that, and I was very, very scared of two things. One was the fact that the Burned Man was now effectively eating my soul. The other was something Adam had said to me last year.

Diabolists go to Hell, Don.

I knew I would never forget those words, and the awful certainty of them.

Adam had been talking about the fallen Dominion then, of course, about how the Dominion had summoned Bianakith to bring Menhit through the Veils and back to Earth from her own dimension to use as a weapon in its heavenly war, but that wasn't the point. Yes, the Dominion had been so far gone that it had resorted to diabolism to achieve its ends, and that had forced its fall once and for all. Yes, Menhit had killed it in single combat and the mouth of Hell had opened up to claim it, but all of that was beside the point too. The *point* was that *I* was a fucking diabolist. I had been for twenty years, and Adam knew that.

Adam never said anything for no reason, and I knew damn well that the smarmy fucker had been aiming that comment at me. I was well and truly on the slippery slope to damnation and I knew it all too well, so no, I wasn't going to start making things even fucking worse for myself by murdering innocent people to feed my fucking heroin addiction. And I *wasn't* going to Hell, not if I had anything to do with it.

I didn't need to, as far as I could see. I was pretty much already living there.

I turned up the collar of my coat and let myself out into the corridor.

One of the local lowlifes was heading towards me with an ill looking mate in tow.

"It's the ratcatcher, ey?" the bloke said. "Awright Ratty?"

I gave him a noncommittal nod and shouldered past him down the hall. The block of flats had been condemned a couple of years ago and was now just sitting there waiting for someone to be bothered to bulldoze it. They would sooner or later, as the council redevelopment work made its slow way across the estate, but not yet. Half the neighbourhood was the same, the buildings deserted except for a few derelicts and junkies. My people.

I trudged down the stairs to where I had set the first trap on the bottom landing. There was nothing in it, but at least the trap itself was still there. I'd had a few nicked after I first started setting them, and I'd had to go around kicking in doors until I got them back. Traps cost money, after all, and there was the matter of respect to consider too. I might have sunk to this but I'd be buggered if I was going to let some half-feral junkie steal from me.

I shoved the back door open and pushed my way through into the overgrown wilderness that had once been a communal garden behind the row of five-storey flats. The second trap was just behind a rusty downpipe, and I could hear the squealing already. I felt a tight grin stretch my face as I crouched down and looked at the rat. It was well and truly trapped, its back broken by the heavy steel bar. I knew how it felt, figuratively speaking anyway. I certainly knew what trapped felt like, with the heroin ruling my every waking hour with a rod of sick need and Menhit somewhere out there in the world, waiting for me to show my face.

I pulled a sack out of my coat pocket and grabbed the rat tightly around the throat before I eased the spring of the trap back and freed it. The fucking thing still tried to bite me but I stuffed it headfirst into the sack and did it up with a ziplock cable tie. That was one.

The next two traps were empty, and I tried to remember how many rats I actually needed for tonight's job. They're not as good as toads, but they were what I had. At least we weren't short of the fucking things around here. I was trying to work out the rat to toad conversion ratio in my head when I realized I couldn't actually remember what tonight's job even was.

I stopped and slumped against the damp grey pebbledash wall, breathing unevenly.

"Fucking hell," I muttered.

I knew there was this geezer, some clap-raddled lowlife pimp who had somehow got wind of what I was and what I could do. He had promised me a hundred quid, I remembered that. I remembered that hundred quid extremely well. I had to... Fuck it. No, it was no good, it was gone. *Bollocks*. A spell, obviously. Not a summoning, I didn't do them any more. Not with the state of my karma I didn't. Just a spell, the sort of minor shit you could do with a rat's lifeblood and a candle. Or maybe it was two rats, I wished I could fucking remember.

Get on with it, the Burned Man growled in my head. *I don't want to be stuck in here when you start going fucking cold turkey.*

"Get the fuck out then!" I roared at it.

I winced when I saw a couple of young women turn and stare at me from the other side of the waste ground, from in front of the flats that were still occupied. The looks on their faces said "crazy old junkie" all too plain.

"Bawbag!" one shouted at me.

The other just took a long drag on her cigarette and shook her head. They turned and hurried away, pushing their charity shop prams ahead of them. I sagged down onto my haunches and put my head between my knees, fighting back tears. How the fuck had I come to this? For the thousandth time that month I thought about taking my amulet off and begging her for help, for forgiveness. For the thousandth time I told myself why I couldn't.

You need another fucking rat, dipshit, the Burned Man told me. *Spell of binding, remember? Fucking hell, you don't, do you, you worthless sack of shit. Two rats and two sprigs of sage. Even you can find fucking sage in this jungle, can't you?*

I sighed and pulled myself back up to my feet. I supposed I could, at that. The amulet weighed heavily around my neck as I followed the side of the building, past the big damp patch where the guttering was broken and the black mould on the wall seemed to be thicker and more poisonous looking every day. I finally found the last trap, and allowed myself a smile as I saw the rat struggling feebly in its steel maw. It was a poor specimen really, small and scrawny and nearly dead, but it would have to do. I bundled it into another sack and went in search of some wild sage.

I was rooting through the undergrowth when I realized

there was someone standing behind me.

"Awright Ratty?" he said.

I looked around and saw the grubby ned I'd pushed past on the landing standing over me. He had a different mate with him this time, both of them wearing greasy tracksuits that reminded me of Harry the Weasel from back in London.

I missed London, where I knew the rules and everything made sense. Up here I knew bugger all, and the whole place seemed to run on some sort of law of the jungle that I still hadn't fully got my head around. London worked on respect, and relationships, and who was connected to who. Here it really was survival of the fittest, or of the least fucking half-dead anyway. I stood up and met their flinty stares.

"Wha's with the fuckin' rats then, ey?" he asked me.

"S'fuckin' weird," his mate said. "Fuckin' rats an' that. You eat them, Ratty?"

I had the two tied-off sacks dangling from my left hand, both squirming vigorously on account of rats who would much rather be elsewhere. *I'd* rather have been fucking elsewhere, to be perfectly honest about it. Pretty much anywhere elsewhere at that precise moment.

"I don't bother you, you don't bother me," I said.

That line of negotiation had always worked on the night creatures back in London, but then even night creatures were capable of simple reasoning. I wasn't sure this pair of rocket scientists were even up to that.

"Away you old cunt," the first ned said, and his hand came out of his tracksuit pocket with a Stanley knife in it. "Yer fuckin' weird."

I took in a breath, and felt the Burned Man rear up inside me. I'd been resisting it as hard as I could ever since I'd pitched up in this little corner of Hell, but right then I was too sick and too fucked off and simply too tired to put up with this shit any more. Karma be damned, if only for a few moments.

I let the Burned Man loose.

Sort them, I thought at it.

"Oh I'm fucking weird all right," I said. "I'm the weirdest old cunt you ever met."

I held the precious sacks of rats down by my side in my left hand and raised my right in front of my face. My grin widened, and I felt the Burned Man take over. My hand caught fire, flames whipping up into the air in front of my face.

"Jesus and Mary!" the second ned shouted, but that wasn't going to help him any.

Not against the Burned Man it wasn't, that was for fucking sure.

"Burn," I whispered.

The one in front of me screamed as the sleeve of his tracksuit caught fire. It went up like a torch, the cheap nylon blazing as he flailed his arms. The knife flew out of his hand and into the undergrowth. He ripped the tracksuit top off and hurled it away from him, screaming and cursing. His bare arm was burned raw and already starting to blister.

The Jesus and Mary shouter was already running away, fucking hard man that he was. I glared at his mewling friend, the one who lived in my block. I'd have some fucking respect around here if it killed me. Well not *me,* obviously, but I didn't care if I had to burn a few of these worthless little scumbags to get what I was owed. I didn't care if I had to burn *all* of them. I remembered other times, another plane, where I had ruled a million souls with a ruthless rod of fire. Talk to *me* like that? They had got off fucking lightly. I could have flayed the skin from their bodies with a look, drowned them in acid for a thousand years...

I shuddered as I recognized the Burned Man's poisonous thoughts. That wasn't me, and I *did* care. I cared a great fucking deal, but the Burned Man definitely did not. Still, I had let it in, hadn't I? Deliberately, that time. Before, it had just shoved its way to the front of my head and taken over when it decided someone needed hurting. This was the first time I could remember actually inviting it. The first time I had deliberately wanted its power. That was a great way to arrest my slide down that slippery slope to Hell, wasn't it?

No Don, no it fucking isn't.

The ned fell to his knees in the undergrowth in front of me, cradling his burned arm and blubbering. The rats squirming in their sacks against my leg brought me back to myself.

"Go on, fuck off," I said. "And enough with the 'Ratty' shit. My name's Drake."

He nodded, speechless with shock and pain and sheer terror.

That's more like it, Drake, the Burned Man thought in the back of my head. *You've got to show these arseholes who's boss.*

Who *was* boss though, me or the Burned Man? I only wished I still knew.

After the ned dragged himself off to lick his wounds I rooted through the undergrowth until I eventually found some sage. I took it and the bagged rats back to my squat, where I dumped the lot on the floor and sat down on my greasy sleeping bag. I had maybe three hours to kill until my client arrived.

I looked at my works, and made myself look away. I wasn't twitching yet, but I knew I would be by the time he turned up. I didn't want to start getting sick while I was trying to work a spell, after all. I looked at the works again.

Have a fucking word with yourself, Don, I thought. I lay down and closed my eyes, wrapped in my coat against the cold. I fidgeted, coughed, fidgeted again. Of course now I had the bloody idea in my head I couldn't think of anything else. I was at absolute rock bottom at this point, in case you aren't quite getting that yet. This was about as miserable as the junkie life got. And yet I still wanted it. I didn't have any choice any more. *Maybe just a little bit.*

I sat up again and took my coat off. My arm was a little worse for wear, but most of the vein was still good. I swallowed, tried to work some spit around my dry mouth. Oh it was no fucking good was it? I was doing it.

I fixed up quickly, just a small hit, rationing what little I had left. I let the needle drop back onto the plate and loosened the rubber tube around my arm, already sinking into warm grey oblivion.

The memories came.

When I ran away from London, I went north. I still had money then, enough for a train to Glasgow and a hotel when I got there. Debbie was supposed to be in Glasgow, but I had no idea where. Debbie had been my girlfriend ever since we were in university together, all those years ago. Well, my very on-off girlfriend to be honest, but we had always been close. She had finally dumped me for good six months before then, after I had accidentally got her kidnapped and tortured by one of the Furies. A Fury I'd been shagging at the time, at that. Long story.

Anyway, I wanted to find her. I was a mess. After everything that had happened it was hardly surprising. Since Debbie left me I had killed one archdemon and got myself possessed by another, then raised a war goddess and sworn to serve her. It had been an eventful few months, to put it fucking mildly. The whole getting possessed thing had been the key point, though. With the Burned Man living in my head I hardly knew who I was half the time. Sometimes I wasn't in control of myself, either. It spoke for me when it felt like it, thought for me sometimes. Sometimes it killed for me, too.

For me, or for itself? I simply had no idea. The Burned Man didn't owe me any favours after all, and I knew damn well that it wasn't my mate. Oh, I might enjoy bullshitting with it sometimes but I never let myself forget what it was. After that business before, after Trixie found out and I had felt it almost turn on her, I knew it wasn't safe. *I* wasn't safe any more, not for her. If I killed Trixie I knew it would be the end of everything. I didn't dare be around her, and she quite obviously didn't *want* me around her any more. So I ran away.

And now I was looking for Debbie. Was it selfish of me to try and find her, knowing what I had become? Yeah of course it was. I'm a selfish bloke, I know that. All the same, I knew the Burned Man didn't have any sort of beef with Debbie, whereas it hated Trixie almost as much as it both respected and fancied her. That wasn't as much as *I* fancied her, admittedly, but then I was also hopelessly in love with her. The Burned Man really wasn't.

It called her "Blondie" and it liked looking at her arse, but I knew that if it thought for one moment it could get away with wringing her neck it wouldn't hesitate for a second. She *had* tried to steal it, to be fair, but all the same...

I didn't have any illusions about getting back with Debbie, and since I had fallen so hard for Trixie I didn't even want to. I just wanted to see her, you know what I mean? Debbie had been my sort-of girlfriend for almost twenty years, but for all that time she had also been my best friend. She had always been there for me, and now that she wasn't I missed her like I'd lost an arm or something. I just wanted to... I didn't even know what I wanted, really. To make sure she was all right, I supposed. To see her again. To see if she had stopped hating me yet.

I had to admit, for all that I was in love with Trixie, I still wondered... oh, I don't fucking know. Debbie was *normal*, you know? Well, as normal as an alchemist can be, I suppose. She was at least human, anyway. She lived for her work, the same as I had, but alchemy exists on the very fringe of the magical lifestyle. If you squinted at it and ignored the blood and toads you could say she was an experimental chemist, I suppose. That was beside the point, though. What I mean is, Debbie had been my last, probably my *only*, chance at a normal life.

Yeah I loved Trixie, but I had loved Debbie once too. In my own shitty way I had, anyway. Sort of. I had never really made any sort of commitment to her but I had always thought that maybe one day we'd make a real grownup go of it, just because that was what you did. I had thought that maybe one day we'd have enough money to get a house together. Maybe we'd even get married and have children, I don't know. After how my dad had been, the thought of having children of my own frightened the life out of me, but it's what normal grownup people are supposed to do, isn't it? Maybe... I couldn't help but think that maybe it would have been my chance. My chance to put things right, for everything I had done over the years.

Whatever, I wanted to find her.

The trouble was, Debbie didn't seem to want to be found. It didn't take me long to find the sort of people who would know where to find an alchemist. I met with a wealthy Wiccan high priestess in a restaurant so expensive the prices made my eyes water, with ceremonial magicians in trendy city centre bars and with various seekers in the friendly atmosphere of nice normal pubs.

Of course they all knew an alchemist, but none of them seemed to know Debbie. That, it seemed to me, was a tiny little bit unlikely. Debbie was bloody good at what she did, and more to the point she didn't really know how to do anything else. Unless she was flipping burgers to pay the rent then she had to be working as an alchemist somewhere in Glasgow. Someone as good at their job as Debbie gets known quickly, yet it seemed that she wasn't. I smelled a rat.

"Listen mate," I said to the dapper little chap sitting across from me in the pub. "I need an alchemist. A *decent* one, you understand me?"

"Aye, I heard you," he said. "And I'm telling you, my pal Chris is the best alchemist in Glasgow."

This guy's name was Willie McLaughlin and he was a seeker of some note. He was wearing a green jacket and a tweed cap and drinking a pint of dark brown real ale, and spinning me a fucking yarn.

"I don't know your pal Chris," I said. "I heard there was this bird moved up from London a while back, amazing with her tinctures and that. Debbie her name is. It's her I want."

"You're Don Drake, are you not?" he said.

I nodded. There didn't seem to be a lot of point in denying it, and it's always nice to be recognized by a fellow professional. "Yeah, that's me," I said. Too late. I could feel the shutters come down behind his eyes.

"Thought so," he said. "Never heard of her."

I knew damn well I was being stonewalled. I sipped my pint of Tennents and glowered at him. Unless I was being more paranoid than usual, it looked like Debbie had spread the word. I could almost hear her telling them that if a Don Drake ever came around asking after her then she didn't exist. I sighed. I supposed I could hardly blame the bloke. She was the best, and if he *did* know her then he would want to carry on being her customer. That, I was starting to suspect, was dependent on him not telling me where she was.

"Ah go on then, fuck off," I said.

He frowned at me.

"There's no need to be like that," he said. "And this is my local not yours, pal."

I coughed. I suppose he had a point – I was forgetting my protocol. I was too used to doing my business in the Rose and Crown back in good old South London where Shirley would forgive me just about anything and big Alf was always on hand to sort out any difficulties that might arise. I wasn't in Kansas any more, that was for damn sure.

"Yeah, course," I said. "Sorry."

Twat, the Burned Man said in the back of my head.

Oh shut up, I thought at it as I got up and put my coat on. *The bloke's got a point.*

He's got a fucking silly hat and no manners, the Burned Man said. *Doesn't he know who we are?*

No of course he didn't, and it was going to stay that way. If he *had* known about the Burned Man living in my head he wouldn't have been likely to have sat down with me in the first place. Running away would have been his more sensible course of action. The Burned Man's reaction to any threat or slight, real or imagined, seemed to be to set fire to something or preferably to someone. That might have been acceptable in the bronze age but it was no way to get business done these days.

Just leave it, I thought. *He's been nobbled the same as the rest of them.*

Debbie didn't want to be found, all right. Or more to the point she didn't want to be found by *me,* that was becoming abundantly fucking clear. I didn't know if Debbie had ever shared my thoughts about the future, and I supposed the fact that we had never really talked about it in the best part of twenty years spoke fucking volumes. Even if she had been entertaining visions of a cottage with roses round the door and all that shit, I supposed her encounter with Ally would have well and truly put paid to that. I could hardly blame her, but that wasn't the point. I wanted to find *her*, and like I said before, I'm a selfish bloke. I'd explain myself when I was looking her in the eye.

CHAPTER 2

Of course it wasn't that simple. Nothing ever fucking is.

I worked my way gradually down the spectrum of Glasgow's magical initiates, from that glittering high priestess through the seekers and magicians until I was all the way down to the scummy sort of shitbags I knew best. All the time I was looking over my shoulder for Menhit's people, waiting for Mazin and his mysterious organisation to show up and spoil my day, but so far I seemed to be getting away with hiding. Thank fuck for that, that's all I could say. The thought of Menhit the Black Lion of Nubia catching up with me was enough to give me nightmares all by itself, and that was *without* everything else that kept me awake at nights.

Christ knew what this pub was even called – the sign outside was too covered in graffiti to read. I was on the outskirts of Glasgow now, in the sort of estate where the television people like to set gritty kitchen sink dramas about razor fights and battered wives. If it hadn't been for the Burned Man seething quietly in the back of my head I would never have dared even set foot in a pub there, but there was something sickly comforting about knowing I could reduce the entire place and all its patrons to sticky ashes if I had to. I didn't want to, but it was still nice to know that I could. That is about where my moral compass was pointing by then, in case you hadn't got the idea yet.

I shouldered my way to the bar and ordered a pint, trying not to sound too English and failing miserably. I could feel the hostility around me in the warm wall of tracksuits and leather jackets, threatening as it pressed closer.

I looked hastily around and found my guy across the room, wedged behind a corner table between the fruit machines and the pool table. I waved and headed over, and when people saw who I was with they reluctantly parted to let me through. This bloke obviously had respect in here, I realized. He was old and balding and scruffy, with a big grey beard and the sort of army surplus greatcoat that only tramps seemed to wear these days. His remaining hair hung in long grey straggles around his face, his scabby bald spot shining in the bright overhead lights from the pool table. He had a bottle of fairly decent whisky on the table in front of him though, with two glasses and a greasy looking deck of cards split in two. He reminded me uncomfortably of Wormwood, for all that he was unmistakably human. His dull, fuzzy blue aura was enough to tell me that.

I sat down opposite him and nodded in greeting.

"You Davey?" I asked.

He returned my nod with a sly, oily smile that said he knew something I didn't.

"You'll be Drake, then," he said.

"Yeah," I said. "You look set up for Fates there, mate. I didn't know anyone played it north of the border."

"Oh aye, a few of us," he said. "If you know where to look."

I nodded again, and wondered why my skin was crawling. Sure he was grotty, but I knew a lot of grotty people. Something about *this* bloke was nasty in a whole new way.

"I was told to come find you," I said. "She told me to tell you 'Kelmeth at midnight, in the shadow of the La'hah'."

Davey snorted. "Someone doesn't fucking like you, do they?"

"A lot of people don't fucking like me," I shot back at him. "Comes with the job, doesn't it?"

"Does it?"

"Oh don't fucking give me that, mate," I said. "Buggered if I know what your little handshake phrase means but I've said it now so I assume you must know who sent me to you. And you're set up for Fates, and you're sitting in a shithole like this. You're my people."

He grinned and poured whisky for us both.

"Oh I am most definitely your people, that's true," he said. "All the same, your name's poison in these parts."

Of course it was. I remembered Vincent and Danny McRoth, and everything that had gone wrong with that job. I remembered the child. I saw his ruined face, and shuddered. Edinburgh wasn't so very far from Glasgow, after all. Of course everyone knew.

"Shit," I said. "Look, about that…"

He shrugged and waved me quiet.

"I'm old and I'm reliably told I'm horrible," he said, giving me a leer that showed me his eight remaining brown teeth. "I don't really give a fuck about all that."

Of course he didn't. This bloke was the very bottom of the chain, the dregs of the magicians' hierarchy. All the same, the lovely aristocratic ceremonial magician who had told me what to say to him had seemed to respect him. In a wary sort of way, anyway. It's often people like this Davey, people like me come to that, that the higher-ups end up having to be scared of. We're the ones who do their dirty work for them, after all. Even so, there was something about him that was just making me itch.

"Fair enough," I said. "So will you help me find Debbie?"

"Why the fuck would I do that?" he asked. "I said I'd meet you, that's all. Maybe I just wanted to meet the famous Don Drake. Maybe I wanted to meet Danny's bane, the child killer."

"Oh fucking look here, that was an accident…" I started, but he waved me to silence.

"Listen for a minute, pal," he said.

He picked up the thicker deck of cards, the suits of the minor arcana, and started to shuffle them noisily. I got the impression he was trying to use the sound to cover what he was saying, and leaned forwards across the sticky table to hear him better.

"You have to understand, Danny McRoth was a bitch," he said. "Her old man wasnae so bad really as black magicians go, but her? Oh, she was an evil cow and no mistake. You maybe did the world a favour ridding us of a necromancer… but then there was that wee boy."

Oh yes, there had been that little boy all right. He had been five fucking years old and my screamers had torn him to bloody rags. I screwed my eyes tight shut and saw his face all over again, the bloody holes where his eyes had been. Cheers Davey, I fucking needed that right now. Oh thanks a bunch, you horrible old wanker.

"Yeah," I said.

"Well that did you no favours with folk around here," he said.

"I suppose it wouldn't have," I muttered.

"Ah but then you see, there's people like me," he went on. "Old Davey's a horrible old cunt, anyone'll tell you that. Anyone except Margarite it seems, as she told you the words to say to me. Silly wee lassie, bless her. That aside, you're here now. Will you play a hand?"

I looked at him. I wasn't born yesterday, and I could feel

the jaws of the trap quivering in the air around me. That, and there now seemed to be a circle of leather jackets and tracksuit-wearers around our table, watching us in hostile silence. Watching *me*.

"What are we playing for?" I asked him.

"Truth," he said. "What else is there?"

Well there was money, as far as I was concerned, but right now it was truth I was after.

"Do you know where Debbie is?" I asked him.

He shrugged. "Play me and if you win you can find out," he said.

"And if I lose?"

"Then you'll have to tell me a truth instead," he said.

I frowned at him. This was feeling more one-sided by the minute, and I knew there really was something wrong about this guy. I just couldn't put my finger on *what*. I wasn't even sure if he actually knew where she was, after all, and if I lost, then Christ only knew what he'd want me to tell him. And of course we were in a pub that was pretty much on the outskirts of Hell and where it seemed he was the only thing keeping me from getting knifed. Oh, how the fuck had I let that Margarite talk me into coming here?

Because she looked a bit like a poor man's version of Blondie and you're a twat, the Burned Man helpfully pointed out.

Oh fuck off, I told it.

It sniggered. *What do you make of old Merlin here?* it asked me.

I don't like him, I thought back at it. *I don't really know why but I just fucking don't, and I like his little ned army even less. All the same, he might be grotty but I think he knows his shit.*

Yup, it said. *Whether he knows where your Debbie is I couldn't tell you, but he didn't just fall out of a tree that's for sure.*

No, I hadn't thought so either. Whatever it was about Davey, whatever I didn't like about him, I could tell that he knew which way was up. I looked at Davey and nodded.

"Go on then," I said. "I'll play you."

He grinned again, flecks of spit bubbling in the gaps between his teeth.

"Thought you might," he said. "You're in here now."

"Don't think that gives you a fucking edge," I said, and I knew that was the Burned Man talking for me suddenly. "Don't you think for one fucking moment that a room full of scummy little neds is going to bother me. We'll play fair or I'll burn this place and everyone in it to the cunting ground, you understand me?"

Davey looked at me, expressionless, and none of the lads looming behind me seemed particularly moved. He didn't look very impressed, I have to admit. He didn't know the Burned Man was inside me of course. No one knew that, except Adam.

And Trixie, I thought bitterly. *Trixie knows.* I told myself to shut up.

All the same, I could tell he was switched on enough to know that hadn't been just a slightly shabby London magician talking to him.

I leaned over the table and got right in his face.

"Danny's bane," I whispered. "Think about what that means."

"Yeah all right," he said. "You can stop showing off now, laddie. Cards, aye?"

The Burned Man left me all at once and I settled back into the seat opposite him, my palms sweating. Fuck, that was me told, wasn't it? The Burned Man had done its full sneering, swaggering, "fuck you, I'll eat you" routine at this Davey geezer and it had just bounced right off him. That didn't exactly fill me with confidence, shall we say.

"Cards," I agreed.

He nodded and started to deal. I watched closely, very

closely. I'm good with cards myself, and unless they're a master at it I can usually spot when someone else is tickling a deck. Davey didn't even seem to be trying. Every card came off the top and there were none of the distraction techniques I was expecting to see, nothing to cover the palming of a card here and there. He actually seemed to be on the level, which surprised me. I cheat like hell whenever I get the chance, personally.

"I'm no a cheat," Davey said, as though he had been reading my mind. "Fates is as much about divination as it is about gambling, and where's the point in trying to cheat that?"

Well of course there were all sorts of reasons you might want to cheat on a divination for someone else, but I wasn't about to get into that. The time I had fobbed Gold Steevie off with a spread that promised him a one-way ticket to Hell if he did something I didn't want him to do sprang to mind, but that was a while ago now and none of Davey's business. Gold Steevie was dead now, anyway, and Davey actually seemed to be on the up and up. I have to admit that threw me a bit. I suspected that might be why he seemed to be even more skint than I was. There was no money in honesty these days, not by a long way there wasn't. Oh fuck it, who was I kidding? He wasn't on the up and up, he was just a better liar than me. That's fucking saying something, believe you me.

I drew my cards up into a fan and looked at them. I had three sixes and two irrelevant bits of crap, but for a first draw that was a blinding hand. I looked at him and tried to keep my face still, feeling the usual tick wanting to beat under my left eye. I forced it to be still. This might be important.

"Card," I said.

He dealt me another and I tossed a useless Two of Cups onto the table between us. I drew a Four of Swords, which was no better.

"I'll stand," he said, for all that he hadn't changed a single card.

Damn it, I thought. *He's got a bloody good hand, or he's bluffing, or he's stupid.*

I was already damn sure Davey wasn't stupid, so that option was out. Was he bluffing? I looked at his bearded face and met his twinkling blue eyes. Davey looked like some idealized nineteenth-century pastoral painting of a tramp, with his big shabby coat and his wiry iron-grey beard and that sparkle in his eye, but I wasn't fooled. It wasn't a glamour, I knew that much. I can see glamours like I can see auras, and they don't fool me for a minute. No, it wasn't a glamour but I fucking knew it was an act of some sort. A low-rent magician like him in a place like this, attended by a mob of half-feral thugs, and I was supposed to think he was on the level? Nah, no chance mate. There was definitely more to Davey than met the eye, and whatever it was I didn't like it. He really did make me feel like I was covered in ants. The sort that bite.

"Card," I said.

He dealt another card, face down on the table in front of me. I threw in a Knight of Pentacles and eased the new card up into my fan. Eight of Cups. That was no fucking help either, then. I had a long swallow of my pint and sighed. I looked down at the cards again, at my three sixes. They would just have to be good enough, I reckoned.

"That's us then," I said. "I'll stand."

He nodded. "Trumps then."

He picked up the slim deck of major arcana and dealt us a card each. The way Fates is played, you can't change your trump once it's been dealt. That's the whole "Fate" part of the game, and it's where the biggest part of the divination comes into it. I eased my card up off the table and looked at it.

Oh for fuck's sake.

I slipped the Lovers into my fan with a weary sense of resignation. That wasn't even funny. Here I was hiding from Trixie and trying to find Debbie who was obviously hiding from *me*, and I drew the sodding Lovers as my trump? Someone was taking the piss, weren't they? The Lovers is the sixth trump so it doesn't even score all that well.

"Well now," Davey said. "We're playing for truth so there's no point in raising and all that shite. The truth is the truth. What've you got?"

I shrugged and laid my hand down on the table. Not a bad hand at all, but not a brilliant one either. Davey smiled, showed me three Kings and the Hermit, and started to laugh.

"What's so fucking funny?" I snapped.

"Your trump," he said. "Lover boy."

"Get fucked," I muttered, but I could see his point.

I helped myself to another shot of his whisky and looked glumly down at the cards. I'd lost, and as far as I could tell it had been fair and square for all that I was sure it had been nothing of the sort. There wasn't much I could do about that really. Whatever he was going to ask me, I'd have to answer him. Whether I actually told him the *truth* might be another matter, of course. I didn't really care one way or another. I just wanted to find Debbie, and it seemed Davey had been my last hope of tracking down someone who might help me.

"So, what do you want to know?" I asked him.

"Ah, now," he said, pouring himself another drink. "Old Davey wants to know a lot of things, but not right now. I think I'd rather you owed me a truth for later."

"Later?" I repeated, frowning. That was more than a bit odd. "When later?"

I hadn't exactly been planning on ever seeing him again if I could help it.

"When it suits me," he said. "When I've heard some other things from other people, maybe then I'll want to hear a truth from you, Don Drake. Until then you can owe me."

"Oh, right," I said.

That was a bloody horrible thought.

I know it sounds weird, but the thought of owing grotty old Davey anything, even information, made me feel uneasy. Still, I could hardly force him to ask his question so there wasn't a hell of a lot I could do about it, as far as I could see.

"Do ye want another?" he asked, pushing the bottle towards me.

Is a bear Catholic? At least I was getting a drink out of him, I supposed there was that. I poured and drank, and looked at him over the rim of my glass. He was still smiling his horrible brown gap-toothed smile at me, and there was that twinkle in his eye again. There was suddenly something fatherly about that twinkle that just pushed all my buttons. I didn't like him and I didn't trust him, and I wasn't at all sure what this kindly old gentleman-of-the-road act was all about but I had to admit it was starting to work on me despite myself. That or there was something in the whisky.

"Ta," I said. "Look, Davey…"

"Aye?" he said, when I tailed off.

"Look, I mean, I wouldn't normally go asking for a favour but… oh fuck it. Look, mate, have you *any* idea where my Debbie is?"

"No," he said. "Sorry."

I ground my teeth in exasperation. Everyone in this bloody freezing, miserable country seemed to be trying to take me for a mug, and it was starting to get on my tits.

"Well what the fuck were you going to tell me if I won?" I snapped.

"I was going to tell you I had no idea," he said. "We were playing for truths, and that's the truth."

God give me strength…

Fatherly or not, he was winding me up now and he suddenly started to make me itch all over again. Whatever he had been doing to me, that sort of shitty reply had broken his spell.

Fair play for hitting the target, I thought, *but you haven't figured me out* that *well, have you? Not as well as you reckon you have, anyway. Fatherly always gets me, you got that much right, but don't take the piss. Don't be like* my *dad or you'll lose me right there, you arsehole.*

I put a hand over my eyes for a moment while the Burned Man sniggered in the back of my head.

Oh I like him, it said. *He's a proper cunt.*

Takes one to know one, I thought back at it. *Just shut up will you?*

"I'll tell you something though," Davey went on, leaning towards me over the table.

"What's that?"

"Edinburgh," he said.

"What about Edinburgh?"

Edinburgh was where Vincent and Danny McRoth had lived. Edinburgh was where my screamers had killed their little grandson and everything in my entire life had gone so horribly fucking wrong. I never wanted to see Edinburgh in my bloody life.

"You should go there," he said.

"Why? Debbie's in Glasgow."

"Is she? You've no done very well finding her so far, have you?"

"I know she came here," I said.

"Aye, but did she stay here?"

"I don't fucking *know*, do I?" I snapped at him. "If I knew where she was I wouldn't be in a shithole like this having to talk to people like you to try and fucking find her, would I?"

I realized I was shouting, and I was suddenly very aware of Davey's henchmen crowding close behind me with violence on their tiny minds. I coughed and lowered my voice. It wouldn't do, not now. Not when any one of that lot would have knifed me in a heartbeat, and Davey was obviously far more respected in here than he looked like he had any right to be.

"Sorry," I said. "I'm a bit… stressed."

"Aye," he said, and topped his whisky up. "You are. You're a fucking rude prick as well."

I blinked at him. I mean yeah, that *had* been a bit rude of me, but all the same. *He* was lecturing *me* on manners, really?

"I, um…" I said.

"It's all right, I'm a fucking rude prick too," he said. He leaned closer, and suddenly the kindly, fatherly old tramp act was a distant memory.

His eyes glittered with anger, and there it was. *That* was the sort of father I remembered, the one with the bloodshot eyes and the hard hand. The one who would backhand a nine year-old kid across the kitchen floor because there was no whisky in the cupboard. Oh yeah, well done Davey. If you were trying to push my "father" button you've fucking managed it in spades, mate, but not the way you wanted to.

"So let me finish with this," he went on. "Tell Margarite that if she ever sends me another worthless wee shite like you I'll boil her in her own piss. Now get out of Glasgow and away the fuck tae Edinburgh where you belong."

Oh don't you fucking worry, I was going. Anywhere to get away from you, mate.

I got up and shouldered my way through his crowd of glowering thugs, and fled.

•••

That went well, the Burned Man muttered when we were safely back in my city centre hotel room.

I had to admit it really hadn't. So much for the lovely Margarite and her "I know a man who knows everything". No love, no you don't. You know a grotty, lying old tramp with a filthy temper who probably cheats at Fates even though he's too good for me to catch him at it. I didn't even know what sort of magician Davey was, but I didn't think he was a diabolist like me. I hadn't quite got that vibe off him, but he was obviously one of the other dodgy sorts. A *very* dodgy sort. Most magicians are basically dodgy, when you come right down to it, but he was something else.

"Load of bollocks," I muttered to myself as I poured a shot of whisky into the plastic tooth glass from the bathroom.

I was buggered if I was paying the prices in the hotel bar so I'd just bought myself a bottle from a late shop on my way back from the horrible pub on the outskirts. Truth be told I was starting to get a bit low on money. This hotel was hardly flash but it was all right, and whilst Glasgow hotel prices might not be quite as eyewatering as they are in London, the place still wasn't exactly what you'd call cheap. I had been there for nearly three weeks now. What with that and food and buying drinks for every magician in Glasgow, not to mention needing to buy myself clothes and a razor and toiletries and all the other shit I hadn't brought when I ran away from London, I had spent a worrying amount of money in a fairly short space of time.

I couldn't even see a way to earn any more. I didn't know anyone up here except the other magicians I had met. I didn't know an alchemist here and I had no prospective clients, and no way to find any without treading on other people's toes. When the money was gone it was gone, and then what was I going to do? There were only so many times I could get away with doing my little trick with the fruit machines before someone caught me at it and I got my head kicked in. I fingered the amulet through my shirt, and sighed. I wanted to take it off and call her name. I wanted to let her find me, and I knew damn well why I couldn't.

The amulet had been pretty much all I had brought with me, other than the clothes I stood up in and all the cash I could get my hands on. I'd had to make the amulet in a hurry and it was a bit of a slapdash job, but it was working so far. It's amazing what knowing someone's true name can achieve if you know what you're doing. I sat down on the bed and sipped my whisky, and thought about her.

Bad idea, I thought, or the Burned Man did. I wasn't even sure which one of us that had been but it was true all the same. The last thing I needed to be doing right then was thinking about Trixie. It sounded like what I *should* be doing was going to Edinburgh.

I didn't want to, but I didn't think Davey had been stringing me along. Oh he wanted rid of me all right, and that was the Burned Man's fault for shooting its mouth off, but all the same his words had had the ring of truth about them.

I didn't know much about Edinburgh. I knew it was Scotland's capital city, obviously, and that it was where all the tourists went. Apparently there was tartan and bagpipes everywhere you went, like some awful Disneyfied vision of Scotland, and I'd already gathered that the good folk of Glasgow regarded the place as something of a joke.

Great.

I'm a city boy, I always have been, and for all that Glasgow was cold and wet even in late spring there was something about its grey austerity that made it feel like home. It was a lot like London, in a way. It didn't sound like Edinburgh was really going to be my sort of place.

I sighed and poured another drink. I was starting to go off Scotland in a big way.

CHAPTER 3

Edinburgh was bloody beautiful.

I got off the train at Waverley station and walked out into the strangest looking capital city I could have imagined. I'd been reading the paper on the train and worrying about Menhit and what the fuck she was going to do to me when she finally found me instead of looking out of the window, so it was all a bit of a shock when I came out of the station. The steps led out onto a road bridge over the railway tracks and on the other side of it was a public park, with what looked like some bizarre sort of Victorian spaceship standing in it. I later discovered that this was the Scott Monument, but right then it looked for all the world like something out of one of Jules Verne's early science fiction stories. There was a busy road with shops and hotels on my right, and to the left the city rose up in a cliff of grand and ancient buildings that ended in a looming basalt crag with a bloody great castle perched on top of it. This was definitely not anything like London.

"Fuck me," I muttered, and almost got run over by an open-topped tour bus as I stepped off the kerb without looking.

The bus was full of tourists wearing brightly coloured anoraks against the weather, which to be fair wasn't any better than it had been in Glasgow. That was enough to reassure me that I was still in Scotland and hadn't stepped through some sort of wormhole into another dimension. Where the bloody hell were the skyscrapers? Where was the noise, and the filth? Was this *really* a capital city?

I crossed the road a bit more carefully this time and headed up onto the main road. There were at least shops there that I'd heard of, although the clean, modern electric tram that slid past made me jump. You didn't get trams round my part of South London.

I found a hotel that didn't look too horrifyingly expensive and checked in, but all the same I was getting more and more concerned about the state of my finances. I'd have to find somewhere cheaper tomorrow, maybe a bed and breakfast or something. I dumped my bag in the room and headed out again.

Of course now that I was here I'd have to start all over again, find the local action and make some contacts. Magicians don't exactly advertise, even in this day and age, but you can usually track them down if you know what to look for. All the same it was a pain in the bloody arse.

I walked aimlessly for a while, getting a feel for the place. I went back over the bridge past the railway station and up an asthma-inducing hill, following the flow of tourists. I actually could hear someone playing the bagpipes somewhere, I realized.

The road wound its way up a hill and into the old part of the city, the long road that led up to the castle. Here it really was Disney Scotland, where every other shop sold tartan knitwear or single malt whisky or cuddly Loch Ness Monsters and all that tat, but it didn't matter. The architecture was breathtaking, most of the buildings easily six or seven hundred years old.

There was an imposing cathedral further up the hill and I headed that way, drawn by the way the top of the tower resembled a crown. Fuck knows why, looking back on it, but at the time it just appealed to me.

I stood outside the cathedral staring up at it and feeling a bit lost. It wasn't St Paul's but it was still bloody impressive in a dour, grey sort of way. I could almost picture Trixie standing on the top of the tower with her flaming sword raised high. God but I missed her.

Oh for fucksake, man up, the Burned Man snorted in my head. *What sort of wet week are you turning into?*

I ignored it and kept walking, my hands buried in my coat pockets and my collar turned up against the damp wind. At least it wasn't actually raining, that was something I supposed. I headed up towards the castle then turned left on a whim. I walked down a flight of steep stone steps under a bridge and into what appeared to be the trendy district. Here it was all street cafes and bars and little vintage boutiques, and thankfully most of the tourist tat seemed to have been left behind.

Now we were getting somewhere. If you want to get to know a place you have to know its people, not its visitors. You don't learn about Londoners by hanging around theatres in the West End, if you know what I mean. I kept walking, looking around but not really taking much in. I carried on for maybe another half an hour, and I didn't know where I was going until I got there. I had only ever seen the place in my scrying glass but something in the dusty recesses of my memory must have been pointing me in the right direction.

This was Vincent and Danny's house.

I stood across the road and looked at it, at the overgrown front garden and the forlorn *For Sale* sign that was leaning at a windblown angle against the garden wall. I imagined the estate agent had probably all but given up on shifting the murder house by now. Even with the Edinburgh property market being how it was, who was going to want to buy a house where three people had been inexplicably torn to shreds by person or persons unknown? Especially when one of them had been a five year-old child. The case was still unsolved. The windows were dark and grimy, unlived in and unloved for over six months now.

"Oh fuck me," I said.

What the fuck are we doing here? the Burned Man asked.

Nothing, I thought. *Nothing at all.*

I sat on a wall and stared across the road at the house. I *was* that person or persons unknown, of course. Well not exactly me, not literally anyway, but I had been responsible for what had happened in that house. It had been me who had summoned the screamers and sent them in there to murder Vincent and Danny McRoth for the crime of trying to muscle in on Wormwood's business interests. It had been me who had had a fight with Debbie that night and hadn't been paying attention to the scrying glass, me who hadn't realized there was a child in the house until it was far, far too late. Me who had tried to regain control of the screamers and save that little boy's life, and who had failed so utterly. My summoning had killed that child, my magic. My diabolism.

Diabolists go to Hell, Don.

Like I say I'd had a row with Debbie beforehand, and at the time the Burned Man had told me that made it her fault. It didn't, obviously, I knew that. It was *my* fault and no one else's, but all the same I couldn't help wondering if that was why I was so desperate to find her. Jesus, was I only doing this because it wanted to find someone to blame?

Bollocks, the Burned Man said. *I'd all but forgotten about it. If that business is still on anyone's mind it's on yours not mine.*

I rubbed a hand over my face and sighed. Of course the Burned Man wasn't dwelling on one dead kid. Why would it? It simply didn't care, about that or much of anything else. It was a fucking archdemon, after all. I leaned forwards and put my head in my hands. Oh God, it was all on me, wasn't it?

Yeah, it really was.

Will you pull yourself together, you maudlin piece of shit, the Burned Man sneered at me. *Fuck knows what we're even doing up here in the land that time forgot but you are well and truly getting on my tits now, Drake. It was just some pointless fucking kid. Get over it.*

That was it.

That was the point where I just fucking broke.

I don't… I don't even know what it was, really. The Burned Man had said worse things to me before, but that one just tipped me over the edge. It was too much, too much of *everything* I think, all on top of everything else. You can only cope with so much. You can grit your teeth and stiffen your upper lip and square your shoulders and all that *fucking shit,* but past a certain point you just break, however strong you think you are.

I had been thinking about Debbie, before, back in Glasgow. I had been thinking about how maybe, once upon a cunting fairytale, we might have had a life together. A house, and children, and one of those godawful garish plastic swings in the back garden that I would have hated the sight of but that would have made me burst with happiness every time I saw my little son or daughter playing on it.

Oh God, that was all gone, wasn't it? All my hopes, all my futures, had died with the McRoth child and the coming of the Furies that I had brought down on myself. It was all gone forever, and so was Debbie. I was so deep in the life now, so far removed from the normality of regular human existence, that simple things like that would never be in my reach. Would Trixie ever give me children? Of course she fucking wouldn't. She wouldn't even sleep with me and I had no idea if we could make a child if she did. We weren't even the same sodding species, after all.

The fucking Burned Man always knew *exactly* where to stab me where it would hurt the most, didn't it? Bastard fucking thing.

It was just some pointless fucking kid.

"Shut up!" I shouted out loud.

A passerby turned and looked at me over his shoulder, then quickened his pace. Over the road I saw a curtain twitch in one of the other houses. It was time to go.

I hurried off down the road, hands in my pockets and my head down. I needed to find a pub, any pub. The trouble was I drank so bloody much these days that I barely noticed it, and booze didn't shut the Burned Man out of my head however pissed I got. There was only one thing that had ever brought me that much oblivion.

When I had been a student, back when the Burned Man had still been training me, it had made me spend a week off my head on heroin. My Crowley phase, it had called it, after the famous magus Aleister Crowley and his drug fiend methods. I had bloody hated it, and I'd never been so ill in my life. But the heroin had brought total and utter oblivion, I remembered that much. I remembered the time last year when Trixie had shot me full of the stuff too. I remembered that all too well, and something deep inside me twitched with the memory, twitched with longing. Maybe I've just got an addictive personality, I don't know, but right then I knew *exactly* what I wanted.

I found a pub and started drinking, and I started talking to people. There's always someone who know a guy who knows someone, you know what I mean? I left that place and

walked to another pub, drank and asked careful questions
and moved on, always heading further out. Edinburgh gets
a lot less pretty the further from the centre you go, in case
you didn't know. I ended up in a dump not much better
than the place where I had met Davey back in Glasgow, and
I found my man.

Of course I had to buy everything, not just the smack
but a syringe and needles as well. *Works,* he called it, and I
remember just hoping that it did.

What the fuck do you think you're doing? the Burned Man
demanded as I rode back to my hotel in a taxi I couldn't
really afford any more.

I'm getting well and truly off my fucking face, I told it. *It can't
hurt can it, just this once?*

The Burned Man snorted.

If you say so, it said.

Of course it fucking hurt. It hurt more than I could have
imagined possible at the time.

I locked myself in my room and cooked up the heroin
in a teaspoon from the coffee service with a cheap plastic
lighter held under it, my belt tied around my arm. When
the time came I jabbed myself inexpertly in the crook of my
elbow and winced, but I'd started now and I was fucking
doing it. Seeing that house had just about finished me, if
I'm perfectly honest about it. I just... I don't know. Looking
back on it I don't know what the fuck I was thinking really.
I think it was a combination of grief and horror and posttraumatic stress compounded by the constant voice of the
Burned Man in my head and the feeling that I didn't even
know who I was any more.

In the last six months I had killed a child and met an
angel, lost a lover and fallen in love, argued with Lucifer,
seen a Dominion die, been betrayed more times than I

could count, sworn service to a living goddess and utterly betrayed the woman I loved. My life was a total and utter clusterfuck.

I pushed the needle home and emptied the syringe into my arm.

I just about had the presence of mind to take the needle out and loosen the belt before the warm, heavy grey blankets came down and I nodded out on the bed.

When I woke up the hotel room was almost dark and he was standing beside the bed, staring at me.

He had no eyes, of course. My screamer had taken those. His face was a torn and bloody ruin, his eye sockets black pits of dried blood. He held out a hand to me, and I almost wet myself.

"I know you," he said, his five year-old voice soft and slightly lisping like young children do, with the hint of a Scottish accent.

"Jesus Christ," I said, struggling to sit up.

"I'm Calum McRoth," he said. "I'm five. I go to Tollcross primary school."

"I, um…" I said, staring at him in open-mouthed horror. "Um."

"A monster came," he said.

"Yeah," I said, lost for words.

"A monster killed Grandma and Grandpa and then it killed me. A bad man sent it."

Oh bloody hell…

"I know you," he said again. "You're the bad man."

"I…" I started, but there was really no answer to that.

I'm the bad man, I thought, and I knew it was true.

The boy's ruined face melted and ran like tallow, and his hands grew and grew as he reached out for me. He had huge, clawed hands, like a talonwraith.

"The monster took me away to where it lives and I changed," he said. "I'm a monster now and I *know* you."

I screamed as his hands found my throat.

When I woke up for real I felt hideous. I gagged on the vinegar acid taste in the back of my throat and cast a panicked look around for the child, but of course there was nothing there. I was alone in the hotel room, just me and my own stink.

I didn't know if it really had been a ghost or I had just been dreaming and had thought it was. I didn't even think I believed in ghosts. All the same I was almost shaking with fear on top of the comedown. I'd had heroin dreams before but never anything like that. I hugged my knees to my chest and sobbed into the pillow.

A monster came. Oh dear God how had I got myself into this fucking mess? *I know you.*

It comes to something when the bogeyman is afraid of the children instead of the other way around. Well, one child anyway. I was the bogeyman, I knew that much, and I hated myself for it.

You fucking wet fart, the Burned Man snorted. *It was a dream, get over yourself.*

Oh joy, it was back. I'd been off the nod for two whole minutes and the fucking thing was already back in my head again, sneering at me. I looked at my works, at the half a bag of heroin I still had left, and for a moment I was tempted to shoot up again just to shut the fucking thing up.

And you need a shower, it added. *You've pissed yourself.*

I realized with a flush of shame that it was right. I bloody had as well. It was a good job the hotel did laundry service. I dragged myself off the bed and looked at the clock. It was the middle of the night and I'd missed any chance of dinner now. So now I was hungry, scared, strung out and reeking of piss.

I sat on the edge of the bed and found myself thinking about Debbie again, about the children we might have had if I had been a normal, decent human being and not the utter cunt that I actually was.

I thought about those non-existent, impossible kids, and I realized that the last man on Earth I would have wanted anywhere near them was someone like me.

The bogeyman.

I put my head in my hands and wept. It wasn't my finest hour, I have to admit.

I didn't know it at the time, but really I should have been counting my fucking blessings while I still had some left – because I soon wouldn't have.

CHAPTER 4

I woke up in the squat and grimaced at the taste in my mouth. I rolled off my greasy sleeping bag and reached for the whisky bottle, taking a gulp to rinse my teeth. My client would be along soon and it wouldn't do to have bad breath. I looked around at the truly disgusting conditions I was living in and snorted. Oh no, bad breath would never do, would it? Not amongst all this finery it wouldn't.

Of course I had gone downhill fucking fast after that first ridiculously unwise night on the smack. The Burned Man had been pissing me off all day and I'd still had another good hit's worth left in the room so that night I did it, and of course the next day I went out and scored some more. The rest, as they say, is history.

Shitty history admittedly, but there you go. If I had been bleeding money before then I was now absolutely haemorrhaging it, and it didn't take long before nice hotels were a thing of the past. It was a fast and nasty descent to skid row, but when I was reduced to squatting in a condemned block of flats on the Muirhouse I knew I had got there. And here I still was six months later, armed with two half-dead rats and feeling half dead myself, waiting to do a spell for a pimp in return for a hundred quid to spend on more smack.

Fuck a duck, how had it come to this? How had I become this fucking worthless?

I remembered the child, the ghost or the dream or hallucination or whatever the fuck it had been back in the hotel that first night I had shot up, and shuddered. I knew *exactly* how it had come to this. I had seen it maybe two dozen times in the six months that had passed since then, and every time I had woken up screaming. My life had become fucking unbearable, and I had reached a point where I just wanted it to *stop*.

I fingered my amulet and I was so, so tempted to hurl it out the window. I wanted to fall on my knees and beg her for forgiveness. She would come to me if I did, I knew she would. Even after six months of hiding from her and despite everything that had happened, she would still come. She was still the Guardian whether she liked it or not. And it had been me who had run away from her after all, not the other way around. It had been me who had run away from her, and from what I might do. It had been as though I was trying to run away from myself. I was still trying, and I was utterly sick and tired of it. I was sick of hiding, sick of being scared. I was sick of *myself*.

Fuck, if I *could* have run away from myself that's exactly what I would have done but wherever you go there you are, as they say. There was only one way I could see to make it end, and I'm sorry but I'm just not that brave. Diabolists may well go to Hell, but I had been raised Catholic and brought up believing that suicides did, too. Suicide is a mortal sin, after all, according to the Church. Did I still believe that? Probably not, but I was scared enough of going to Hell as it was. I couldn't take the risk, and to be blunt I didn't have the balls to do it anyway.

Getting all fucking deep and religious on us now, are you? the

Burned Man sneered in my head. *You're about as deep as a puddle of piss. You need to pack that in and get your shit together if you want this fucking money.*

I wanted the fucking money. Of course I did. I was down to my last half a gram. I *needed* this money. I needed the smack. There was no kidding myself any more, I wasn't just doing junk to keep the Burned Man out of my head and I hadn't been for some time. Maybe to start with but that had been then, and *then* was in the past. Now I was well and truly addicted and I was doing it because I fucking had to.

I put my head in my hands and tried not to cry.

"Yeah," I said out loud. "Yeah, I need to do this."

Well get off your fucking arse then, you worthless bag of shit, the Burned Man said in that gently coaxing way it had. *He's coming.*

I dragged myself up off the sleeping bag and scrubbed my hands over my bearded cheeks and back through my long hair. God, I must look like a fucking tramp. I remembered horrible old Davey back in Glasgow, and how I'd thought *he* looked a state. I was in a much worse state than him by now, that was for bloody sure. At least I still had all my teeth, which was more than he did. That was something, I supposed.

That's it Don, look on the bright side, I told myself. *You haven't got hepatitis yet either but it's probably only a matter of sodding time.*

That might have been a blessing, in a way. Hepatitis is fatal if it isn't treated, and at least if disease took me there would be no sin. Just the blessed relief of an end to it all.

I told myself to shut up and had another gulp of whisky while I waited. I had a client coming, and that was important. Business was important. It was time to pull my sorry shit together and do some real work.

Of course, I fucked it up.

There was a thump on the door a couple of minutes later,

and I opened it and let my client in. I had thought my old clients back in London were sleazy but they had nothing on this geezer. He was probably somewhere in his late thirties, with pinched, acne-scarred cheeks and long straggly hair that didn't quite hide his bald patch. He was wearing a shabby brown leather jacket and stonewashed skinny jeans and pointy toed cowboy boots like tossers wore back in the Eighties. Pretty much everything about him said "cheap pimp" – which was exactly what he was, of course.

"You must be Joe," I said.

"Joey, aye," he said. His breath could have stunned a buzzard at twenty paces. "You Drake?"

I was almost ashamed to admit it to this horrible wanker but I nodded all the same.

"Yeah," I said. "Step into my office."

I held the door open for him to walk into the squat. I saw his twitchy gaze dart around the room, taking in my grotty sleeping bag and the nearly empty bottle of whisky, the stubs of candles on the floor and the saucer with my works on it. He knew what he was looking at all right, I could see it in his face.

"Aye, right," he said. "So my pal Lambo, he says to me you're a man who…"

He tailed off, and I could see he was staring at my works again.

"Who what?" I prompted him.

He flicked his horrible long greasy hair out of his face and glared at me.

"Was Lambo taking the piss?" he demanded.

I shrugged. "Might have been," I said. "That would depend on what exactly he told you, wouldn't it?"

"You're supposed to be a warlock, aye? A man who can make shite go away an' that. All I'm seeing is another fucking junkie."

Fucking *warlock*. I hate that bloody word. I glared at this Joey prick and gave the Burned Man a mental kick up the arse.

"That right?" I said. I raised my right arm and the Burned Man sniggered in my head and obligingly set my hand on fire for me. "You see a lot of fucking junkies do this do you, Joey?"

"Fucking shite!" Joey said, taking a step backwards. "Aye all right big man, I believe you."

I showed him a cold smile and let the flames die away.

"Right, now we've finished measuring cocks I believe you said a hundred quid," I said.

"Aye, right," he said. "When you've done it."

"Before I do it," I said.

He met my eyes for a minute, then nodded and pulled a thin fold of money out of the pocket of his jeans and held it in his hand.

"This arsehole that's hassling my girls, you can make him fuck off then?" he said. "Binding, I think Lambo called it."

"I can do that," I said.

I wished I had the slightest memory of who he actually wanted me to get rid of. I wished I even remembered who his mate Lambo was, for that matter. My memory was a bit patchy by that point, it has to be said.

"So how do we do this?"

"Did you bring something of his?" I asked. "Or a photo of him, anything like that?"

I would have asked for that, surely? Please tell me I hadn't been so off my face when I had spoken to whoever I had agreed this with that I had forgotten to even ask for a magical focus. There was no way it was going to work without one, after all.

"A photo, aye," he said. "On my phone."

I shut my eyes and pinched the bridge of my nose between

my fingers. I could hardly burn his fucking phone in the candle flame could I? God help me but modern technology was fucking up everything to do with magic, I swear it was.

Oh sod him and his phone, I'd have to bluff it. I needed that hundred quid.

"That'll do," I lied.

Obviously it wouldn't do at all, but this twat didn't know that. A focus is an important part of what's called sympathetic magic, in case you didn't know. If you want to bind someone to stay away from someone else, like I did here, then one way to do that is to take something that symbolized them, like a lock of their hair or a photograph of them or whatever and burn it in the flame of a ritual candle while you perform a banishing. Power your working with some lifeblood and the appropriate herbs and put a bit of your Will into it and you've got a pretty solid spell right there. Without a focus you were just staring at a blood-covered candle and some salad garnish, and feeling silly.

Of course the only lifeblood I had was going to come from two mangy rats that were probably already dead by now, and all I could do for a focus was to wave the bloke's mobile bloody phone about over the candle and hope for the best. I supposed it *might* work, but by then I didn't really care whether it did or not.

"Give it here then," I said. "And the money."

He gave me a wary look but handed over phone and cash together. I stuffed the money in my pocket and fiddled with the phone for a minute before I got it to wake up. He had hundreds of photos on there, most of them of skinny, ill looking women with no clothes on.

"Give us a fucking clue mate," I said, passing it back again.

"Oh, fuck," he said. "Yeah, here."

He passed it back to me, and the screen was now showing a picture of a rough looking bloke with deep scars at the corners of his mouth. Oh joy, a Glasgow smile. That was always a good sign. I nodded and gestured for him to get out of my way while I squatted down in front of one of the candles. I took my lock knife out of my pocket and clicked it open, then reached for the rat sacks.

Neither of them were moving any more, which didn't bode too well for the health of their contents. Still, when I cut the bag open and pulled out a dead rat Joey looked suitably impressed. Or horrified – I wasn't too sure which and I didn't really care. I held the rat up over the candle and Joey looked like he thought he was getting a real magician for his money, which was the important thing. So much of this game is showmanship, it really is.

I muttered under my breath and cut the sad, dead rat open with my knife, letting its congealing blood spatter over the candle. I did the same with the second dead rat then lit the candle with a cheap plastic lighter and burned a couple of sprigs of sage in the flame. Once everything was suitably smoky and rank smelling I passed the phone over the flame while I muttered some more, whatever bollocks came to mind. It didn't really matter what I said, there wasn't a hope in hell of this working now with no lifeblood and only a stupid fucking mobile phone to work with. Oh sod him, he'd paid me already and he was horrible anyway. I couldn't care less if it didn't work.

"...name of Astaroth and Asmodeus, be thou bound by my Will and the blood of these beasts to stay away from the plaintiff Joseph forever unto the end of time," I finished, and hurled what was left of the rats dramatically across the room.

I nodded with feigned satisfaction and stood up.

"That'll do it," I said.

"You sure?" he asked, looking warily at my bloody hands.

I grinned at him.

"Would I lie to you?"

He gave me a queasy smile and left.

As soon as I was sure he'd buggered off I put a shirt on and went out to score. One good thing, probably the *only* good thing, about this hellhole I was living in was that you didn't have to go far to find a dealer. I made myself keep twenty quid back for food and spent the rest of it on gear. I got back to my squat a couple of hours later and by then I was already starting to feel a bit twitchy. Jesus, the sick need was coming on quicker and quicker every time now.

I fixed up in a hurry and lay back on my sleeping bag with a sigh of relief as I felt the grey blankets of sweet oblivion coming down. My amulet lay heavy on my chest, making me think of her. Oh God I missed her so badly. I pulled the sleeping bag around me against the night's cold. As the heroin darkness came down over me, I remembered how we had parted.

I had been sitting in my workroom flicking through one of my grimoires, pretending to feed the Burned Man and killing time while I waited for Trixie and Adam to finish talking in my office. We had just got back from Wormwood's club, on the night that Mazin had turned up at my door and announced that he and his Order of the Keeper worked for me now.

That was the Order of *Menhit's* Keeper, in case you don't remember. Menhit, the ancient Nubian war goddess who I had allowed myself to be browbeaten into swearing service to, remember her? Menhit, who I was fucking terrified of. Mind you, she *had* just killed a fallen Dominion and saved all our lives, so it was no wonder I had been feeling a little bit in awe of her at the time, and that was without the whole "actual living goddess standing right there in front of me" thing. Long story, as I said.

The fetish of the Burned Man didn't actually need feeding

any more, of course. The Burned Man itself was now inside my head, and instead of the blood that the fetish had drunk it was sustaining itself by slowly eating my soul. The fetish stood on the ancient altar at the end of my workroom where it always had, only now it hung lifeless in the tiny chains around its wrists and ankles. It was inanimate and thick with dust, and it obviously hadn't moved for weeks.

And that was when Trixie barged in and finally saw it.

"Oh Thrones and Dominions, what did you *do*?" she said, but by then she knew.

And then of course the fucking Burned Man decided to wake up and speak for me. I lurched to my feet and grinned at her.

"Hello Blondie," I said.

I have no words to describe the look on Trixie's face.

Oh she knew what I had done all right. She knew because Adam had gone and bloody told her, the smug bastard. He had told her *exactly* what I had done. He had told her all about how I had accidentally invoked the Burned Man. About how it was now living in my head and how I couldn't get rid of it, and no doubt he had also told her how it was controlling me half the time.

Adam, if you don't remember, was the name that Lucifer was going by on Earth these days. He wasn't exactly my mate, to put it fucking mildly.

I'll make you more powerful than you can possibly imagine, the Burned Man had told me once, and it had certainly done that. In a manner of speaking, anyway. The Burned Man never said anything it didn't mean, but sometimes the meaning you think you hear isn't the meaning you actually get, if you understand me. Oh I was powerful now all right. I had an archdemon living in my head, after all.

I had an archdemon living in my head, and it was fucking awful.

"Trixie..." I started, but it was far too late for that and I knew it.

"No! No, Don. Not that *thing*, inside you. No!"

Her long evening dress swirled about her ankles as she stormed out and slammed the door of my workroom behind her.

I sank to my knees and stared at the dusty, inanimate fetish of the Burned Man.

"Oh God help me," I said.

It's too fucking late for God now, the Burned Man said in my head. *Too late for piety by a long way. You shut that fucking door the day you took up with me, you daft prick.*

I hung my head and whimpered.

Diabolists go to hell, Don.

Adam had told me that, and I supposed he should know. I fought the sharp sting of tears and made myself go after Trixie. Of course Adam was long gone. He'd sown his seeds of discord and dissent and fucked off as usual, the wanker. Trixie rounded on me with a face like thunder.

"How *could* you?" she demanded.

"I didn't have any fucking choice," I said. "Bianakith was killing you. I... I didn't know what else to do."

"I'm a soldier," she said. "I am an angel of the Heavenly Host, a Sword of the Word. I fight battles, that's what I'm *for!* If I die in one, then there we are. There's *no* excuse for freeing that... that *thing!*"

"You're *that thing*'s Guardian, in case you'd forgotten," I snapped back at her. "Your Dominion tasked you to–"

Oh fuck me no. Oh shit that was *exactly* the wrong thing to say, wasn't it?

I knew it was the moment the words left my mouth, but as always that's a moment too late. Trixie slammed a hand down on my desk so hard it smashed in half.

"My Dominion has *fallen!*" she screamed at me.

She threw her head back and shrieked. My office window exploded and blew out into the street below.

I felt the Burned Man rear up inside me.

I went ice cold and burning hot all over, all at once, and flames roared up out of my hands. I snarled at her like an animal.

Like a demon.

Stop it! I screamed at the Burned Man, feeling like my skull was going to burst. *What are you doing? Stop it!*

I hurled my Will at it in desperation, mentally throttling it as hard as I could. My sudden fury died down and the flames went out, but I felt utterly drained by the effort of keeping the monstrous thing under control.

My shoulders sagged and I looked helplessly at Trixie. She stared back at me with a mixture of horror and blind rage on her face.

"I…" I said.

Trixie tuned on her heel and stormed out of my office. I heard the front door slam shut behind her, and I collapsed onto the sofa and put my head in my hands. What the fuck had I become?

I didn't know, but I knew one thing. I was dangerous. The Burned Man had no love for Trixie, I knew that much. I did though. I loved her more than anything, and I had almost hurt her.

Again.

It wasn't even the first time. I remembered the time I had been ambushed by Miss Marie's so-called Initiates of the Melek Taus. After killing them the Burned Man had almost turned on Trixie as well, as though it had gone berserk. It had been as if the killing frenzy had overcome it and it didn't know when to stop. This time had been much worse though. This time it had come horrifyingly close to just attacking her out of hand.

I wasn't having that.

No I wasn't, but I wasn't at all sure I was strong enough to control the Burned Man either. I remembered my attempt to banish it when I first realized that it had possessed me, and what a miserable failure that had been. No, I wasn't going to match the Burned Man in a straight battle of Will, that was for sure.

Still, a man in my line of work knows more than one way to skin a toad.

I walked back into my workroom and rummaged through the drawers of my cupboard. I knew this was cowardly, and I also knew it was going to hurt me as much as her. More so, probably. God only knew I didn't want to do it, but I didn't want the Burned Man to hurt Trixie either. More than anything I didn't want that. I found the things I was looking for and put them on the altar in front of the dead fetish.

Years ago people used to think pebbles with holes in them were magic. They aren't, but they're nice and easy to hang from a cord or a necklace or whatever so they make great amulets. I threaded this one onto a leather cord and picked up my scalpel. One quick nick of the back of my hand was all it took to make my blood well up, enough to dip a small artist's paintbrush into. I gritted my teeth as I used the brush to draw the necessary sigils on the pebble, muttering her true name over and over again under my breath as I worked.

I slipped the leather cord over my head and stuffed the amulet down the front of my shirt. An amulet of binding charged with my own lifeblood and the sigil of Trixie's true name would be enough to keep her from even finding me, never mind coming anywhere near me. I knew it would work, I had made one once before. That hadn't ended entirely well, all things considered, but I figured things were a bit different now. This was for *her* safety this time.

I emptied my desk drawer of all the money I had, then

caught sight of Trixie's eyewateringly expensive handbag sitting on the floor beside the sofa. It was testament to just how upset she had been that she had left without it. I had a brief moment of guilt, but made myself ruthlessly suppress it.

Her good as much as mine, I told myself as I raided her bag. There wasn't much in there, just her silver cigarette case and a slim gold lighter, a packet of tissues and a thick roll of cash that looked like it was probably a good five or six grand's worth. I pocketed the money and left the rest. She always seemed to be able to produce more money whenever she wanted it but woe betide the man who took Trixie's smokes away from her. I touched her cigarette case fondly for a moment, feeling tears well in my eyes. It was so much a part of her it was almost like stroking her face.

God, was I really doing this?

Was I really leaving her?

I have to, I told myself. *It's not safe for her any more. Or for me, for that matter.*

If I really had gone for her I dread to think what would have happened. The Burned Man was a murderous psychopath, but to be perfectly honest so was Trixie.

Angelus Mortis, I remembered Janice calling her. The Angel of Death. Maybe she wasn't exactly that, not literally anyway, but she wasn't bloody far off it. If I had gone for her I don't really know *who* would have won but it was a pretty sure bet one of us would have ended up dead on the floor, and there was no way I was going to let that happen.

I had obligations here in London, I knew that. There was Papa Armand for one thing, and more to the point there was Menhit, who had appointed me her Keeper of the Veil. I never had got to look at Mazin's book so I still wasn't too clear what I had actually agreed to there, but whatever it was, I was backing out. Menhit might frighten the life out of me but at that precise moment all I really cared about was keeping Trixie and myself alive.

Was that cowardly? Yes I'm afraid it fucking was, but I was doing it anyway.

Sorry my love, I thought sadly as I put her bag down again. *I have to*.

I put my coat on and fled.

CHAPTER 5

When I woke up I was fucking freezing. I had been dreaming about the fucking child again, or maybe it had even been there while I was on the nod. I really had no way of knowing, but it never got any less ghastly whether it was real or not. I gagged on the vinegar aftertaste of the heroin, something I didn't think I'd ever get used to. It took me a moment to work out why I was so cold. Eventually I realized it was because I was half bloody naked and lying on top of my sleeping bag instead of in it.

I sat up, and realized I wasn't wearing my shirt. That was more than a bit odd, as I was damn sure I'd still had it on when I shot up. I scrubbed my hands through my hair and blinked, shivering violently, but the squat was in pitch darkness. That figured – by the time I had got rid of Joey the pimp it had been getting late, and then I'd gone out to score and come back to shoot up and then I had been on the nod for however long it had been. It was the middle of the bloody night. Even so, when had I taken my shirt off and why the fuck wasn't I in my sleeping bag? I never shot up at night without getting in first. That was how people froze to death in their sleep.

I crawled into the horrible nylon bag and pulled it around me, huddling and shivering until I'd worked a bit of warmth back into myself. Something felt even more wrong than usual but I put it down to the comedown and the cold and the general fucking awful state of my life in general. It took me about half an hour to realize what it was.

My amulet was gone.

I sat bolt upright and started scrabbling around on the floor for it, my hands shaking. I knocked over the whisky bottle and cursed fluently and at length until I finally found a candle and my lighter. I got the candle going and started to look properly, and that's when I noticed my door had been kicked in.

Jesus, I'd been on the nod so hard the noise hadn't even woken me up. I stumbled onto my knees, half tangled in my sleeping bag, and spotted my coat and shirt thrown carelessly on the floor a few feet away. My works were still there, but my smack and the last of my money was gone. All my lovely new stash, gone.

"Fuck," I whispered.

No smack and no amulet. No smack and no money to buy more.

Oh fuck…

Someone had quite obviously robbed me, but why the bloody hell had they taken my amulet? It was only a pebble on a rotten bit of leather, worthless to anyone but me. How would someone even have known I was wearing it under my shirt?

They already knew you had it, the Burned Man said.

"How?" I asked out loud.

How does anyone know anything? it said. *Some cunt told them.*

I swallowed and made myself think. Someone had wanted my amulet, because someone had told them I had it. The amulet was worthless in itself so they didn't want *it* exactly, they must have just wanted me to *not* have it. And they'd nicked my smack as well, which either made them some special sort of sadist or someone who'd either wanted it for themselves or to sell on, which narrowed it down quite a bit.

Joey. My money was on that Joey creep. He knew as much about magic as I imagined he did about quantum physics, but this Lambo character who had put him on to me obviously knew which way was up. If he knew what I did for a living, then I was damn sure he knew what an amulet was too. I just wished I could remember who the fuck he was.

Lambert, the Burned Man said. *It's short for Lambert. Daniel Lambert, if my memory doesn't fail me.*

Of course its memory didn't fail it, the little git never forgot anything. I nodded slowly. I vaguely remembered a Danny Lambert. He was a seeker I had met briefly in Edinburgh while I was still seriously looking for Debbie, before my whole life went down the toilet in such a spectacular fashion and I stopped looking for anything except more heroin.

Danny Lambert knew I was a magician, but the only way he could have known about the amulet was if someone had told *him.* And, now that I thought about it, it didn't matter how long the chain of someone-told-someone was, it must have started somewhere. There was only one person who could have originally known or at least guessed that I was wearing that amulet.

And that person was Trixie.

"I have to get that amulet back," I said. "Right fucking now."

I couldn't just make another one, it didn't work like that. Oh you can make hundreds of amulets for general things, like good luck or protection from the Evil Eye or whatever, everyone can wear one of those if they want to. But an amulet for binding a specific person away from another specific person? Nope.

There could only be one of those at a time or it wouldn't work. This was the second one I had made to bind Trixie from me, admittedly. It had only worked a second time because the first one had been destroyed when the council finally got around to dynamiting the condemned building where I had abandoned it while the Furies were torturing me. Unless the second one was also destroyed I couldn't make a third that would actually work. I had to get the original back and that was all there was to it.

And how the fuck are you going to do that? the Burned Man sneered.

I got up and pulled my shirt and coat on, still shivering, and picked up the sputtering candle. I stuffed a few more candles and the lighter and my knife into my pockets, and walked out into the hallway.

"The old fashioned way," I told it.

I started kicking in doors.

The first two flats were empty. In the third I found two grotty junkies huddled in sleeping bags, snoring on the nod.

"Oi!" I shouted.

I gave one of the sleeping bags a kick, and the Burned Man took the hint and obligingly called up the flames from my right hand. That was a hell of a lot better than my candle, so I chucked it into a corner and let it go out. The junkie I had kicked struggled to sit up, a hand over his face to protect his eyes from the light of the leaping flames that were roaring up from my hand. *Her* face, I corrected myself. Oh crap. I hated to see women in this state, almost as much as I hated to see *myself* in it.

"Bloody nightmares," she muttered.

"I'm a bloody nightmare all right," I said. "I'm looking for a pimp called Joey. Sleazy looking, dresses like it's 1988. Where do I find him?"

"I dunno, I'm no on the game," she said, and laughed

bitterly. "Who'd have me?"

She lay down again and turned her back, obviously writing me off as just another hallucination. She was nodding again in seconds.

I cursed and crossed the hallway, and booted open another door. The flat was empty. Jesus this was going to take all night at this rate, and I was pretty sure I didn't *have* all night. If I had called out to Trixie I knew she would have been there in a flash, but even without me doing that I didn't think it would take her long to find me now that I had lost the amulet. Assuming she still *wanted* to find me, of course. It occurred to me that I might be seriously flattering myself here, but I couldn't take the risk. She *was* the Burned Man's Guardian, after all, and I suspected that meant she didn't have a lot of choice. She would come whether she wanted to or not. She *had* to.

I hurried on down the corridor, flames trailing from my hand as I kicked in doors at random. I was getting desperate and I knew it. I do rash things when I'm desperate, in case you hadn't noticed. There could have been half a dozen outlaw bikers crashing for the night in one of those flats, or some headcase with a meth problem and an Uzi. Neither of those things were impossible around here, not by a long way they weren't.

Slow down and fucking think it through, I told myself. *Joey's a pimp. Pimps have toms. Toms need somewhere to live and work.*

A house then, but where? The Muirhouse estate is fucking huge, in case you didn't know. Half of it had been redeveloped into endless rows of new council houses and half of it was still like this, old and grim and falling to bits. If Joey was remotely competent at his job he'd have his girls in the new bit somewhere, but where? I had to find a lead, find someone who would know. I remembered the grotty ned from that morning, the one whose arm I had set on fire.

I reckoned he might well know, and I knew which squat was his.

I hurried along the corridor to his door and smashed it in with my boot.

"Oh Jesus Ratty, don't hurt me no more!" he wailed.

He was already awake, sitting up in his sleeping bags with filthy rags wrapped around his burned arm, sweating and looking feverish. The silly sod obviously hadn't been to the hospital, probably on account of all the drugs in his system and how he didn't want to breach the probation he was almost certainly on. I had to admit I felt a little bit guilty now, looking at the state of him. Only a little bit, though.

"I'm looking for Joey the pimp," I said.

He blinked in surprise, cowering from the fire that still blazed up from my right hand.

"Joey?" he asked. "Dinnae go to Joey, his tarts have all got the fuckin' HIV an' that."

"I don't want his fucking tarts..." I started.

"I should hope not," a voice said from behind me.

I froze as I realized I could suddenly smell Russian tobacco. *Oh God...*

I turned slowly, my hand still burning. She was standing in the doorway wearing jeans and low-heeled boots and a leather coat, her beautiful blonde hair loose around her face. A long black cigarette was smouldering between the fingers of her left hand, and in her right she held a sword.

For a moment I thought she was going to go for me, and I just simply didn't care. I was so far gone, at the very rock bottom of despair and addiction and torment that I just wanted it to *end*, right there and then. Hepatitis might not have come for me but I would have welcomed anything to make it all stop, even Trixie's blade.

The thought of her standing there looking at me, the thought of what she must be seeing, filled me with so much shame that I just couldn't bear it.

"Which one of you am I talking to?" she asked, her voice sounding strained.

I swallowed.

"Trixie, it's me," I said. "It's Don."

She nodded, the flames from my hand reflecting in her beautiful blue eyes.

"Put the fire out, Don," she said. "If you still can."

"I… Shit, yeah, sorry," I said, giving the Burned Man a mental kick.

It resisted for a moment, but for all that I knew it didn't like Trixie, I suspected it was a bit scared of her too. So it bloody well should be. The flames disappeared, and left us in darkness. Trixie produced a torch from her coat pocket and turned it on, and I saw that she had made her sword go away. For now, anyway.

"I can control it," I said, although I wasn't at all sure that was true any more.

That was why I had run away in the first place, after all, but looking at her now I was so pleased to see her I just wanted to cry. Whether or not she was pleased to see *me* still remained to be seen.

"I see," she said, and that could have meant anything at all. "Don, what on earth are you doing in this horrible place?"

I cleared my throat, feeling a fresh wave of shame sweep over me. "I, um," I said. "Um, I live here."

"Here?" she echoed.

"In a squat down the hall," I muttered. "Things, um, haven't been going very well recently."

The ned sniggered. I had almost forgotten about him, but now any guilt I might have felt for hurting him was fast vanishing.

"Aye, he's Ratty the ratcatcher," he said. "Ratty the weird

old junkie. He's nae better than the rest of us, hen."

I could have strangled him. I mean I was going to have to tell her, I knew that, but I had hoped I could maybe break the news a bit more gently than that.

"Be quiet," was all she said, and something in her voice shut the little bastard up. "Don, come with me."

She led me out of the ned's squat and along the corridor and down the stairs, and all the way there she didn't say anything else and I didn't dare speak at all. We went out of the front door and into the small patch of wilderness that passed for a garden between the flats and the road. Trixie sat down on a low wall. It was cold and dark, and half the streetlights weren't working. I sat beside her, pulling my filthy coat around me against the chill night air. I didn't think I'd ever felt more ashamed in my life.

"Mazin will be here soon with the car," she told me. "I telephoned him an hour ago, as soon as I was sure I knew where you were."

"Right," I said, wondering if she knew how long it took to drive from London to Edinburgh, even in the middle of the night.

"We were in Glasgow anyway," she said. "It's not all that far away."

"Oh, right." It wasn't, to be fair.

I just didn't know what to say to her. I hadn't seen her for six months and I was horribly conscious of how I looked and smelled, and never mind that it was only going to be a few hours before I started twitching for smack.

Then I was going to get ill. Really ill.

I was penniless and I just couldn't bring myself to ask Trixie for drug money. I still had *some* pride, after all.

Or so I thought at the time, anyway.

Even if I *had* had any money, I couldn't see Trixie letting me go off and score. There was nothing to be done and that was all there was to it.

"We were in Glasgow because I had a telephone call from a man there who said someone who worked for him called Daniel Lambert had found you," she went on. "I had to go and see this man to find out who Daniel Lambert was, and to give him the reward."

"Right," I said again.

What fucking reward?

She carried on as though I hadn't spoken. "While we were there Daniel Lambert called again and said he had arranged for your amulet to be taken, and to be ready. I came as soon as I could, Don. I came as soon as I was allowed to."

It took me a moment to realize she was crying. Very quietly, but she was definitely crying. I wanted to hold her, but I didn't quite dare. For one thing I really wasn't sure where we stood right at that moment, and for another I could smell myself and I very much doubted she would want me to touch her in my current state. I put my grimy hand over hers on the wall instead, and she didn't seem to mind that.

After a few minutes she stopped crying and spoke again.

"He told me it was funny because he'd met you months ago, before he knew anyone was looking for you, and by the time he found out about the reward he didn't know where you were any more," she said. "It took him weeks to track you down, he said."

"Who was he?" I asked, for want of anything better to say. "The man in Glasgow, I mean?"

"His name was Davey," she said. "I didn't get a last name."

Davey. Oh that's just great. Grotty old Davey had got Danny "Lambo" Lambert to set Joey the pimp on me to steal my amulet. *Cheers Davey, you horrible old git. I fucking owe you one.*

Although, thinking about it, that meant grotty old Davey got to tell Lambert what to do. I still didn't really remember

Lambert very well but I knew I had met him somewhere in the middle of Edinburgh – somewhere decent, not out here in the badlands of the outskirts. That ought to make him several cuts above Davey in the general pecking order, but apparently it didn't. I shivered. Not for the first time I found myself wondering who Davey was, and exactly what it was that he did. I wasn't sure I wanted to find out, to be perfectly honest. I had a nasty feeling I really wouldn't like the answer.

"Here's Mazin now," Trixie said, and I forgot all about Davey as a bloody great Mercedes pulled up at the kerb in front of us.

It was one of the really huge posh ones, a *Maybach* I think they're called, eighteen feet of glossy black land yacht with tinted windows and an engine that purred like a contented tiger. I hardly ever get to drive a car but I do like a nice motor, you know what I mean?

Mazin got out of the driver's seat, walked around the car, and bowed low to us both.

"Lord Keeper," he said. "Madam Guardian."

I couldn't have looked or felt less like a lord at that precise moment, but all the same I couldn't help but smile. It was as though angels had come and rescued me from Hell. Which, to be fair, was pretty much exactly what *had* just happened.

Well, *an* angel anyway. I still wasn't too sure about Mazin.

"Hi Mazin," I said.

He was tall and broad shouldered and sort of Arabic looking, wearing a butter-soft leather jacket over jeans and a white shirt. I had only met the geezer once before and I didn't know him at all, but apparently he was in charge of my "people". I still had no fucking idea what that even meant – everything had gone to shit so quickly after he first turned up that I hadn't had time to find out. The gist of it seemed to be that he was the boss of whoever the people were who had worked for Rashid, who had been my predecessor as Menhit's Keeper of the Veil. Apparently I had inherited Mazin and his whole organisation when Menhit had murdered Rashid and pretty much ordered me to take his job. I still didn't really know what that meant either, come to think of it, or even if I still *had* the job after walking out on it and disappearing after barely a month in office. I must admit I had been rather hoping that she had fired me in my absence – at least that way I wouldn't have had to see her again. I supposed this meant that she hadn't.

"Hello," Trixie said. "We should go. The car will be conspicuous here."

That was a bit of an understatement really, and if it hadn't been four or five in the morning we'd probably all have been robbed or shot or something by now. Well I mean obviously we wouldn't, not with Trixie there, but you know what I mean. There would certainly have been a scene, and no one wanted that.

"Of course, Madam," Mazin said.

He opened the back door of the car for her, then led me around the other side and ushered me in beside her. The door closed with a heavy clunk and I sat back into a cushioning dream of quilted cream leather. The car had two individual rear seats rather than a bench, with footrests and armrests and a big raised console thing between them. It was a bit like how I had always imaged being in a private jet must be.

I rubbed my hands over my bearded face in stunned astonishment. This was... not how I had expected the rest of my day to go. Mazin got into the driver's seat and the car's interior lights gently dimmed as he closed his door. He slotted the transmission into drive and eased the huge car away from the kerb.

I looked out through the tinted window and watched the

Muirhouse estate slide past. I had pretty much expected to die there, had started wanting to in fact, and now here I was being chauffeured away in a limousine. This really, *really* wasn't anything I had been expecting. It was wonderful, except for one tiny little thing.

I could feel the first twinges already, the early warning signs that I was going to start twitching in a couple of hours. And then I was going to start hurting.

Badly.

One thing at a time, I told myself. *Fuck that and just enjoy the ride. You're saved.*

CHAPTER 6

I wasn't saved.

Oh fuck me no, I was a very long way away from that. I vomited for the sixth time in an hour, shaking and sobbing pitifully as I spat rancid, stinking bile into the toilet bowl. I had a blanket wrapped around my shoulders and I was shivering with cold and pouring with sweat at the same time, out of my mind with a desperate, frantic animal need. My stomach cramped and clenched, and if there had been anything left in there I honestly would have shit myself. Again. It wouldn't have been the first time in the last three days, I'm ashamed to say.

If someone had offered to kill me I would have cheerfully let them. If someone had offered me heroin I would have done anything, and I mean *anything,* to get it. I was a wreck. A tortured, screaming, hallucinating, pitiful wreck.

For God's sake can't you do something? I begged the Burned Man for the hundredth time that day.

Still no, it said. *I'm suffering too, you cunt. I fucking told you not to get hooked on that filthy shit.*

It had, to be fair. When I first started my slide into addiction it had raged at me about it, and the more it had raged the more I wanted to get off my face to shut it up. That had been a self-fulfilling prophecy and no mistake.

I clutched the toilet and gagged, wanting to tear it off the floor and hurl it through the wall. Anything to make me feel better. Anything to stop the agonising need.

Trixie and Mazin were ruthless.

For all that Trixie was naive about certain things I was pretty sure Mazin wasn't, and someone had obviously explained this to her well enough. We were holed up in a beautiful fourbedroom Georgian apartment in Edinburgh's New Town, a whole floor of one of those grand grey terraces. It was all huge rooms and marble fireplaces, high ceilings and towering velvet drapes over the windows. I would have gone back to my filthy squat on the Muirhouse in a heartbeat if I could just have had some fucking smack.

"Just a little bit," I sobbed, and puked again. "For fucksake it's not fair, I *need* it!"

I was crying again. Jesus wept, I know I haven't ever been exactly what you'd call an upstanding citizen but I didn't think I'd ever been as pathetic as this in my life. Had I really thought I still had some pride? Not any fucking more I didn't.

The apartment was locked down like the world's poshest jail and they wouldn't let me out for a second. The windows didn't even open, which meant the whole place now stank of Trixie's cigarettes despite the best efforts of the air conditioning system. I couldn't imagine how much this place must be costing or who was paying for it, but that really was the least of my fucking worries at that point.

I convulsed helplessly, my head swimming. I was starting to see things again, I knew I was. That was bad. I had seen the child twice so far since I had been going cold turkey.

It had been fucking plaguing me ever since that night in the hotel room where it had literally frightened the piss out of me, but two dozen times in six months was one thing.

Now it was tormenting me almost every fucking day, when I had more than enough woes of my own. *Why?*

I simply had no idea, and I still didn't know if I really believed it *was* the ghost of the McRoths' grandson or not. In fact I doubted it, but it didn't really matter in the great scheme of things. When I saw it… yeah, let's just say it was real for me at the time when it was happening. It was fucking terrifying, that's all I can say, but all the same I was getting well and truly fucked off with it now. It wasn't as though being dragged naked through Hell by the withdrawal was bad enough, I had to have some snot-nosed ghost giving me grief as well? Fuck that.

I seemed to have finally stopped throwing up so I dragged myself back into my bedroom and up onto the gigantic bed. The bathroom was en suite so it wasn't too far to crawl, I supposed that was something. The bed was at least a king-size, probably whatever the next one up from that is called. I flopped onto the sweaty Egyptian cotton sheets and pulled the blanket around me, shivering and crying.

This was fucking inhuman, and I would have given *anything* to make it stop.

"I know you," a soft voice said from beside the bed.

"Oh piss off," I groaned.

The thing was, I was so fucking ill and pitiful and sorry for myself that I couldn't spare any mental energy to waste on fear any more. It was a hallucination of a dead child, or the ghost of a dead child, or whatever it fucking was but he was dead either way and I wasn't, for all that I was fucking praying for someone to put me out of my misery. The bottom line was there was nothing I could do for him now and if he wanted to hurt me he'd have to get in the queue behind the fucking withdrawal that was hurting me more than I had ever dreamed it was possible to be hurt. Even my fucking *bones* hurt.

There is no flu on Earth that feels this bad, trust me. My leg kicked involuntarily as another spasm of muscle cramps hit me, and I only wished I could have kicked the ghost in the face to shut it up.

"You're a bad man."

"I know and I don't care!" I screamed at it. "Fuck off!"

The door opened and the child vanished as Trixie walked in.

"Are you all right?" she asked. "You were shouting again."

I sat up in bed and stared at her.

"All right?" I yelled. "Am I fucking all right? Do I fucking *look* all right, Trixie? *Do* I?"

She gave me a sad look.

"You will be," she said. "Soon, I hope. There's someone here to see you."

I could have strangled her. If the Burned Man hadn't been suffering almost as much as I was, I really think it might have gone for her throat right there and then, but thankfully it kept its mouth shut for once. All the same, the last thing on God's green bloody earth I wanted right then was a visitor.

"I'm not really in the fucking mood for visitors," I said through gritted teeth.

Trixie walked into the room and closed the door behind her.

"I'm afraid it's not really optional," she said. "Menhit is here."

My heart almost stopped. I didn't think I *could* have felt any worse right then but suddenly I did. *Menhit* was there? Of all the people I didn't want to fucking see, Menhit was right at the top of the list.

"Tell me you're kidding," I said.

"No, I'm afraid not," she said. "Mazin and I have, let us say, phrased our explanation carefully."

You've lied through your teeth to her, you mean, I thought. *Thank fuck for that.*

The door opened again and Menhit swept into the room closely followed by Mazin.

Menhit, the Black Lion of Nubia. Menhit the Slaughterer. Mother of War. She Who Massacres.

Menhit the living goddess.

I nearly shit the bed, or at least I would have done if there'd been anything left in me to come out.

To be fair she didn't look *quite* as much like a resurrected Nubian war goddess as she had the last time I had seen her, but she was still terrifying. She was well over six feet tall, black as a desert night and visibly muscular even in a well-fitted business suit, but at least her eyes weren't glowing with that unnatural golden light any more. That made her a little bit easier to look at, but not a lot. I could still feel the air in the room growing tight the way it does before lightning strikes. Her hair hung about her face in a hundred thin black braids that brushed her shoulders as she strode towards the bed.

"My Keeper has been poisoned?" she demanded.

Trixie gave me a long look, and swallowed.

"Yes, Mother," she said at last, "he has. In a manner of speaking. He was taken away from us by a poison of the modern world."

Menhit nodded and I stared up at her broad, flat features. She really *did* look like a lion, I thought. I started to sweat all over again. Dear God but she was scary. I mean so was Trixie of course, but I was used to Trixie. Sort of, anyway. I was also hopelessly in love with her, which obviously made quite a bit of difference. I was simply terrified of Menhit. Papa Armand must be off his head, sleeping with that.

Menhit, in case you don't remember, really was an actual living goddess. Menhit had slain the fallen Dominion in single combat. Menhit was death walking. She was magnificent and she was terrible and just her very presence made me want to piss myself with fear. *That* is what a real live goddess is like, believe you me.

She was also my boss.

"Mother," I managed to croak, bowing my head to her in respect. "I beg your forgiveness but I am… unwell."

That was the Burned Man talking, of course. It was surprisingly good at the diplomatic shit, I had to give it that. I let it speak, just grateful that I didn't have to.

"Who is responsible for this outrage?" Menhit demanded. "I will rip their heart out and eat it."

Oh shit, that was an awkward one. I mean obviously *I* was responsible, but I could hardly tell her that. Thankfully the Burned Man could put a positive spin on anything when it had to.

"Those responsible are already dead," the Burned Man said for me, and I realized it was right.

Those responsible for my posttraumatic stress and subsequent addiction were definitely already dead, because I had fucking killed them. That was the whole problem, but as usual what the Burned Man said was technically true if not entirely said in the spirit of good faith. Christ, I don't think the Burned Man would have known the spirit of good faith if it had bitten it in the arse. All the same, that really didn't matter so long as it stopped Menhit from tearing my head off and shitting down my neck.

Menhit nodded her head in understanding, however misled.

"This is good to know," she said. "I am pleased that my Keeper has taken his own revenge on those responsible. That shows initiative, and the ability to act. These are traits I value in a Keeper."

I let her have her delusions of my competence. No one

had actually lied in this conversation, and if we were talking a little bit at cross-purposes then that wasn't my fault.

"Thank you, Mother," I said. "Although I must confess the poison is causing me some discomfort."

Some discomfort? Some fucking *discomfort?* I was past caring about mortal sins by now, and if I had had any way to kill myself I honestly would have done, just to make it stop. *Discomfort* had to be the understatement of the fucking decade, but all the same I knew the Burned Man wanted this to stop as much as I did. All I could do was let it keep talking and hope for the best.

"I see," Menhit said.

She was standing right beside the bed now, towering over me. She reached out one large hand and put it on my forehead. I managed to stop myself from cowering, but only just.

I heard Mazin gasp. Somehow I got the feeling that Menhit didn't usually go in for healing people, or even touching people come to that. Not unless she was about to hurt them very badly, anyway. She was war personified, after all, and war isn't really about helping people whatever shit the politicians might like to have you believe. I realized I was holding my breath, and I didn't seem to be able to stop.

"He is unwell," Menhit said after a moment. "An illness I do not recognize."

No, they hadn't invented heroin back in the bronze age, had they? I thought. *Did they have* any *sort of addiction back then, though?* I didn't know, but I hoped not. If she realized what was actually wrong with me I was going to be in a truly immense amount of shit, I knew that much. The prospect of being in the shit with Menhit didn't even bear thinking about.

"Something of the modern world as I said, Mother," Trixie said, and I noticed the nervous tremor in her voice. "I am sad to say it is beyond my abilities to help him."

I winced. There were a number of ways I could take that and none of them were good. Menhit just nodded.

"Few things are beyond *my* abilities, Guardian," she said, "although healing is not my forte. If I do this he may experience some distress."

Distress? I had a nasty feeling that was an understatement of the same magnitude as *discomfort* had been, and that alone was enough to make the shakes come back. I shuddered helplessly on the bed, starting to go into spasms all over again.

"He will cope, Mother," Trixie said, as though they had both forgotten I was actually right there in the fucking room between them. "Please, do what you can."

Menhit nodded again, and I felt a bolt of pure magic shoot down her arm and into my head.

I shrieked.

Some. Fucking. Distress.

Yeah, it was safe to say I experienced some fucking distress all right. I have no idea what she did to me but it fucked me up good and proper. My head was all over the place, and I mean that quite literally. I don't know how much you know about astral projection but I'm going to take a guess at not much. The first time you experience true astral projection – the out-of-body-experience type, not the navel-gazing-and-making-it-up type I mean – it's bloody terrifying.

Imagine you're a balloon, weightless and at the mercy of the wind. Now release that balloon into a hurricane. You can't control yourself and everything happens in a headlong rush, only this balloon isn't even solid and it can fly through walls and ceilings if the wind blows it that way.

Now, I didn't just fall out of a tree and I had done conscious astral projection before. Well, I'd had it done to me anyway, so I wasn't quite as helpless as the poor kid who spontaneously leaves his body in his sleep one night and prays to all the gods he's ever heard of to make it stop and never happen again. All the same I can't say it was exactly my strong point, and it's never been something I've learned to enjoy.

I felt sick as I shot through the ceiling of the bedroom, flashed through the building's attic and out into the overcast Edinburgh night. I realized immediately that whatever Menhit had done to me had torn my astral body out of my physical one and basically just thrown it into the air like a discarded wrapper. I could only assume this was a side effect of her brutal healing magic, which was probably so bloody hideous my astral form had fled my body to get away from it. A lot of the accounts you read of spontaneous astral projection are from people at death's door in hospitals, after all, looking down at themselves on the operating table and all that. I could only assume this was the same sort of thing.

Whoa there, Don, I thought, consciously slowing my careering astral form before I went into the stratosphere. I managed to get some sort of control and after a while I was able to make myself float unsteadily along above the street.

Astral projection sounds cool, and people who are really good at it can do useful things when they're out and about in their astral bodies. When you're out of your body you can theoretically go anywhere you want to, see anything you want to see. You could supposedly drift through the walls of the Pentagon or the GCHQ Doughnut and peek at whatever the hell they do in there, if you wanted to. *Remote viewing*, the spooks call that, although the jury's still out on whether they can really pull it off or not. I still suspect most adepts just spy on whoever they happen to fancy taking a shower, to be honest. Either way I'm *not* good at it, and I don't like it.

I tried to remember how this worked. You have to sort

of swim, if that makes sense. You're not solid, not even a shape really, although normally your mind fills in the gaps and makes you see a ghostly form of yourself. I think you'd just go nuts otherwise, being a purely disembodied consciousness. No one's really ready to cope with being a ghost, are they? I looked down and yeah, I could see a semi-translucent version of myself, sort of silvery and shiny and embarrassingly naked. I have to admit I don't look good naked, but then most people don't.

There was a bright silver cord extending from just below my bellybutton and down into one of the roofs below me. That was good, that meant Menhit hadn't completely severed my astral body from my physical one. If she had I knew I'd have been dead in a few hours, but with the silver cord intact both body and soul were at least still connected if nothing else. Also, of course, it meant I could find my way back.

This is a bit fucking different, innit? I thought at the Burned Man. *I haven't done this since you were teaching me.*

Of course the Burned Man had made me astrally project when I was still a student, back before Professor Davidson died, and it had dragged me straight into the summoning and sending business. Astral projection is a useful skill that any true adept should know how to do, but all the same I had never really got the hang of it and I can't do it by myself. The Burned Man had been able to coax me out but on the rare occasions I had attempted it since then I'd had no joy. All the same, now that I was getting the idea I found it wasn't as bad as all that. The Burned Man was curiously quiet, though.

Mate? I thought. *You awake in there?*

There was no reply. I made myself sink slowly down through the air until I was sort of perching on the roof of the house that contained our apartment, my non-solid arse hovering just above the chimney pots. I formed the astral equivalent of a frown and dug around inside myself, looking for the Burned Man.

It wasn't there.

Well fuck me, isn't that interesting? It seemed that when I had invoked the Burned Man I had drawn it into my physical body but not my astral. The two overlap each other most of the time of course, to the extent that the vast majority of people don't even realize they *have* an astral body and that they're two different things. They are, though. And if the Burned Man wasn't in my astral body...

Jesus wept, I could have kicked myself all the way down the street and back. I could have been doing this instead of filling myself with poison to get away from the little shit. If all I had to do was leave my body... I thought about that for a moment.

It couldn't be that easy, could it?

I didn't see why not. I mean yeah, I couldn't actually do it by myself but if this was the result then I was bloody well going to make myself learn how.

I sat back against the chimney I couldn't feel and looked up at the sky, feeling truly relaxed for the first time in months. The sky was a solid bank of cloud, reflecting the streetlights of the city back down at me in a dull orange glow. Stars would have been nice, but I suppose you can't have everything. It was wonderful just to be away from the Burned Man for a little while. I loved Trixie dearly but I had to admit it was nice to be away from her too – I know we'd only been back together for a few days but I had been so fucking ill that her stern refusal to let me out of her sight had been really starting to get on my tits. I knew she was only trying to get me off the smack but... shit.

Smack.

For the first time in months I had just thought about

smack without my mouth watering with need. I plucked up my courage and thought about it again, deliberately this time. I thought about using. I thought about shooting up, the needle pushing its way into my diseased arm, and the whole idea felt utterly repellent. There was no longing there at all, not even any desire.

Fuck…

My astral body wasn't addicted to anything, of course, and whatever Menhit was doing to me down there seemed to have already cleared my mind if nothing else. I was so, so relieved. I felt happy for the first time in six months. That lasted about a minute and a half, by my reckoning.

"I know you," a soft voice said beside me.

If I had been inside my skin I'd have jumped out of it, let me tell you. I shot up off the chimney pots and stared down at the ghostly figure of Calum McRoth standing on the roof looking up at me. No five year-old should be that scary, but he was.

"You're the bad man," he whispered, and he reached up towards me.

His arms grew and grew, talons extending from his hands while I felt like I was mired in treacle. All that balloon-in-the-wind shit was just gone and I was stuck, helpless as he reached for me with those awful claws.

Fucking do something! I shouted at the Burned Man, before I remembered it wasn't there.

I had got so used to having the little bastard in my head that I had come to rely on it in times of need, I realized. And now it wasn't there, and I was all on my own.

All on my own with the ghost of the child I had killed.

CHAPTER 7

"Get away from me," I shouted at it, or tried to anyway.

An astral form can't shout, of course. Or even really speak, come to that. Even so, it seemed to hear me the same way I could hear it.

"I know you," it whispered as its taloned hands closed around my throat. I struggled, tried to swim my way up into the air, but it was no good. The ghost or whatever the hell it was belonged on this plane and I really didn't. I was out of my element, quite literally, whereas it had all the advantages. It shot towards me, its freakishly extended arms seeming to retract into itself as it drew closer until its blind, bloody eyes were only a few inches away from mine.

"You're the bad man," it said, its voice now a low growl of menace.

No five year-old kid had ever sounded like that.

I tried to fight it but astral bodies aren't physical and my size and relative strength made no difference whatsoever. Astrally, this dead little kid was a lot stronger than I was. Or whatever was *pretending* to be this dead little kid, anyway. I still didn't believe this really was Danny McRoth's grandson, but at that precise moment it was a bit fucking academic.

Whatever this horror was, it was choking the life out of me and I had no Burned Man to help me.

I spun helplessly in the air, the apparition now on top of me. In my astral form I had no actual throat, of course, and no need to breathe anyway, but that didn't seem to matter. It was all just symbolism and it was killing me one way or another, I was all too aware of that. I couldn't banish it – on the astral plane we were both spirits, so where would I have banished it *to?*

I did the only thing I could think of.

I pulled on my silver cord and dived for my body. The ghost and I both plummeted through the roof of the house. I could see myself thrashing helplessly on the bed, my mouth locked open in what looked like a silent shriek of agony. Menhit was still bent over me, holding my head with one hand while Trixie and Mazin held me down between them. Did I really want to go back into that body? No, I really didn't, but the child was clawing at me now, spitting with murderous hatred, and I knew it was only a matter of minutes before it finished me. Fuck it, I didn't have any choice. I'd just have to.

I dropped back into my body and the agony hit me like a freight train. I was suddenly staring up into Menhit's broad, flat face, her pitiless eyes looking down at me. It felt like every bone in my body was being stretched until it cracked and split, the joints screaming and tearing. My back arched and one foot came free of Mazin's grip. I kicked him full in the face, unable to stop myself. Trixie threw herself across me and pinned me to the bed. Something tore in my back and my vision greyed out with pain. I screamed like an animal being butchered alive.

I didn't know where the ghostly child had gone and I didn't care. I couldn't think. I couldn't see, I couldn't breathe. I couldn't *stand* it, simple as that.

Whatever Menhit's brand of primitive healing was, she was going to end up killing me at this rate. My eyes were actually bulging in my head, the pain was so excruciating. I bit into my tongue and my mouth filled with hot blood, choking me. Somewhere in the back of my mind I could hear the Burned Man howling. I'd never heard *that* before.

That's how bad it was.

I blubbered and sobbed, bloody spittle frothing on my lips and tears streaming down my cheeks. I pissed myself, and I screamed until my throat bled.

And suddenly it stopped.

Menhit lifted her hand from my forehead and straightened up, and I collapsed onto my back, gasping and sobbing. Trixie got off me and went to see to Mazin who was nursing a nosebleed from where I had kicked him. I gradually got my breathing under control and did a mental damage assessment. Now that the agony had stopped I actually seemed to be in pretty fair shape, all things considered. My bones had stopped aching at least, and my stomach wasn't cramping any more. The fever had gone too, and if anything I was feeling a bit chilly lying there in nothing but my piss-sodden boxers. I had a suspicion I'd just gone through a month's worth of withdrawal compressed into a handful of minutes. I didn't actually know how long it had been since she started but it couldn't have been more than a quarter of an hour at the most.

"The poison has worked its way out of his system now," Menhit said.

"Thank you, Mother," Trixie said.

She left Mazin holding a handkerchief to his face and stood to give Menhit a short bow. I blinked and shuffled backwards out of the soggy patch until I was sitting up against the pillows.

"Yeah," I croaked, trying to work some bloody spit around

my mouth. "Thank you. Mother, I mean."

Menhit nodded.

"Be more careful in future, my Keeper," she said. "I should hate to find you had been poisoned again."

She hadn't said anything about it but there was something in her tone, something in the flash of her eye, that made me suspect that perhaps she hadn't fallen for Trixie and Mazin's carefully phrased explanation after all. I wondered if the healing had really needed to hurt as much as it had, or if that had been her idea of teaching me a lesson. I didn't know but it wouldn't have surprised me one little bit.

Menhit was no one's fool, after all.

"I understand, Mother," I said, and she gave me a cold smile that made me shudder.

Oh yeah, we understood each other, didn't we? That smile said that if I went back on the smack she would fucking crucify me. Literally, I imagined.

I sighed and looked at Mazin.

"Sorry about that, mate," I said. "I wasn't myself for a bit there, I'm afraid."

"There is no need to apologize, Lord Keeper," Mazin said, wiping his nose again with the bloody hanky. "I am just glad to see you returned to us."

I nodded. *I* was fucking glad to be returned to the civilized world, I have to say. I'd done smack before, when the Burned Man was training me, but these last six months had been my first real exposure to the proper junkie lifestyle. It was utter shit, believe you me.

Never again, I told myself, and I meant it.

The best thing, the most *wonderful* thing, was that I didn't even want to. Menhit must have done more than just rush me through withdrawal, as I knew damn well that a lot of junkies kept relapsing however many times they went cold turkey. The need never really went away, so I gathered, except it seemed like mine had. I can quite honestly say that if Mazin had put a bag of gear and a set of works in front of me right then I'd have thrown it at him. That's what a goddess can do when she wants to. I just hoped that it was going to last.

It *was* going to last, I promised myself. Never again. Now I'm not always great at keeping promises, I'll grant you, but I meant this one.

I sighed. That meant I had no fucking excuses now though, didn't it?

Menhit had cured me. She had taken away my addiction in a few short minutes of blinding agony, and in doing so she had taken away my last hiding place. Without the drugs to hide behind any more there I was, exposed in all my pitiful cowardice and weakness. With nowhere left to hide, I had no option but to face myself.

I knew I had to face up to what I had done, stop wallowing in self-pity and take some responsibility for once.

Whichever way I looked at it, it was time to start putting my life in order.

They let me go and have a lovely long shower after that, and generally clean myself up a bit. I still had the fucking awful beard and straggly long hair I'd grown while I was living like a feral animal but at least now it was a *clean* fucking awful beard. That was something, I supposed. I rubbed my hair with a towel and wrapped another one around my waist and was about to leave the bathroom when I realized I could hear raised voices coming from the bedroom.

"...possibly let this happen?" Menhit was demanding.

"...apologize, Mother," I heard Trixie replying, only catching snatches through the closed door. "...a disagreement. I left the Keeper's side in a moment of anger... bound me away from him with an amulet... last half year to find him and… bindings broken but–"

"I don't care about your disagreement!" Menhit interrupted her, shouting now. "*My* Keeper, reduced to a crawling wretch enslaved to chemical poisons? What sort of Guardian *are* you, to allow this?"

There was a sharp crack. I winced as I realized Menhit had just hit Trixie. I wanted to storm in there but really, what the fuck could I do? This was like my mum and dad all over again, but my dad had only been an abusive cunt of an alcoholic. Menhit was a *goddess* for fucksake, a really bloody dangerous one. I hid in the bathroom and felt nine years old all over again, ashamed and scared and wanting to help my mum and knowing damn well there was absolutely nothing I could do about it.

"This will *never* happen again, do you understand me?" Menhit raged.

"Yes, Mother."

That was Trixie, obviously, and she sounded cowed. She sounded the same way she had when Adam had been bullying her, come to that. I remembered the way that arsehole had pushed her around, and that made my hands curl into fists. I *wasn't* nine years old any more. I was a grown man and a magician and I wasn't fucking having it. Not all over again I wasn't, goddess or no goddess. It didn't matter how scared I was of Menhit – I owed it to Trixie, and most of all I owed it to my poor mum.

All the same, I'd have to be bloody careful about this.

I opened the bathroom door and strolled into the bedroom like I hadn't heard any of it. Trixie was just getting up off the floor from where Menhit had obviously knocked her down, but I made myself pretend not to notice that. I pretended not to notice the ugly red mark on her face, either, just the same as I had always pretended not to notice Mum's frequent black eyes and split lips. There were only so many doors a woman could walk into, after all, only so many times she could fall down the stairs. After a while it had been easier to just stop making her lie about where the bruises had come from. I was only nine years old, for fucksake. Whatever you may think of me now, please forgive a scared little boy for that, at least.

"That feels better," I announced, as cheerfully as I could manage. "I still look like a bloody tramp though. Trixie, I know you don't want to let me out of your sight but now I'm healed is there any chance you could take me to see a barber?"

"Have someone call here," Menhit said. "One does not go to service people, Keeper. They come to us."

"Um, OK," I said. "That costs more though and I'm afraid I, um… well, I'm sorry Mother but I don't have any money. None at all."

"Don't be ridiculous," Menhit snapped. "Talk to Mazin, he will arrange whatever you need. That's what he's *for*. Now that you are healed, Keeper, I expect you to take your people in hand. There have been shortcomings that must be addressed, and I may have need of you soon. All of you."

I saw her give Trixie an icy look, but I ignored it.

"Yes, Mother," I said, bowing my head to hide the look on my face.

One does not go to service people. Oh, doesn't one? For fucksake. She must be driving poor Papa Armand round the bend by now.

"I must leave," Menhit said. "I am expected back in London and the aeroplane will be waiting for me. Put your house in order, Keeper, and await my summons."

With that, she swept out of the room. I watched through the bedroom doorway as she was greeted by two men I hadn't even realized were in the flat, big black men in expensive looking suits. They radiated danger in a way that said "mercenaries" loud and clear. Where the bloody hell had she got them from? They both bowed to her and escorted her towards the hall, out of sight. The plane would be waiting for *her*, I noted. Jesus wept.

I waited until I heard the front door open and close with a heavy thump that spoke of steel reinforcement, then turned to Trixie.

"Bloody hell," I said. "What the fuck have we got ourselves into with her?"

"You've only had a few days of her in total," Trixie said. "I have had the pleasure of her company for the last six *fucking* months."

I blinked in surprise. Trixie hardly ever swore. She put a hand to her face and covered the red welt with her palm.

"Jesus, I'm sorry Trixie," I said. "I am so, so sorry. About Menhit, and… and about everything."

I knew that was lame but what else could I say to her, really? She wasn't my mum, she was a Sword of the Word for fucksake. She could stand up for herself, I knew that. But she hadn't, had she?

"Even Armand was close to the end of his tether before she left him," Trixie said. "She got herself banned from Wormwood's club months ago, and Armand and I were almost banned along with her just for being in her company. Wormwood was absolutely furious."

"What the hell did she do?"

Wormwood was quick enough to kick out people he didn't like, but Papa Armand was one of his best customers, after all. He was so rich that Wormwood practically let him have the run of the place so long as he kept spending money.

"She killed a waiter."

"She did *what*?"

"With her bare hands," Trixie said. "He brought her the wrong drink, something she didn't like, so she tore him in half and pulled his spine out through his stomach. Literally."

"Fucking hell!"

"Yes, quite," Trixie said. "It was… very unpleasant to watch."

There was no way Wormwood could have overlooked that, whoever she was. I was just grateful that none of his staff were human. Trixie had killed a good number of demons herself over the centuries, of course, and if *she* was saying this had been unpleasant then… yeah. I swallowed, and tried not to think about it.

"She moved out of Armand's apartment shortly afterwards," Trixie went on, "and I think by then he was pleased to see her go. She's installed herself in a mansion in Surrey now, surrounded by these new hired bodyguards she has acquired."

"Oh," I said. "Right."

Menhit had left Papa Armand, then. That was probably for the best, all things considered. If she had been doing things like that then I doubted he was missing her.

"Why, Don?" Trixie demanded suddenly.

Her hand fell away from her face and I saw that the mark was already fading. She did heal very quickly, I reminded myself, not that that made it any better or gave Menhit any right to hit her in the first place.

"Um," I said.

I sat down on the edge of the bed and put my head in my hands. What the bloody hell could I say to her? I could hardly tell her the truth, after all. I had run away because I was scared that I would hurt her. Her, a Sword of the Word?

Trixie was basically an angel of death, and *I* was scared I'd hurt *her*?

Yeah, that'd go down fucking well. Of course when I say "I", what I really mean is the Burned Man, but that was academic really.

"I was scared," I admitted at last.

That was true enough. I remembered the flames roaring up out of my hands, the snarl on my lips, but I also remembered her smashing my desk in two with the flat of her hand. I remembered my office windows exploding into the street all by themselves as she screamed with rage. Yeah, one of us would have certainly ended up hurt all right, but I had to admit that it might well have been me. Even the Burned Man respected Trixie, after all, and sometimes I got the distinct impression it was a little bit scared of her too.

Which was hardly surprising really – I knew *I* was. I had to confess to myself that I was very scared of Trixie for all that I loved her, and of course *that* had really been why I had run away, whatever I'd been telling myself all these months. I sighed. That still wasn't right, was it? I mean yes, I was scared of what she might do, of course I was, but most of all I was scared of what she might think of me.

"Scared," Trixie echoed. "You were scared. Don, you'd had the Burned Man inside you for *weeks* by the time I found out about it. Plenty of time to get used to the idea, I would have thought. How was that reason enough for you to leave me? To run away into the night and leave me alone with that... that harridan?"

I wasn't sure I was used to the idea *now* to be honest, but that was irrelevant. She had completely missed the point.

"Trixie," I said slowly, "I was scared of *you*."

She stared at me.

"Oh," she said at last.

Now that I'd said it out loud I knew it was true. I mean yeah, there *was* a chance the Burned Man might go for her in a fit of rage but in the cold light of sobriety I realized it was actually a pretty slim one. The Burned Man was violent and vindictive and horribly powerful, but it wasn't exactly what you'd call brave. Trixie was a Sword of the Word, a soldier of

Heaven. Killing demons was what she was *for*, and it bloody well knew that. No, now that I really thought about it I had to admit that I didn't think the Burned Man would pick a fight with Trixie if it didn't have to.

I licked my lips. Jesus, I could be such a fucking coward sometimes.

"Yeah," I said, and put my head back in my hands.

She came and sat beside me on the bed, and put her arm around me. That was so nice I just sort of sagged against her, feeling all the pain and misery of the last six months well up all at once. I let her hold me while I tried not to cry like a baby.

She stroked my hair and sighed.

"I love you," she said. "You do know that, don't you?"

I pulled back and stared at her in open astonishment. No, no I fucking well *didn't* know that, actually.

I loved *her*, I knew that all too well and it wasn't so very long ago that I had made an utter arse of myself trying to prove it in bed one night. She had made it very plain indeed what she had thought of that, and other than one other time when she was basically going nuts after her Dominion fell, the subject had never come up again.

"Good God, do you?" I blurted like an idiot.

Trixie gave me a smile that was as close to shy as I think I'd ever seen her look.

"I think this is where you're supposed to say it back," she said.

"What?" Oh fucking hell I was on a roll today wasn't I? Move over Frank Sinatra, the real Mr Smooth just got into town. "Oh hell, oh Trixie of *course* I love you."

I hugged her again and tried to kiss her, but she turned away so I only got her cheek.

She cleared her throat.

"We aren't having another misunderstanding, are we?"

she said. "I *love* you, Don, but that's not the same as wanting to mate with you."

Mate with you. Jesus, she knew how to pour cold water on a mood didn't she? What a truly bloody awful expression that was. I sighed and forced myself to remember that not only was she not human, not only was English not even close to being her first language, she was also probably old enough to remember the pyramids being built. She was certainly old enough to be my great-grandmother about a hundred and fifty times over. At least.

"Um, yeah, sure," I said, and coughed. "Sorry. It was just a bit of a shock, that's all."

She smiled at me again.

"Of course I love you, we fought a Dominion together," she said. "You slew Bianakith to save me, and you damned yourself to do it. And we're both in this together with Menhit."

Well, we certainly seemed to be in it together with Menhit, but her other two points gave me pause. Adam had fought the Dominion with her too, and got himself sent back to Hell for his troubles. I had always thought she was a little bit in love with Adam, so I wasn't sure where that left *him* in this weird little triangle we seemed to have going on. And... I had damned myself, she said. That was exactly what I had been afraid of.

Diabolists go to Hell, Don.

I remembered Adam saying that to me all too well, but then he *would* say that, wouldn't he? Trixie made it sound like a certainty, like a foregone conclusion, and that was without her knowing that the Burned Man was slowly eating my soul as well. Maybe I still hadn't fully grasped just how much shit I had got myself into, and how hard it was going to be to climb out of it again.

I got up and walked over to the window, suddenly

embarrassed that I was still only wearing a towel. I stared out at the wide street below, at the elegant Georgian terrace across the road that was probably a mirror image of the one we were in at the moment. I was feeling horribly shut in all of a sudden. I could feel Trixie watching me.

"Are you all right?" she asked me.

"Yeah," I said. "I'm going to get dressed."

"I'll make coffee," she said.

She left the room and shut the door behind her, and I rested my forehead against the armoured glass of the window with a weary sigh. Nothing ever got simpler, did it?

CHAPTER 8

By the time I'd got some clothes on and wandered through to the kitchen Trixie had made coffee and was sitting at the table smoking one of her long black cigarettes. Mazin was with her, and he got up and bowed when I entered the room.

"Lord Keeper," he said.

"Mazin, mate," I said. "Enough with the bowing, all right? It's a bit weird and it's starting to get on my tits now."

"I apologize, Lord Keeper," he said.

He stood there looking awkward for a moment, then sat down again.

I took a third chair and pulled a cup of steaming black coffee gratefully towards me.

"Ta," I said.

Trixie shrugged and tapped the end of her cigarette into a heavy crystal ashtray.

Oh great, we were *all* being awkward. Every time Trixie and I tried to have any sort of heart-to-heart we ended up awkward instead. Why did this have to keep happening?

Fuck it. The atmosphere was uncomfortable now and not just on account of Trixie's smoke. I needed to talk about something. Anything.

"Look," I said after a moment, "who the bloody hell is paying for all this?"

"All what?" Trixie asked.

"Everything," I said, waving a hand vaguely at the apartment. "This place. The Mercedes. Menhit's fucking private plane. Even Papa Armand isn't *that* rich."

"No of course he isn't," Trixie said, "and no one would expect him to pay for this apartment anyway. This is for your benefit, Don."

"Well I know *I'm* not sodding paying for it," I said. "I haven't got a brass farthing."

Mazin cleared his throat as though asking permission to speak. I glanced at him and he inclined his head with a smile.

"My Lord, your predecessor founded my order in part to look after the financial interests of the Keeper. We have a long history as merchant traders and bankers, and these days we administer a modest hedge fund and have a wide portfolio of diversified investments whilst also maintaining a lively trade in commodity futures and–"

I waved him to silence. He might as well have started talking in Arabic for all I understood what any of those things even were.

"So we've got money?" I asked him.

His smile widened. "Yes, Lord Keeper, we have money."

"How much money, exactly?"

"It is, ah, hard to say at any given moment," he said. "The market fluctuates and futures especially have a largely speculative element, so–"

I waved again. The whole stockmarket thing had a largely bullshit element as far as I had ever been able to tell, but there we were. It seemed to work, after a fashion anyway, so what did I know?

"Are we in the realm of 'lots'?"

"At the last quarterly accounting the Order of the Keeper

had a net worth of seven hundred and eighty-four million American dollars," he said. "We are, if the Madam Guardian will pardon me, in the realm of 'shitloads'."

I gaped at him.

Wow.

I started to chuckle. I had to admit I rather liked Mazin, and the fact that he seemed to have just told me I was a multi-millionaire was making me like him a whole hell of a lot more.

Hang on a minute Don, I cautioned myself. *Your* job *is a multi-millionaire, not you. Don't get carried away.* I was right of course, and that brought me right back around to thinking about what this fucking job even was.

I may have need of you soon, Menhit had said. *Await my summons.*

Need of us for *what,* exactly? I dreaded to bloody think. She was a war goddess after all. Anything *she* needed us for was unlikely to be to do with flower arranging and kittens, that was for fucking sure.

"Mazin," I said, "what exactly do we do? The Order of the Keeper, I mean. What's it *for*?"

"You should read the book," Trixie said.

I remembered Mazin giving her this mysterious book just before Adam had shown up and spoiled everything and I had had to run away. I'd never even had the chance to open it, of course, but I knew Trixie would have read it cover to cover several times by now.

"Yeah I really should," I said. "Have you got it with you?"

"No," she said, and it seemed that was all she was going to say on the subject.

"Right, OK," I said, rubbing my temples with my fingertips. "That's helpful. Mazin, you have a go. Simple question – what do we do?"

He shrugged. "Anything the Mother asks us to," he said.

"I don't really know any more, other than that. For as long as our written history goes back, the order has assisted your predecessor the Lord Rashid in maintaining his work and keeping it secure, to keep the Mother safe beyond her Veil. Since your predecessor's sudden demise and the Mother's decision to rejoin us on this plane we have been at, ah, something of a loss. I look to you for direction now, Lord Keeper."

Oh fucking hell, do you?

"Right," I said.

I wondered how much Mazin actually knew about my predecessor's "sudden demise", and whether he had the faintest idea that Menhit had murdered Rashid herself. Or that Menhit's supposed "decision" to come back to Earth had been nothing of the sort, and that she had actually been forcibly dragged here by the schemes of a fallen Dominion. I looked Mazin in the eye and decided that no, no he hadn't got a fucking clue.

Of course he hasn't, I thought. *That would have made this easier, and nothing's ever fucking easy is it?*

"Right," I said again. "Direction, right. Well all right then, first thing – giving Menhit whatever she wants sounds like a bloody good idea. So long as she doesn't want to buy a fucking aircraft carrier we can probably afford it."

"Yes," Mazin said, and from the earnest look on his face I could see that the poor bastard was being completely serious.

"I doubt she wants an aircraft carrier, mate," I said. "Don't worry about it. I shouldn't think she even knows what one is."

"I wouldn't bet on it," Trixie said. "She has had six months to become accustomed to the modern world, and she's no fool."

"No, no of course she's not," I said.

That made me think, of course. I had actually only met

Menhit a couple of times before today, both times very shortly after her return to Earth. She had been scary as fuck and a royal pain in the arse even then, but she had also still been half dead from culture shock. Things didn't work like they had in bronze age Nubia any more, to put it bloody mildly. Still, if she had really had enough time to adjust, and by now I supposed she probably had, then that meant she was going to be even more of a walking nightmare than before. Poor Trixie had probably had one hell of a six months with her.

"Do we actually *know* what she wants?" I asked. "I mean, why is she even still here?"

"I have no idea," Trixie said. "Menhit has never really confided in me, I'm afraid. I don't think I'm worthy of her confidence, in her eyes anyway. She didn't even see fit to tell me that she intended to come here in person."

In a private fucking plane no less, the Burned Man thought at me. *Her ladyship doesn't do things by halves, does she?*

I almost jumped out of my seat. It hadn't said a word since I had returned from my involuntary astral projection and I had almost managed to forget the bloody thing was there.

Doesn't look like it, no, I replied.

Who the fuck charters a private plane just to get from London to bloody Edinburgh?

A goddess does, I thought.

It was silent for a moment.

Fair point, it conceded.

"She, um…" I said, darting a sideways look at Mazin, "she seemed to bring some opinions with her, too."

"Yes," Trixie said, and I noticed how her fingertips brushed her cheek as she said it.

The mark was almost gone now but she obviously hadn't forgotten about it.

She belted Blondie, didn't she? the Burned Man sniggered. *I like her already.*

No you don't, I reminded it, and I could feel it mentally shrug.

She's growing on me, it said.

I sighed. I supposed she probably was, at that. The Burned Man was a contrary little bastard at the best of times. It wouldn't have surprised me to discover that Menhit was exactly its type.

"Right, well," I said, and scrubbed my hands back through my horrible long hair. "What about that barber? I'm sick of looking like a bloody tramp."

"I can arrange to have someone suitable visit here, Lord Keeper," Mazin said at once, as though he'd been prepped for the question.

He probably had been, knowing Trixie.

"Ta," I said.

I wanted to get out of the apartment really, but only because I was feeling shut in and the whole place stank of Russian tobacco. No air conditioning system could cope with the amount of fags Trixie smoked when she was bored. No other reason. I wasn't looking to score or anything.

I *wasn't.*

You sure about that? the Burned Man asked me.

Fucking positive, I said. I knew the Burned Man wasn't at all keen on me doing smack, and I also knew it hadn't enjoyed Menhit's idea of healing any more than I had. I considered my options for a moment, and made a decision.

I'll make a deal with you, I said. *If you catch me trying to buy any more of that shit, stop me. Hurt me if you have to.*

Can I? it asked, a little bit too eagerly for my liking.

Yes, I said. *Just don't let me do it.*

I could almost feel it smile.

Deal, it said.

Right, good. That was that then. I knew damn well the

Burned Man would keep up its end of *that* deal if only out of spite. I told myself it was worth it in the long run and swallowed the end of my cooling coffee.

Trixie stood up and stretched.

"I'm going to take a bath," she announced, and strode from the room.

I waited for her to retire to her own bedroom before I leaned towards Mazin across the table.

"I need you to do something for me," I said quietly.

Trixie had hearing like a bloody bat, and I didn't want her hearing this.

"Of course, Lord Keeper," he said. "I will telephone for a barber at once."

"Not that," I said. "Well yeah, do that as well. This fucking beard is driving me nuts. There's something else though. I need you and your boys to find someone for me. Can you do that?"

He smiled and spread his hands.

"Of course," he said again.

When I had had something to eat and the barber had been and gone I had another long hot shower just because I could, then stood and admired myself in the mirror. Well I say admired but I suppose there was little enough to take pride in really. I've always been a fairly ordinary looking bloke but I must have lost at least thirty pounds while I had been living rough, and I hadn't exactly been fat to start with. I could see every one of my bloody ribs, and my left arm was a mess of needle tracks. I could only hope they would heal up with time, or I wouldn't be wearing T-shirts in public again.

At least I looked like myself now and not like some horrible homeless junkie. I was clean shaven and my hair had been cut so that I was able to comb it into some semblance of tidiness for once. I have this awful habit of pushing my hands back through it when I'm thinking so it never stayed tidy for very long but at least it was out of my eyes now. I'd take that.

"God, that's better," I said to myself.

"Yes, it is," Trixie said from behind me. "A lot better."

I was stark bollock naked, and suddenly finding her in the bathroom with me was something of a shock.

"Um," I said, keeping my back to her. "I, um, did you need something?"

"No, I'm fine," she said, and turned and strolled out of the room again.

Well that was bloody embarrassing. I just wished I knew where I stood with her. She loved me but she didn't want to shag me, apparently. Did that just mean she was chaste or did she mean she loved me like a brother? Like a son? Or, given that she was well over two thousand years old, like a great-great-great-God-knows-how-many-times-over-grandson? I really had no fucking idea.

Trixie was *weird*, there was no other way of putting it. I mean, don't get me wrong, I loved her and I bloody well wanted to shag *her,* but then I always had done. Fat lot of good that had done me so far.

Do you reckon Adam's had her? the Burned Man asked.

No he fucking hasn't, I snapped at it without thinking.

I mean, in all honesty I had no idea, but I doubted it somehow. I just really couldn't see Trixie going in for sex, however sexy she might be. The Burned Man sniggered in my head and I realized the bloody thing was winding me up. It must be getting bored.

Stop taking the piss and make yourself useful, I told it. *What the bloody hell is Menhit up to? She killed the Dominion so why hasn't she fucked off home again if she likes it there so much?*

Who killed a Dominion? the Burned Man asked. *That'd be*

quite some fucking achievement, believe you me. No, it fell and when she defeated it in combat she cast it down into Hell the same way that it cast down Adam, but no one's been killing any Dominions around here. I don't even know if that can be done on this plane, and even if it can be she hasn't fucking done it.

I blinked. Well, that was interesting. If by "interesting" I meant bloody horrifying, I supposed. So that awful fucking thing was still alive down there somewhere in Hell?

Oh joy.

This just kept on getting better. I sighed and pushed my hands back through my hair, messing it up already. Oh what the hell did it matter what my sodding hair looked like? I padded naked into the bedroom and put some clean clothes on, then wandered through to the living room. Trixie was standing by the windows smoking, and she looked lost in thought. I tiptoed back out of the room to the kitchen where Mazin was talking quietly on his phone.

"Put everyone on it," he was saying. "The Lord Keeper's express request. Yes, spend money you fool, that's what it's there for. I don't care what it costs, grease some palms. Don't disappoint me."

He touched the screen to hang up and put the phone back in his pocket, and bowed to me.

"It is in progress, Lord Keeper," he said.

I nodded. "Ta," I said.

I was going to pull him up on the bowing again but I just couldn't be arsed. If it made him happy then I supposed it wasn't hurting anyone.

You're getting to like it, aren't you? the Burned Man said.

I ignored it and put the kettle on. If I wasn't too up myself to make my own coffee then I wasn't going to let some bowing go to my head.

"There is coffee in the machine, Lord Keeper," Mazin said.

I blinked and realized that the filter machine had a jug full of fresh black coffee sitting in it waiting for me. It stank of Trixie's fags so badly in there I hadn't even smelled it.

"Right, thanks," I said, turning the kettle off again.

No, you're not too up yourself to make your own coffee but then you don't have to when you've got bowing flunkies to do it for you, the Burned Man sniggered.

Sometimes I really couldn't figure the Burned Man out. I remembered it complaining about how we were still poor and stuck in South London when in its opinion we should have been living in Monte Carlo, but now that we actually *were* rich all it seemed to want to do was take the piss.

What is your problem? I thought at it. *You do realize we've finally got everything you've been bitching at me to get for all these years, yeah?*

Have we? it said. *Go on then, go out and buy a fucking Bentley if you think you can actually get your hands on any of that cash. You liked that one you nicked off Gold Steevie, didn't you? So why not get one for yourself?*

I looked at Mazin, and paused for a moment. The Order of the Keeper was seriously minted by the sounds of things, but I still didn't even really know what that was, never mind how to actually get at any of the money. Mazin obviously held the purse strings, and for all that he technically worked for me I somehow couldn't see him giving me two hundred grand to go out and blow on a motor. Maybe it was time to start testing the waters.

"I could do with some new clothes," I said. "There's a Harvey Nicks round here somewhere, that'll do. Do I get a credit card or something?"

Mazin blinked at me.

"I can have a tailor call here, Lord Keeper," he said. "No need to trouble yourself."

"I quite like shopping," I lied. I mean obviously I fucking hate shopping, but he didn't need to know that. "I don't mind going myself."

"Service people come to us, Lord Keeper," he said with a small smile. "We do not go to them."

Yeah, so her ladyship said, the Burned Man said.

"Fair enough," I said. "Look, how about if I want to go for a drive? I haven't even got a motor any more. I quite fancy getting a–"

"I would be honoured to drive you in the Maybach," he interrupted, and unless I was mistaken I thought I could detect a slightly terse edge to his voice.

"Thanks, but what if you're not here? Can I borrow the keys?"

"If I am away on business I will be in the car," he pointed out. "Another car and driver can easily be arranged if you require them."

Right, that was me told then, in a very polite but firm sort of way. I was starting to realize that the Burned Man was right. However much money there might be, it certainly wasn't *my* money. In fact it looked like I wasn't going to get a hell of a lot of freedom at all.

Still, I supposed I could hardly blame Mazin. He was the head of this Order of the Keeper so he had probably been in Rashid's service for a long time, quite possibly all his life in fact, and then suddenly Rashid was dead and *I* was his boss. I was a total stranger to him, and a very recently reformed junkie at that. No, I supposed in his position I wouldn't be giving me piles of cash either.

"Cheers," I said, as though I had just been making conversation. "A tailor would be good."

I supposed that if I could get some new suits out of the deal if nothing else then that would at least be an improvement on the nondescript shirts and trousers that had been provided for me in the apartment. I had noticed that there was no coat and not even a jacket in the wardrobe in my room. It

was as though it had been taken for granted that I wouldn't
be going outside any time soon.

They can't keep us locked up forever, I thought. *Not when
Menhit wants us for something.*

Yeah, but for what? the Burned Man asked.

Now that, of course, was a fucking good question.

CHAPTER 9

I put up with it for another six days before I finally lost my shit at Mazin.

"Enough!" I yelled at him. "I'm fucking going out. I'm bored out of my fucking skull shut up in this sodding flat, and the air in here is thick enough to gag a fucking vulture. Get out of my way!"

I was wearing one of the gorgeous new suits his tailor had delivered yesterday. The bloke must have been working around the clock, but I dare say Mazin had made it worth his while. I had a very nice new black cashmere overcoat on as well – I was all dressed up and I sodding well *did* have somewhere to go, actually.

It was called the pub.

Any pub, I didn't care. Being the multi-millionaire Lord Keeper of the Veil had turned out to be a bag of fucking shit so far, and I had simply had enough of it. Menhit still hadn't got back in touch and I was starting to feel like a prisoner, kept on ice until I was wanted. I simply wasn't having it any more.

Mazin was standing between me and the front door. He was trying to look tough, but he was shit at it and he couldn't hide the nervous expression on his face. He knew what I could do, or he must have had a rough idea anyway. That, and even if he didn't exactly respect *me* he at least respected the office I held. All the same, he obviously had his orders. I felt a bit bad for the poor bastard, but only a little bit. One way or another I was going out of that door if I had to go straight fucking through him to get there.

"It's all right, Mazin," Trixie said from behind me. "I will accompany the Lord Keeper."

Mazin visibly relaxed as Trixie walked towards us wearing her long leather coat over jeans and a white jumper.

"Very well, Madam Guardian," he said.

"Right," I said, looking at her. "Yeah, ta."

I have to admit I was a bit surprised. I wasn't sure if she was just trying to keep the peace or if she was feeling cooped up as well, but I was bloody livid that he was taking her authority over mine. *I* was supposed to be the boss here, after all.

Well no, I supposed that wasn't quite right, to be fair. When Rashid had been the Keeper he had been Boss Almighty over these guys, but then for one thing Rashid had been a magic immortal and for another Menhit had been little more than a legend to them. They had followed their goddess through blind faith and the power of Rashid's money and influence rather than any real evidence of her actual existence. Now that Rashid was dead and Menhit was very much alive and right there in front of them the whole chain of command seemed to have gone to shit.

Menhit herself was the boss here now, and I had no idea what she might have told them about me. All the same, if Mazin was prepared to let me out with Trixie holding my hand then I'd take that. I really didn't want to have to hurt the poor guy but I *was* going, one way or another. A man can only take so much, after all.

He stood aside and finally opened the hallowed front door. That thing had taken on an almost mystical importance to me, like it was a portal to another world. I supposed in a way that's exactly what it was – a portal to the *real* world, away from the constant fear and batshit craziness and endless tedium that being part of a goddess's entourage seemed to entail.

I let Trixie lead me out onto the landing and down three flights of broad, curving stairs to the ground floor lobby. We reached the outside door and she turned and looked at me.

"Don, what exactly are we doing?" she asked me.

"I dunno," I said. "I just had to get out of there for a bit. I mean don't get me wrong, I like Mazin, but there's only so much bowing and scraping I can take. I want a pint and a game of cards and a bit of banter with someone, anyone. I want to be *alive* again, you know what I mean?"

I hadn't really meant to say that last bit but now that I had I knew it was true. I had been a walking corpse for six months and since then it was like I had been embalmed or something, preserved in extremely expensive aspic. I wanted to *live*.

"Yes," Trixie said, surprising me. "I do know what you mean. I've been very bored cooped up in there."

"Shit yeah, me too," I said. "How about we go and have a few beers somewhere and just… I dunno. Live."

She smiled at me and reached into her handbag. She pulled out a fat roll of notes, probably a couple of grand at least, and pressed it into my hand.

"You'll need this," she said. "I don't mind paying at all but ladies don't go to the bar, remember?"

I grinned and stuffed the money into my inside pocket. I'd never get my head around that but if she didn't want to go to the bar that was up to her. I brushed my fingertips one more time over the thick roll of cash and wondered how much smack that would buy. I wondered, but only in an academic sense. I was about ready to murder someone for a beer but I had no interest in heroin at all. Damn, Menhit's healing might have nearly killed me but it had fucking well worked, I had to give her that much.

Don't forget our deal, the Burned Man said. *If you go near that shit again I fucking* will *hurt you, I mean it. I have your permission to now, Drake, and I'll use it the first chance I get.*

I ignored it. I *wasn't* going near that shit again and that's all there was to it. All the same, I supposed I had to admire the Burned Man's honesty. It was normally incapable of directly hurting its owner, I knew that, but then I *had* given it permission in that specific situation. I took a moment to wonder what being hurt by the Burned Man might actually entail, and quickly wished I hadn't. It didn't really bear thinking about, which I supposed was the whole point of the exercise.

"Come on then," I said to Trixie, "let's go get a beer or ten."

She pressed the button to unlock the front door of the building and we stepped outside into blessedly fresh air. Edinburgh air actually *is* fresh, unlike London air. I don't know if it's because the city is so close to the sea or just because the wind is so fucking strong it blows the pollution away before you notice it, but there's a cleanness to the air there. A bitingly cold, painfully damp cleanness, but a cleanness all the same. After God only knew how long cooped up in that dry fug of central air and Trixie's cigarette smoke it was like smelling heaven.

"Bloody hell that's marvellous," I said, taking a deep breath.

"What is?" Trixie asked me.

"Just being outside," I said.

I knew part of that was the Burned Man talking. It

had been imprisoned in the fetish for thousands of years after all, no doubt being moved from one magician's dark, smoky workroom to another over and over again down the centuries. I remembered how good it had felt just to be outside the day after I had invoked it, before I even knew what had happened. Being shut up in Mazin's hermetically sealed apartment had been starting to make me feel the same way.

Bloody hell am I seriously starting to sympathise with the Burned Man? I wondered. *That can't be good.*

No it probably wasn't, but then nor were a lot of other things. Fuck it, so what?

"Buy a girl a drink?" Trixie prompted with a smile.

I shook my head and blinked. Shit, yeah, we were going to the pub weren't we? I had just been standing on the front steps of the house, breathing. Sometimes it was all too easy to get lost in my own thoughts, or the Burned Man's. I'd have felt a lot more comfortable if I had still been able to tell them apart but I'm afraid that wasn't always the case any more.

"I'd love to," I said, and I really meant it.

I was, if truth be told, a bit pissed. The pub wasn't that far away from our apartment but Edinburgh's New Town all looks very much the same, a grid pattern of lots of great sweeping Georgian terraces all built of the same grey stone and broken up by endless little green parks surrounded by identical rows of black iron railings. I wasn't too sure I could have found my way back on my own by that point.

Still, I didn't have to care about that just then. I returned to our table with another pint and gin and tonic, on a tray this time with four whisky chasers for good measure. I unloaded the mismatched glasses in front of Trixie and grinned at her.

"I thought we weren't doing chasers?" she said.

Of course what she meant by that was she thought I *shouldn't* be doing chasers. However much Trixie drank she never seemed to get drunk, more was the pity, but I really did. I shrugged and winked at her.

"In for a penny," I said, and necked my first whisky.

She shrugged and did the same.

"If you say so," she said.

We drank in companionable silence. I wanted to talk but I had no idea what to say to her. Everything was so mixed up in my head I couldn't even get my own thoughts straight, never mind express them in a way that approached coherent. I wanted to know what the hell Menhit expected me to do for her. I wanted to know what Mazin was hiding and why he wouldn't let me near the money, and I wanted to know what was in that book he had given Trixie. I wanted... oh fuck it let's be honest, what I *really* wanted to know was exactly what Trixie had meant when she said she loved me.

I took a pull on my beer and had just about worked up the nerve to ask her when two men walked into the pub. There was nothing odd about that in itself, I grant you – we were in the heart of the New Town and the pub was busy, with people coming and going all the time. Only these two blokes were a little bit special.

"Oh shit," I whispered.

Trixie raised an eyebrow at me but she had more than enough experience to know not to look around.

"Two geezers with dark red auras just came in," I said in a low voice.

"I'm sorry?" she murmured, leaning towards me to reach for her second whisky. "Did you say *red* auras?"

"Yeah," I said, and sat casually back in my chair to keep an eye on them. "Yeah, I did."

Now as I might have said before, everyone's aura is a sort of dull, fuzzy blue. Everyone *human* that is. Trixie's wasn't of course; Trixie's was a dazzling white that was a pack of fucking lies, but then Trixie wasn't human. Nor was I entirely these days, come to that, although I knew the Burned Man kept itself well hidden. And if I knew my arse from my elbow, these two blokes weren't either. Not even a little bit.

They were both tall and fair haired, one in jeans and a leather bomber jacket and the other in a long black overcoat. They were both wearing sunglasses though, and that jogged my memory. The only time I'd ever seen a red aura before had been on a bloke called Antonio who I had fleeced at cards one night last year in Wormwood's club. I never had found out exactly what he was, but I remembered his aura and that his eyes had also had a dull red glow to them. That and he'd been shit at Fates and had accused me of cheating, which had led to him being thrown out of the club in short order. Still, that was beside the point – the point was, whatever he had been I'd have put good money on this pair of jokers being the same thing.

I sipped my beer as nonchalantly as I could and watched them head to the bar, both still rather conspicuously wearing their sunglasses. They each bought a pint of lager and turned to stand with their backs to the bar, holding their beers and not drinking them as their heads slowly turned left and right, scanning the room.

Trixie's foot nudged mine under the table and I glanced at her.

"They look like they're hunting," she murmured, "Probably for us, although I don't understand why they can't see my aura."

Oh how nice to be able to just *assume* we were the ones being hunted for. I was well and truly back in the life now, wasn't I?

All the same, I knew she was almost certainly right. I felt

that now-familiar nudge in the back of my head that meant the Burned Man had mentally shoved past and started talking for me.

"They can't see your bullshit fake aura because I'm hiding it, the same way I hide mine to make numbnuts here look like he's still as normal as he gets," it whispered in my voice. "And I've put a glamour on you to make you look a bit less… you. All the same Blondie, you might want to get ready for a scrap. They're bound to twig sooner or later."

Trixie's mouth twisted in distaste at hearing the Burned Man speak through me, but at the same time I couldn't miss the sudden glint in her eye at the prospect of a fight. She really had been as bored as I had, shut up in that apartment, and I knew how much she enjoyed her work. Well, the violent parts of it anyway. She really is a fucking case, bless her.

"Mmmm," she said.

I looked at her and saw the Burned Man was right. I can see straight through glamours so I hadn't noticed before but now that I was looking for it I could see it well enough, and I knew that was what everyone else would be seeing whether they liked it or not. Her hair was a couple of shades less blonde, almost mousy in fact, her eyes now a pale, watery blue instead of their usual piercing sapphire, and it had made her figure appear a little less, shall we say, conspicuous than usual. I still thought she was gorgeous, though. I really did love her, I have to admit.

There was a group of lads a couple of tables away from us, builders or plumbers or something by the look of their work clothes, and for all that it was only mid-afternoon they were quite noisily pissed. A bunch of pissed-up Scottish lads in the same pub as two blokes who wore sunglasses indoors was never going to end well, was it?

It didn't.

"…think he's in the fucking *Matrix*?" I heard one of them

laugh, his voice getting louder as the one in the overcoat turned to stare at him. "Tae the fuckin' blue pill and fuck off, y'wanker!"

"Oh dear," Trixie said. "That might not have been entirely wise."

She really did have the gift of understatement sometimes.

The bloke in the bomber jacket was beside their table in three long strides, the pint glass falling from his hand to shatter on the hardwood floor in a fountain of unwanted lager and broken glass. The landlord bawled something unintelligible but by then it was far too late. Oh dear, we were all taking the red pill, weren't we?

Bomber jacket reached across the table and grabbed the one who had shouted by the throat, yanking him bodily out of his chair. He hauled him over the table, scattering drinks in all directions, and pulled him up into a vicious punch that sent him flying back the way he had come until his head met the wall with a solid thunk.

All hell broke loose.

The rest of the lads, five or six of them, reared up with glasses and bottles in their hands, and the other red-aura bloke in the overcoat waded in to join his mate. Someone screamed and I heard someone else shouting about calling the police.

"Oh fuck this," I said.

"Yes," Trixie said, and stood up.

Now I must admit when I'd said "oh fuck this," I'd meant "let's leg it while we've got the chance," but of course Trixie meant "oh good, let's have a huge conspicuous fight," so that was that down the shitter then. She was over the table before I could stop her, the Burned Man's glamour shredding away from her as she went into action.

Oh bugger, I thought.

Fuck it, she's gone, the Burned Man muttered. *I can't hide her if she's going to do this sort of shit in front of people. There are limits, even for me.*

Trixie flowed between the Scottish lads like they weren't even there and shoved the two red-aura geezers backwards with a hand on each chest.

"Looking for me?" she asked, her own aura blazing white and a smile of fierce joy on her face.

At least she hadn't produced her fucking sword, I supposed there was that to be thankful for. This place was full of civilians, after all. One of the lads tried to come past her with a broken bottle in his hand.

"You're all right love, let the boys sort it–"

Trixie back-elbowed him in the face without even looking, dropping him on his arse in a puddle of spilled beer.

I necked my other whisky and got up.

"Leave us to it, boys," I said. "The grownups are talking now."

They looked at me and I felt the Burned Man allow a few wisps of smoke to curl up from my fingertips. The lads backed away, muttering, then turned and fled. People were streaming out of the pub all around me now and I could hear the landlord on the phone to the police.

Trixie was facing down the two mysterious hunters, her hands held low but ready. Whatever they were, she was obviously confident she could take them on unarmed if she had to.

She's always confident, the Burned Man sniggered. *Proud, you might even call it.*

Shut up, I thought, but I knew it was right.

Overconfidence had bitten Trixie in the arse once before, after all, and the end result of that had been fucking catastrophic. It had for me, anyway. That was how I had ended up possessed by the sodding Burned Man in the first place.

"Blade of Heaven," one of hunters said, the one in the overcoat.

"You know me," Trixie said. "I don't know you."

"We are soldiers of the Fallen," bomber jacket growled. "You can call me Mikael if you must have a name, bitch."

"And you can call me *ma'am*," Trixie snarled as she pivoted on one foot and kicked him so hard he flew five feet through the air.

He crashed into a recently vacated table and showered glasses and drink everywhere as the wood split beneath him from the impact. The other one took a cautious step towards Trixie and reached into his coat.

Oh shit, I thought, expecting him to produce a shooter, or at least a weapon of some sort.

Trixie tensed but his hand came out holding, of all things, a business card. He handed it to her with a short bow.

"The Lord Adamus sends his respects, Angelus," he said.

Of course we legged it pretty sharpish after that, before the Old Bill turned up. I felt a bit bad about the state we had left the pub in but then we hadn't started the fight and at least no one was dead and nothing was actually on fire this time. That was pretty good going for us.

"What the bloody hell," I asked Trixie as we settled into a corner table in another pub a mile or two away, "was that all about?"

She took the card out of her pocket and passed it to me.

"Adam was saying hello," she said.

The last time Adam had said "hello" to me in that tone of voice he had tried to have me killed by an elderly Satanist and his telekinetic dead wife. I supposed we had got off lightly this time, all things considered.

The card was thick and obviously expensive, a plain eggshell off-white with inky black script that simply said

Adam with a telephone number underneath the name. I shrugged and gave it back to her. I was tempted to keep it so she didn't call him but if I couldn't trust Trixie then… well, of course I could trust Trixie. I knew that.

"And those two laughing boys? Any idea what they were?"

"Two of the Soulless," she said, keeping her voice down. "Soldiers of the Fallen, they call themselves. They're nothing much really in the great scheme of things. They tend to be a lot of show and bluster but not much to worry about unless there are an awful lot of them. They're the spirits of the damned, of demon worshipers who made pacts of servitude in the afterlife in exchange for power and riches during their mortal lifetimes. That's how they end up. Their demonic masters make use of them on Earth sometimes but they seldom give them much power in case they start to think they can break the terms of their pacts."

"Oh, right," I said.

That wasn't exactly how it was explained in the grimoires. I knew of a couple of people who were in for a bit of a surprise when they finally kicked the bucket, that was for sure. All the same, I supposed it was better than burning in a lake of boiling acid for a thousand years or whatever.

Diabolists go to Hell, Don.

If Adam thought I was wearing a red aura for him he had another think coming. That wasn't going to fucking happen, whether he liked it or not. At least, I sincerely fucking hoped not, but Trixie had worried the shit out of me all over again now.

You damned yourself to do it.

Fucking hell…

"I think I played cards with one of them last year, at Wormwood's place," I went on. "A geezer called Antonio. I wondered then what he was."

Trixie blinked at me.

"Did you?"

"Well yeah, I think so," I said. "Same dark red aura, glowing red eyes. He was shit at Fates though."

"And you didn't think to tell me at the time?"

I shrugged. "He was just another mug punter," I said. "I didn't think it was important."

"Well it might have been," she said, and took an irritated sip of her gin and tonic. "Don, you can't know *what's* important unless you tell me what's happening."

Oh is that fucking right? the Burned Man sneered in my head. *Cos I just got off the fucking banana boat did I, Blondie?*

I think Trixie was making a conscious effort to forget that the Burned Man was there inside me. I did that too sometimes, I had to admit. I looked up and met her eyes.

"All right, you tell *me* something," I said. "What did you mean when you said you loved me?"

Trixie pinched the bridge of her nose between finger and thumb.

"Not now, Don," she said.

"No fuck it, now," I insisted.

I was drunk enough to push my luck just that little bit too far.

"No!" she snapped. "Not when I heard that *thing* speaking with your voice not half an hour ago."

"Trixie…" I started.

"Not. Now. I'm going for a smoke."

She picked up her cigarette case and stalked out of the pub.

CHAPTER 10

Of course that well and truly pissed on the mood, so we drank up and left after that. I have an absolute gift for fucking things up, I'm sad to say. If there's a wrong thing to say you can pretty much guarantee that I'll say it, and at exactly the worst moment too. We walked in uncomfortable silence all the way back to the apartment. I couldn't bring myself to call it "home".

Home had been my office in nice familiar South London where everything made sense and I was, or had at least once been, my own man. I wasn't any more, that was for damned sure. I was Menhit's man now, or the Burned Man's or Trixie's or even Mazin's for that matter. I was getting well and truly fucking sick of it all, I knew that much.

I thought about my office, and wondered if it even still *was* mine. I hadn't paid any rent for what, at least seven months now, after all. I dread to think what might have happened if Mr Chowdhury, my landlord, had decided to kick me out. What would he have made of all my stuff? I had some rather... well, eclectic things in that office, after all, even once you got past the grand summoning circle I had carved into the floorboards of the workroom. There was the dead fetish of the Burned Man for one of course, chained to its altar, not to mention a Blade of Unmaking and a hexring and a warpstone and various other bits and bobs best not mentioned tucked away in my cupboards. Oh bloody hell, I hadn't even *thought* about that!

I shot a sideways look at Trixie, at the grim set of her jaw and her tight-lipped expression, and decided that now probably wasn't the best time to ask. I swear there's some special afterschool class that only girls go to where they get taught how to do that facial expression. I've never met a woman who couldn't do "the face", my own dear mother included, and I'll bet damn good money you know exactly what I mean.

I sighed. To say today hadn't really gone to plan would be a fucking understatement. We were in our street now, only a few yards away from the steps up to our building. I reached out and put a hand on Trixie's arm to stop her.

"Look," I said when she turned and glared at me, "I'm sorry, OK?"

"You're sorry," she said in a flat voice. "You're sorry you let that awful thing loose and you're sorry you let it take you over, or you're sorry I found out about it? What are you sorry *for* exactly, Don?"

I winced. That was a good question, I had to admit. I wanted to lie of course, to say something sweet and glib that would win her around. I always want that because I'm lazy and it's just fucking easier, but this time I already knew I was going to be out of luck before I even tried. I gave the truth a go instead.

"All of it," I confessed. "I mean, obviously I never wanted it to happen in the first place but... well, you know *why* it happened, and why I had to do what I did. And once it *had* happened... Yeah, I *did* hide it from you. I hid it as long and as hard as I could, Trixie, I admit that. I was ashamed, you understand? I knew how you felt about the Burned Man, and I knew how *I* felt about *you*, and…"

I tailed off helplessly, standing there in the street still holding her arm. God but it was cold out there.

"I see," she said, for all the help that was.

"Um," I said. "I, um…"

Trixie leaned forwards and kissed me lightly on the forehead.

"Thank you for being honest for once," she said.

She turned away and started walking towards the house again, leaving me almost too stunned to follow. I really didn't understand her sometimes, not even a little bit. Ah well, a kiss was a hell of a lot better than the backhander I had been half expecting. It wouldn't have been the first time she had belted me, after all.

I shook the memory off and followed her up the steps to the front door. We went up to the apartment and Trixie let us in with a key I knew damn well I was never going to be allowed to have. I sighed as the door thudded closed and locked itself behind us. It was only about eight o'clock in the evening but I was drunk and tired and more than a bit shaken up, and I couldn't even face the thought of eating.

"I think I'm just going to turn in," I said. "Night."

Trixie gave me an unreadable look

"Yes, it is," she said, and went into the sitting room.

I sighed again and took myself off to bed.

I did the bathroom thing and undressed for bed, feeling decidedly weird. I was hanging up a two thousand quid suit in a multi-million pound apartment in which I was effectively being kept prisoner by the woman I loved and a man who allegedly worked for me. I stood there naked in the bedroom and scrubbed my hands over my face, trying to make sense of things. I suppose my head was still fairly scrambled from all the smack I had done over the last six months, not to mention whatever the fuck Menhit had done to me to get me off the stuff, but all the same I felt like my grip on reality was getting too bloody shaky for comfort.

What were the Soulless doing after us? I asked the Burned Man.

I could almost feel it shrug.

How the fuck do I know? it said. *Probably what Blondie said, just saying hello on behalf of the Lord High Lucifucker.*

I snorted with laughter despite myself. I knew the Burned Man liked Adam even less than I did, but then it at least didn't have to be scared of him. I really sort of did, all things considered.

Yeah I guess, I thought as I got into bed. *He's never going to fucking leave me alone while I'm with Trixie, is he?*

Nope, the Burned Man said.

It went quiet after that, which gave its parting statement a sense of awful finality.

Well, there was that then. Lovely. I turned the light out and made myself go to sleep.

I woke up about midnight when Trixie got into bed beside me.

I almost died. I was stark naked under the duvet for one thing, and I really hadn't expected this to be the night she would decide to start sleeping with me again. Of course when I say "sleeping" that's exactly what I mean, and nothing else. She had made *that* very clear one night last year.

She was wearing a demure nightgown and I knew damn well that sleep was all she wanted, but apparently she wanted some company too.

"Hi," I said, too embarrassed by my nakedness to turn over to face her.

"Shhhhh," she said. "Go back to sleep. I was just lonely, that's all."

Of course that was all, I knew that. I closed my eyes and willed myself back to sleep.

Pillock, the Burned Man said, but I made myself ignore it.

I drifted in and out, painfully aware of Trixie breathing beside me, of the warmth of her. I would only have to wriggle backwards an inch to have her backside pressed against mine. Which would, of course, have been a fucking stupid thing to do. I dozed, thinking about the Soulless and wondering what the fuck Adam thought he was playing at this time.

Surely he knew Trixie would eat them alive? Of course he did, I realized – they were throwaway soldiers to him, nothing that mattered. He knew Trixie would walk through them the same way he had known I would take care of Charlie Page and his weird telekinetic dead wife. Of course I almost *hadn't,* but I'd be buggered if I was ever going to let *him* know that. No, it seemed this was just how Adam did things. Feints and jousts and pointless, egocentric posturing. Fuck, but he really was a prick.

I felt the Burned Man nodding in agreement with that sentiment, and sleep took me again.

The next time I woke, the early pre-dawn light was filtering through the heavy drapes and Trixie was breathing deeply in her sleep beside me. I was lying on my back. My eyes flickered open, and I saw the bloody holes of the child's eyes staring down into mine.

I gasped, hardly daring to move as I realized it was squatting on the bed on top of me.

"The fuck now?" I said.

"I know you," it said, a thin line of drool hanging from its ruined lips. "You're the bad man."

Oh here we fucking went again. I really had had enough of this thing now, guilt or no guilt. Whatever it was, I had my shit pretty much back together again and I was about ready to give the little brat a spanking. It was time to put my life in order, I had told myself, and this looked like a bloody good place to start.

"She's the bad lady," it whispered.

I blinked at it. Well I supposed *that* was fucking new.

"What do you mean?"

"The bad lady," it said again, and I swear to God it looked scared.

This ghost or apparition or demon pretending to be a ghost or whatever the fuck it was, this thing that had grown hands like a talonwraith and tried to strangle me on the astral plane, saw Trixie lying asleep beside me and I *swear* it looked scared of her.

"She's the bad lady," it whispered again, staring at her.

Oh fuck this. Just *fuck* it, I'd had enough. We weren't on the astral now.

I summoned my Will and banished the horrible bloody thing as hard as I could. It screamed as it turned translucent, seeming to stretch and grow thinner as I forced it out of this plane. *Nowhere left to hide.* That meant I was back out in the open, and it was well and truly time to be myself again. I could do that.

I'm back, motherfucker.

The ghost quivered for a last moment and vanished, leaving a thin wail of anguish hanging in the air like an echo.

I looked at Trixie but she was still sound asleep. I almost wondered if I was dreaming, but I needed to piss too badly for that. I slipped out of bed as quietly as I could and padded barefoot and naked to the bathroom to do my business. I thought about how I had banished the apparition, and how easy it had turned out to be without the deadly embrace of the heroin sucking the Will out of me.

Yeah, I was back all right. And it felt *good*.

When I came out of the bathroom again Trixie had her eyes open.

"Everything all right?" she asked me.

"Yeah," I said. "Um, call of nature."

"Oh," she said.

She turned over and seemed to be asleep again in seconds. I got back into bed and lay there awake for what felt like a long time.

She's the bad lady. What the fuck had all that been about? I had killed the McRoths' grandson before I even knew Trixie was alive, so how the hell did the ghost have the faintest idea who she was? Guilt by association with me, perhaps?

Although now I came to think about it, I remembered that wasn't strictly true. The first time I had seen Trixie had been the morning before the disastrous hit on Vincent and Danny McRoth, I reminded myself. That little fact had caught me out once before and I wasn't going to let that happen again. All the same, so what? The McRoth kid hadn't known her from a hole in the ground, which made me even more sure the apparition wasn't the ghost it was pretending to be. So what the fuck *was* it?

I had no idea, but I was damn sure it wasn't a natural manifestation, and that meant some cunt had set it on me for a reason. All the same, I knew that lying there tying my head up in knots thinking about it wasn't going to help. I sighed and turned on to my side, facing away from Trixie, and forced myself to go back to sleep.

When I woke up it was nearly lunchtime, and Trixie was gone. I wondered if I'd dreamed the whole thing. I thought maybe I had. I certainly *hoped* so. That horrible apparition chasing me was bad enough, without it suddenly seeming to know who Trixie was as well.

It's just your conscience talking, I told myself as I got up and headed towards the bathroom.

Oh yeah? the Burned Man asked. *Only I saw it too, and I*

haven't got *a fucking conscience.*

I sighed. Of course it hadn't. Not even a little bit it hadn't, but it *had* been seeing the apparition as well.

So what is it then? I asked. *I don't think I believe in ghosts.*

Me neither, it said. *It's a* thing *though. A* mean *thing, well disguised by someone who knows what they're doing. You watch yourself around it, Drake. I hope you got rid of it for good and all that time, but if it comes back again you fucking watch yourself. It'll bite you if it gets the chance.*

Yeah, well no shit. I'd kind of already figured that much out for myself.

I sighed and got under the shower. Whatever; I'd worry about it after I'd sorted myself out a bit. I had a good long shower to wash it all away, and afterwards I even shaved and everything. New day new start, and all that shit.

I came out wrapped in a big fluffy bathrobe and padded through to the kitchen in search of coffee. I found Mazin waiting for me there.

"Lord Keeper," he said with a deferential bow of his head.

He poured coffee into a fine china cup for me. You know, so I didn't have to strain myself I supposed. For fucksake.

"Morning," I said. "Where's Trixie?"

"The Madam Guardian is out on business, I believe," Mazin said.

I frowned. I didn't know what business Trixie had to be out and about on, but the thought of it didn't give me a warm feeling. Trixie's business was hurting people, as a rule.

"Oh," I said. "Right."

I sat down at the kitchen table with my coffee and Mazin leaned close to me.

"We have another little piece of business of our own, Lord Keeper," he said.

"We have?"

"You asked us to find someone for you," he reminded me.

"She has been found."

I blinked. *Christ, that was quick,* I thought. I had taken me six months to not find Debbie, and now it seemed Mazin and his people and his money had done it in a week. They would have found *me* despite my amulet if I hadn't sunk so far under the radar that I was practically living in the fucking netherworlds. The money was the key, of course. Money opened doors, greased wheels, loosened lips. Money made life easier, that's what it was *for.* I sighed. The Burned Man had always said as much, and I realized now that it had been right.

Thank you, it said in the back of my head. *It's about bloody time you started listening to me again.*

I ignored it and looked up at Mazin.

"Where?" I said.

"Not far," he said. "A nice bungalow near the National Gallery of Modern Art."

I'm not exactly arty and I wasn't too sure where that was but in Edinburgh a nice bungalow meant both "outskirts" and "one of the posh bits". It sounded like Debs had done well for herself over the last year or so. And so she should, thinking about it. Debbie was a bloody good alchemist. Up here, away from all the baggage of London, she had obviously made a fresh start for herself. Away from *me,* more to the point. Did I really want to go and inflict myself on her all over again?

I didn't really know *what* I wanted, but I knew I had to see her. Maybe to make sure she was all right, maybe just to see if she had stopped hating me yet. I couldn't shake the thoughts I had had before, about that nice normal life I was never going to get now. Losing Debbie had come to symbolize the loss of that life, for me. Did I think seeing her would somehow give me back that chance? I didn't know, but I couldn't help thinking it was something more than that. I didn't know what, not really, but I knew I *had* to see her.

"Right," I said to Mazin. "Let me get some clothes on and have a bite to eat, then you're driving me over there."

"And the Madam Guardian?"

"Won't be coming with us and doesn't need to know about it," I said firmly.

I gave him a look that I knew he didn't want to argue with, and after a moment he nodded.

"As you say, Lord Keeper," he said.

An hour later I was in the back of the huge Mercedes as Mazin drove us expertly through the early afternoon traffic. We headed west and over the Water of Leith into tree-lined streets of neat stone houses. This area was money, that much was plain, but in a very Scottish sort of way. There was nothing flash on show but everything was neat and modest and restrained, the cars on the drives all very expensive without being showy – Range Rovers and Jaguars rather than Ferraris, if you know what I mean. After another ten minutes or so Mazin pulled up at the kerb outside a smart detached bungalow with a big garden. He turned to look at me over his shoulder.

"Should I come with you, Lord Keeper?"

I was about to say no but… well, it had been a long time since I had seen Debs and we hadn't exactly parted on good terms. What if she didn't want to see me? Hell, for all I knew she could have married a twenty stone psychopath by now. I resented it, but I nodded all the same.

"Yeah," I said. "To the door, anyway. Then we'll see."

Mazin nodded and got out of the car. I waited for him to open the back door for me, then I stepped out into the late morning wind. I had spent the entire drive mentally rehearsing what I was going to say to her. I was wearing one of the new suits Mazin's tailor had run up for me, and my gorgeous new coat. What with "my man" opening the door of the two hundred grand car for me, I was feeling quite well to do all things considered.

I straightened my lapels and strode up a long stone path to the front door of the house with Mazin at my heels and my heart in my mouth. I mean shit, I might look like a millionaire now but I was still *me*, you know what I mean? I knew that was exactly what Debbie would see when she opened the door. Just me, not the suit or the car or the pretence. And that was even assuming she *did* open the door.

I rang the bell and waited. I could hear a baby crying somewhere, but other than that the street was quiet. I had just about decided she was out or hiding or something when the door eventually opened.

"Debs," I said. "I, um. Hi."

So much for my rehearsed speech then. That had been a fucking waste of time and no mistake.

"Oh fucking hell," she said.

We stared at each other, and no one fell into anyone's arms.

"Um," I said again. "How are you?"

She sighed. She looked tired, tired like she hadn't slept for a week. There were dark circles under her eyes and her auburn hair was pulled back into an unkempt ponytail that said she just couldn't be arsed any more. Even more than she usually couldn't, I mean.

"Christ," she said. "What are you *doing* here? And who the hell is he?"

Always answer the easy question first, that's my advice.

"This is Mazin," I said. "He works for me."

"Oh," she said. "Right."

"Look, can I come in?" I said. "Just me, I mean. Mazin will wait in the car."

If Debs even glanced at the car I missed it. So much for looking impressive, not that it really did in this neighbourhood. Her nextdoor neighbour probably had something almost as good, and she had never cared about cars anyway.

"I suppose so," she said.

She stood back from the door to let me in and just as I stepped over the threshold the baby started crying again. This time I realized the sound was coming from inside the house. Debs ushered me in and shut the door in Mazin's face without blinking. I sighed and let her show me into a sitting room that was mostly given over to some sort of huge, weird chemistry experiment. Some things never changed, I thought.

"Sit down and don't touch anything," she said. "I'll be right back."

I perched on the edge of a brown leather sofa and stared at the miles of glass tubes and pipes and valves and beakers and God-only-knew-what that were set out across two dining tables pushed together. Bunsen burners hissed and things bubbled and steamed and dripped, and I had no idea what any of it was. Debbie is seriously clever, in case I hadn't mentioned it. A puff of purple smoke vented from a valve somewhere in the middle of the huge contraption, making me jump.

She came back a moment later, and she had a baby in her arms.

I stared at her. It was a little girl, maybe six months old, wrapped up in a pink blanket with pictures of white bunny rabbits on it. The baby was still crying, her face scrunched up pink and red and tearful. Debs took something out of her pocket and slipped it into the baby's wet, toothless mouth, and a moment later she was quietly content. Debbie *is* an alchemist, after all.

"Um," I said.

Debbie had a baby girl.

I did a quick bit of maths. The last time I'd been to bed with Debs was maybe three months before we split up. Which was about a year ago now.

She had a baby girl.

A six month-old baby girl. Nine months of pregnancy meant…

Oh fuck me.

"Is…" I started.

Is she mine? I had been about to say, but that would only have started her screaming at me. As far as I knew I was the only boyfriend Debbie had had since we were at university together, the poor cow. Of course the baby was mine.

"Is this really happening?" I asked instead.

"It's already happened, Don," Debbie said. "It happened six months ago, in Glasgow General. It hurt like all hell for twenty sodding hours, and you weren't there."

I stared at her.

"Did you want me to be?" I asked. "I mean Christ, Debs, I didn't even know."

"No," she said. "No, you didn't know, and no I didn't want you there. Not really." She swallowed and looked down at the baby. "Sort of, anyway. I mean maybe part of me did, I don't know."

I smiled awkwardly at the baby. I know fuck all about kids, and I certainly never really thought I'd be a father. I had entertained fantasies, perhaps, but I had never believed in them. Not really. What the bloody hell did a father even *do*? I mean, I knew what *my* dad had done. He'd gone to work and then he'd got drunk and then he'd battered my mum, or me, or both of us. No, I wasn't going to be a father like *my* dad, that was for bloody sure.

Aren't you? the Burned Man sneered in the back of my

mind. *You sure about that?*

Shut up, I told it.

"Can I hold her?" I asked.

"No," Debbie said.

"Right," I said. "Right, OK. Fair enough. I... Jesus Debs, I didn't... I didn't have any fucking idea."

"I know," she said.

I looked at her then, sitting opposite me on a dining chair with that tiny little person cradled in her arms.

"Did *you* know?" I asked her. "Before you left, I mean?"

"Yes," she said. "I knew, Don. I wasn't showing then but I was eleven weeks gone when your slut almost tortured me to death. Of course I knew. I knew, and every minute of it I was terrified for my baby."

She was never going to forgive me for Ally, was she? No, of course she wasn't. Why the bloody hell would she?

"You didn't tell me," I said.

"No," she said again. "No, I didn't. It was never really the right time, and then... well. You know what happened."

I remembered finding Debbie tied up in the back of the van where Aleto the Unresting had taken a bullwhip to her. Yeah, I knew what had happened all right, and that was *before* everything that had happened since then. At least Debbie didn't know about the rest of it.

"Yeah," I said, feeling utterly helpless.

I mean, I could hardly blame her for not telling me. I'm not what most women would regard as a catch, to put it mildly. And after Ally then... well yeah. I had to admit I could see her point.

"What do you actually want, Don?" Debbie asked.

I looked at her, and at the baby, and I realized I had no fucking idea. I didn't know *how* to be a father. But I wanted... oh fucking hell, I wanted to learn.

"Do you need anything?" I asked after a long, painful

pause. "Money, or… or anything."

"No," she said. "I'm perfectly capable of providing for my own daughter."

"Right," I said.

I scrubbed my hands over my face and sighed. *My* daughter, I noticed. Not ours, *hers*. No, I hadn't missed that. What was I even doing there? I honestly had no idea. I had wanted to see Debbie, sure, but this had thrown an almighty spanner in the works. I was a father now, that had to mean something. Didn't it?

Maybe not to her, but it did to me. Seeing that little baby girl was like seeing light at the end of a very long, very dark tunnel of depression and addiction. I could have got down on my knees and thanked the God I had lost faith in that I hadn't taken my own life after all.

"Look, I mean… how do we do this?"

"*We* don't do anything," she said. "You crawl back under your rock and I carry on doing what I've been doing for the last six months, and everything goes back to normal. I don't want you here, Don."

Fucking charming that is, the Burned Man thought, and I must admit I had to sort of agree with it. A bit, anyway.

"Look, Debs," I started, but she cut me dead with a look that could have frozen a blast furnace.

"You don't," she said, slowly and clearly, "get to walk in here and be Daddy. You don't get to do that, Don."

I sighed. No, no I supposed I didn't.

"Right," I said. "Can I, you know, at least be in touch?"

She looked at me for a long moment, then her shoulders slowly seemed to relax. A bit, anyway.

"I suppose so," she said. "You already somehow know where I live. Look, give it a little while. Let me get used to the idea. After that, well, we'll see."

I nodded and stood up.

"Right," I said. "Well, I can't say fairer than that I suppose. I'd better be off but, yeah, I'll be in touch."

Debs followed me down the hall to show me out, but she didn't say anything until I was out of the door and starting back towards the waiting Mercedes.

"Don," she called after me.

I turned back, a smile forming on my face. Bless her, she always had been a bit of a soft touch. I knew she'd come round.

"Yeah?"

"Her name is Olivia, not that you asked," Debbie said, and shut the door on me.

Oh fuck, I hadn't had I?

I got into the car and slammed the door behind me.

"Go," I growled at Mazin, and closed my eyes as the huge car pulled away from the kerb.

Nothing *ever* got simpler.

CHAPTER 11

Of course Trixie was waiting for us when Mazin let me back into the apartment. She didn't look best pleased.

"Where have you been?" she asked.

"Out," I snapped at her.

Mazin looked from me to Trixie and back again, and I realized if I didn't tell her then he would.

"Sorry," I said. "It's been a long day already."

"Oh?"

I ushered her into the sitting room, away from Mazin, and sat down on one of the sofas with a long sigh.

"I went to see Debbie," I said. "I had Mazin's boys track her down for me."

Trixie lit a long black cigarette and paced over to the locked window.

"I see," she said.

"Not like that," I said. "I mean, not like a boyfriend or anything. You know I love you, Trixie."

"Yes," she said. "I know."

"I mean, I just wanted to... I don't even know. Just to make sure she was all right, I suppose."

That was bullshit and I knew it, but how could I possibly

explain to Trixie my longing for a life I couldn't have, with a woman I didn't even want any more. I could barely explain it to myself, and if I had told Trixie that what I really wanted was that life but with *her*, I think she would have laughed at me. I don't think I could have stood that.

"And is she?"

"Well, um," I said. "I mean yeah, I think so. She's, um, she's had a baby, Trixie. My baby. A little girl. From before. I didn't know. That she was having a baby, I mean."

That was possibly the most garbled explanation anyone has ever given, but Trixie seemed to understand.

"I see," she said. "What are you going to do about it?"

"I don't know," I said. "Not a lot, probably. She didn't exactly make me feel very welcome."

"No, I don't suppose she did," Trixie said.

She picked up an ashtray and sat down opposite me with it balanced on her knee.

"Yeah," I said, and put my head in my hands.

"Do you know anything about being a father?" Trixie asked.

"Well I've got a fair idea of how *not* to do it," I said. "Other than that, no. Not a clue."

Trixie nodded. "I thought not," she said, which wasn't exactly reassuring. "Does Debbie have everything she needs? Is the child loved, and well provided for?"

I thought about the nice house in the nice area, but the thing that really came to mind was that pink blanket with the bunny rabbits on it. I felt my eyes stinging.

"Yeah," I said. "She's loved, and she's fine."

"Good," Trixie said, and nodded. "Then that's taken care of. If you want advice Don, I'd say leave it be. For now, anyway."

"Yeah, that's pretty much what Debs said," I said. I sighed and changed the subject. "Where have you been anyway?"

"London," she said.

I blinked. She had been to London and back in a couple of hours, from Edinburgh? I remembered that she seemed to effectively be able to teleport, for all that I had never actually seen her do it. I *had* seen Adam do it though, and he had even taken me with him once. It was possible, I had to admit.

"Oh," I said. "Why?"

"I went to meet Adam," she said, and I almost wished I hadn't asked.

"Right," I said, hoping my voice didn't sound as strangled as it felt. "Um, why?"

"I wanted to know what Menhit is planning," she said. "I thought he might know."

"Oh," I said again. "And, um, did he?"

Trixie sighed and blew smoke up at the ceiling.

"Not really," she said. "But he thinks it might be something to do with my Dominion. He doesn't think it's dead, Don."

"No," I said, "I don't think it is, either. The Burned Man said much the same thing, in fact."

Trixie gave me a look, and I winced. I knew she hated the thought of the Burned Man living in my head. It did though, so there we were whether she wanted it mentioned or not.

"I see," Trixie said.

"I think…" I said, "I think Menhit cast it down into Hell, but that's all. It's probably still alive down there by the sounds of things."

"I doubt she likes to leave a job half done," Trixie said.

I swallowed. No, I didn't think she did either.

"Well there's fuck all we can do about it."

"Mmmm," Trixie said.

I looked at her, waiting for her to say more, but it seemed that was going to be the end of it.

"What else did Adam have to say for himself, then?" I

asked her. "What about those dickheads in the pub?"

"The Soulless?" she asked. "Yes, he sent them. I asked him and he didn't deny it, Don."

"What the fuck *for?*"

"Adam… well, Adam does that sort of thing," she said, and I'm sorry but that sounded a bit lame to me. "He enjoys, I don't know– theatre I suppose you might call it."

He's a fucking ponce, the Burned Man thought, and I had to agree with it.

"Has he been sending anything else after me?" I asked her. "You know, for the fucking *theatre* of it?"

"I don't think so," she said. "He would have wanted to boast about it if he had, I'm sure."

Yeah, I supposed he would have done at that. Wanker. I thought about the child again, and how it had looked scared of Trixie when it saw her. No, I supposed that probably *hadn't* come from Adam, come to think of it. It would have been expecting Trixie if it had, after all. So what the fuck was it then, and more to the point who was controlling it? I was convinced someone was – I still wasn't buying it actually being a ghost, but it was definitely *something*.

"Why do you ask?"

I sighed. Fuck it, now I was going to have to tell her wasn't I?

So I did.

"It sounds like a talonwraith," Trixie said, when I was done.

"Yeah I know it does," I said, "but it can't be. I mean, I can see straight through glamours and all I was seeing was that poor kid, only… you know. Wrong, and dangerous, and scary. If it was a talonwraith I'd have *seen* a talonwraith, or at least its aura anyway. Talonwraiths are invisible after all, and come to think of it I met the bloody thing on the astral as well and I should have been able to see a wraith there well enough. Only I didn't."

"Could a strong enough magician have done something else to hide it?" Trixie asked me. "Something other than a glamour I mean?"

I frowned. "Maybe," I said after a moment. "I mean, I'm only going on theory here. If someone knew what I had done, and how much it had fucked me up, and if that person had got close enough to me to skim my mind and lift the memory and maybe imprint it somehow onto their summoned talonwraith then… oh fuck it Trixie, I don't know. That's proper fucking magus stuff. I don't know anyone who could actually do it. I know damn well *I* couldn't."

"But it can be done?" she said.

I nudged the Burned Man.

Yeah, it can be done, it told me. *That's heavy mojo, though. Actually manifesting someone's nightmares in physical form is proper magus stuff, like you said.*

"Yeah," I said. "Yeah, in theory it could be, anyway."

"It sounds like you've made another powerful enemy then," Trixie said.

Oh fucking joy. Didn't my life just keep on getting better and better?

I got up and paced over to the window. It was getting dark outside. I found myself wishing there was some booze in the flat. There wasn't, I had already looked. Repeatedly.

"I want a bloody drink," I said. "Do you want to go out for dinner or something?"

"Not really," Trixie said.

I turned and looked at her then, and noticed for the first time that she looked a bit out of sorts. I couldn't help wondering what else Adam had said to her while she had been in London.

"Are you all right?"

"Not really," she said again.

She wasn't meeting my eye, I noticed, and even though she had just put a cigarette out she was already lighting another one. I went and sat beside her on the sofa.

"What's up?" I asked her.

She sighed and blew smoke at her boots, still not looking up.

"Adam said…" she started, and trailed off. "Oh, it doesn't matter."

Oh for fucksake, I'd heard enough of "Adam said" last year to last me a fucking lifetime.

"You can't trust that prick," I told her. "Come on Trixie, you know what he tried to do to you."

"Yes, I know," she said. "And then he fought a Dominion with me. That has to be worth something."

Of course I love you, we fought a Dominion together, she had told me. And yeah, so had Adam. I knew that. To be fair it was true as well, but Adam had been doing it for his own reasons, as she bloody well knew. Trixie could have a very selective memory sometimes, I had to admit.

I pinched the bridge of my nose between finger and thumb and bit back the urge to have a go at her. It wasn't worth it, I knew it wasn't. Fuck but I wanted a drink.

"Look," I said after a moment, "it's been a hell of a day. I've just found out I'm a father, for fucksake. I can't be doing with Adam now, and I really want to wet the baby's head, you understand me?"

Trixie finally looked up then, if only to give me a bewildered look.

"You want to do *what*?"

I laughed. "It's an expression," I said. "Wet the baby's head. It means… actually I don't know what the fuck it means, it's just something people say. You have a few beers to celebrate the birth, yeah? It's like a tradition."

"Oh," she said, obviously none the wiser. "Take Mazin,

I'm not in the mood."

I sighed. Going drinking with Mazin didn't really sound like it was going to be a lot of fun but I supposed it was better than not going drinking at all. I left her to brood and went and rounded him up.

"We're going down the pub," I told him. "Wet the baby's head, and all that shit. Trixie's orders."

I know that was stretching the truth to breaking point but Mazin just nodded and put his coat on.

"As you say, Lord Keeper," he said, giving me a short bow.

"Right, two things," I said. "Anytime we're going out on the piss together you call me Don, and you don't bow under any circumstances. You get me?"

He inclined his head in a nod that was as close to a bow as it could get without actually being one. I ignored the Burned Man's sniggers and let Mazin unlock the front door. This was going to be a barrel of laughs, I could tell.

It wasn't.

For one thing Mazin didn't fucking drink, which I supposed with hindsight I should have seen coming, and for another he had no conversation whatsoever. We were sat in a posh bar a few streets away from the flat, me with a pint and two whiskies in front of me and him with a glass of orange juice. Orange fucking juice, I ask you. He seemed content enough to sit and watch me drink, to be fair, but I've always regarded drinking as more of a team sport than some sort of performance art.

I supposed I might as well make the effort to get to know him now we were there.

"What do you do for fun, Mazin?" I asked him. "When you're not working, I mean."

"I am usually working, Don," he said.

I blinked. That was it, was it? That was the full fucking

extent of his answer? And they say the art of conversation is dead.

"You got a family?"

"No, Don."

Jesus wept. He hadn't got an inch less formal either, he was just saying "Don" instead of "Lord Keeper". I found myself missing Trixie very badly indeed. She was just so easy to talk to, and to listen to as well. Mazin was neither of those things.

"Right," I said. "Well, I mean neither have I. Not really. Just my mum, and I haven't seen her for a few years now. My dad's been dead since I was a kid. Mum's married again now but he's just some bloke she met in a pub, not real family. You know what I mean. And here I am now suddenly a dad myself."

I necked one of the whiskies and took a long swallow of my pint. Mazin sipped his orange juice and didn't say anything.

"I suppose I really ought to go and see Mum one of these days," I went on. I was babbling now, talking for the sake of it. I knew I was, but I needed to fill the silence. "I mean I don't really like Steve, this geezer she married, but he's all right really I suppose. He's not like my dad was, anyway. Doesn't knock her about and that. He's just a bit of a twat, you know what I mean?"

Mazin gave me a bland look, and I couldn't help thinking I was wasting my breath. I finished my pint and picked up the other whisky.

You do know coppers do this, right? the Burned Man asked me. *Keep quiet so you feel the need to talk, in the hope you say something useful. How much do you really trust this geezer?*

I blinked. I supposed I had no idea, really. I mean yeah, Mazin worked for me and was in charge of all that lovely money I apparently couldn't have any of, and I assumed he actually did all of the things it apparently said he did in the book I fucking *still* hadn't been able to read, but... Why? Because he had done all that for Rashid, and his order had been doing it before him for fuck only knew how long. I supposed so anyway, but then I wasn't Rashid. Rashid had been an immortal of God only knew how much power, whereas I really wasn't. I was just the poor bastard Menhit had decided got the job after she murdered my predecessor.

"Shit, am I boring you Mazin?" I asked. "You ain't saying much."

"My apologies, Don," he said. "I am not a talkative man, but I very much enjoy listening to you."

Do you? Do you really, or are you playing me like a copper would?

I went to the bar and got another round in. He was having another sodding orange juice whether he liked it or not. Live a little, Mazin, it'll do you good. Push the boat out and have a two orange juice night.

I turned back to our table with the tray in my hands, with two pints and two whiskies all for me and another miserable sodding orange juice for Mazin on it. I nearly dropped the whole fucking lot on the floor when I saw who had joined us.

We were in a posh, swanky bar in the heart of Edinburgh's exclusive New Town, two streets away from a branch of Harvey Nichols. The last person I expected to see sitting there was Davey.

Grotty old Davey belonged in places like that flat-roofed hellhole on the sink estate at the edge of Glasgow, not here. Davey looked and smelled like a tramp, with his long greasy grey hair and his scabby bald spot and his unkempt beard. He was even still wearing his horrible old tramp's greatcoat.

There were doormen at this bar but somehow he'd managed to walk in anyway, like they simply hadn't seen him. Perhaps they hadn't, at that. I still didn't even know what sort of magician he was, but I had a growing suspicion that he was very, very powerful – who knew *what* he could do, when he bent his Will to it. I dreaded to bloody think, to be honest.

I looked at Davey, and my imagination ran riot. I don't know why, but I could suddenly picture him presiding over some awful, depraved sort of Roman circus where men and women and animals tore each other to pieces for the amusement of a baying mob.

He looked like he would have been at home in a place like that, standing behind the emperor's throne like Rasputin and whispering lies in his ear. The very thought of it made me shiver. He turned and grinned at me, treating me to a view of his eight remaining brown teeth.

I put the tray down on the table and he helped himself to a pint and a whisky from it, and only then did I find myself wondering why I had bought two pints at once. Two shots maybe, but I like my beer cold so I never get two pints in at once or it gets warm before I can drink it. Only just then I had, and I hadn't even given it a second thought at the time.

That, now that I thought about it, was bloody odd. Fucking hell, Davey was a subtle bugger, wasn't he? Whatever sort of magician he was, he had obviously been tweaking my head before I even saw him. *Get me a drink, you cunt,* I could almost hear him thinking, but by then of course I already had.

"Thank you kindly," Davey said. "Have a seat before you fall on your arse, Donny boy."

I sat down and glanced at Mazin. He looked like he'd been hit between the eyes with a brick, and I wondered if he even knew Davey was there. Probably not, thinking about it. I picked up the remaining beer and tried to play it cool.

"All right, Davey?" I said.

"I am, and thank you for asking," he said.

He took a swig of his pint and his eyes twinkled at me over the rim of the glass as he did the same kindly, fatherly old-gentleman-of-the-road act he'd been doing before. My skin crawled just looking at him, the same way it had back in Glasgow. I ignored it and focussed on *him*, hard this time. I knew there was something about this bugger that wasn't right, and I was determined to find out what it was before it bit me on the arse. His aura was the same dull, fuzzy blue it had been before, the same boring human colour as yours or mine. There was something *wrong* about it, though...

I wasn't even sure what I was sensing. It was like if you run your fingertips over a smooth wooden surface and there's a tiny little splintery bit, not sticking up enough to snag your skin but enough that you can sort of just about feel it even though you can't see it for looking. Davey's aura was sort of like that. Human, sure, but there was something so *fucking* wrong about it. Something hidden, lurking beneath the surface like sharks in deep water.

"Are you done?" he asked. "I don't like being inspected."

His accent was weird too, I realized. He sounded Scottish most of the time, but sometimes it was more Irish or even a little bit Welsh. Native Gaelic speakers sometimes sound like that when they're speaking English, in case you didn't know, although having Gaelic as a first language these days is pretty bloody unusual.

"I'm fine mate," I said, meeting his twinkling blue eyes. "Do I have to say 'Kelmeth at midnight, in the shadow of the La'hah' again? Because I still don't know what that means, and it sounds fucking stupid anyway."

"Aye maybe it does, but you remembered it for six months just the same, didn't you?" he said.

I blinked. I supposed I had at that, or the Burned Man had anyway.

Was that you? I asked the Burned Man, but it ignored me.

"Whatever," I muttered. "What the fuck are you doing here, Davey?"

"You owe me a truth," he said.

Oh fuck, so I did. That had been so long ago I had almost forgotten about it. I owed this frightening, grotty, not-at-all-what-he-seemed tramp magician a truth, and it sounded like he was finally about to call it in. That was just what I needed. I kicked Mazin under the table, and he blinked at me.

"Thank you, Don," he said, and picked up his fresh orange juice.

"Mazin, this is Davey," I said.

Please tell me you can fucking see him too, I thought.

"Good evening, Davey," Mazin said, giving the old man a nod.

Well I supposed that was something. At least I wasn't totally off my nut and he really was actually there. Davey grunted and otherwise ignored him.

"A truth, Donny boy," Davey said.

I shrugged. "Fair enough," I said. "You won it fair and square, as far as I could tell. Mind you, I still think that just means you're better with cards than I am."

"Better *at* cards, maybe," Davey said. "I told you, I'm no a cheat."

You did tell me that, I thought, *and I didn't believe you. I* still *don't fucking believe you.*

"Go on then, what do you want to know?"

Davey laughed, and I could see his spit bubbling up in the gaps between his few remaining teeth. Oh, he really was a delight wasn't he? No he really wasn't, but again I could feel that thing I couldn't put a name to, that slight edge like a splinter in the smooth finish of his persona. That fucking *wrongness* that I couldn't quite describe, the thing that made me want to just run the fuck away from him and not look back. His persona was about as real as the wood trim in a cheap car, I was sure of it. He was hiding something, and I didn't like not knowing what.

"Oh, old Davey wants to know a lot of things," he said, and I was sure he'd said that to me before too.

"I bet he does," I said, getting pissed off with him now. I mean fuck it, yes he was scary but so was I, when I wanted to be. Well, when the Burned Man wanted to be, anyway. "Where to have a fucking wash might be one of them."

The Burned Man might have gone quiet on me but I knew it was still in there and it would be ready to come to life if this all went pear shaped and I got myself into a situation where I needed it. At least, I sincerely *hoped* it would be. I was starting to rely on the damned thing too much, I knew I was.

"And what might you mean by that?" Davey asked me.

I sighed. I had come out to wet my baby's head, not get into an argument with this horrifying old git. Mazin might have been shit company but at least he wasn't Davey, you know what I mean? I really wanted the old bugger to just fuck off.

"Nothing," I said. "Just ask your bloody question and do one, all right?"

"Now, that's not very polite, is it?"

"It's not meant to be," I said.

"You're a fucking rude prick, as I think I told you before," Davey said. "It's all right though, I don't mind. I've dealt with ruder pricks than you over the years, and broken them on my wheel. I'm not impressed, Donny boy."

His wheel? I thought, suppressing a shudder. *Jesus, why does the sound of that make me want to pull my own eyes out? Who is this bloke? What fucking wheel?*

Something shoved me in the side of the brain as the Burned Man woke up.

Trust me, you don't want to know, it said.

I was about to speak when it mentally barged past and took over.

"Now you listen to me, you fucking dirty old hippy," it said with my voice. "You might be old and you might be famous, but you ain't *me*, you understand? *Fuck* your wheel. I'll boil you in your own piss and pour vinegar into your rotting carcass while you bow down before my harpies for a thousand years before I'll tell *you* anything. Do you *fucking* understand me, you dirty old *cunt*?"

Davey blinked at me, and then he started to laugh.

"Thank you," he said. "There's my truth, right there. I've got the truth I was looking for."

"You've got fuck all," I said.

"I've got *you*, Burned Man," he said. "I knew it, I fucking well *knew* it back in Glasgow. There you are, you odious little piece of shit. There you are, stuck in this poor bastard's head."

We have been fucking had, I thought at the Burned Man. *Or rather* you *have. You fell right into his fucking lap, didn't you?*

Shut up, it muttered, which told me all I needed to know.

"Jesus Christ, Davey," I said, and that was me talking now. "Who are you, really?"

"Oh don't you worry about me, Donny boy," he said. "You've got your own fish to fry. You've got obligations, haven't you? Your precious mad goddess for one. She'll be wanting her pound of fucking flesh afore long, don't you worry."

Oh dear God, how the hell did he know about that? I had to admit that if Davey was clued up enough to have recognized the Burned Man just from hearing it speak then he probably knew pretty much everything. I supposed I might as well try to make the best of that.

"What, though?" I asked him. "What does she even want?"

I looked inside myself and I could feel the Burned Man sulking, somewhere deep down. I didn't think it would interrupt me again, and Mazin was still looking stunned and useless. Christ knows what Davey had done to him but it had obviously worked. I had no idea who he was supposed to be, for all that the Burned Man had called him famous. All the same, the Burned Man obviously knew who he was so he must be *someone*, if you know what I mean.

"What does she want, besides war and destruction you mean?" he asked. "Worship, I imagine, but she's got a fat fucking chance of that now. There are computer game characters with more worshipers than Menhit these days. No, I think the main thing on her mind is revenge. That Dominion who dragged her back to Earth is still rampaging around in Hell and I can't see her resting until it's done for, once and for all."

I stared at him. Trixie and I had been close to coming to that conclusion, but all the same. How in the world did she think she could kill it now?

"You think she wants to attack Hell?" I asked him, keeping my voice as low as I could.

He might be ghastly but he obviously knew things, and I wanted to know what. All the same, there were people staring at us as it was and the last thing I wanted was anyone overhearing that sort of talk.

"Menhit would attack fucking Mount Everest if she thought it had insulted her," Davey said. "She Who Massacres, they used to call her. The Slaughterer. That Dominion thought it could order her around, thought it could use her as a weapon for its own ends. Do you have *any* idea how much that fucked her off, Donny boy?"

I reached for my beer and drained most of it in a long, shaky swallow. How the holy *fuck* did he know any of this? Who *was* this horrible old wanker?

I kicked the Burned Man for an answer, but it was either sulking or hiding and I got nothing back. Mazin was staring at Davey now, the mention of his goddess's name having obviously pulled him out of his trance. He didn't look best pleased, but I knew the poor bastard had no idea how far out of his depth he was with Davey. Hell, I knew *I* was out of my depth, come to that.

"Right, well," I said, before Mazin could say anything we might both regret. "That's my daughter's head wetted as much as it's going to get I think. We ought to be off."

Davey gave me a long look, and chuckled.

"Aye, I think you did," he said. "Maybe have a wee chat with your pet angel, eh Donny boy? Give some thought to what you've let yourselves in for. And remember, my wheel is always waiting."

I resisted the urge to give him a sour look. Whoever he was, I was damn sure Davey was a far stronger magician than I was. That, or he was something else entirely, which would probably have been even worse. That splinter in his aura was still nagging at me, making me wonder what exactly I'd find underneath if I picked at it.

Don't do that, the Burned Man said. *Not now. He's not kidding about his wheel.*

I had no idea what this wheel even was, and I had a strong suspicion that I *really* didn't want to ever find out. If the Burned Man said I didn't want to know then... yeah. It had to be bad. That, and there was something in the Burned Man's tone that made me take it very seriously this time. It obviously took *Davey* seriously, and that was good enough for me.

Actually, come to think of it that was bloody worrying. The Burned Man didn't take *anyone* seriously except for Menhit, and maybe Trixie. That meant Davey must be a very big deal indeed.

What wheel? I asked it again, but I got nothing back this time. Sometimes the Burned Man could seem to disappear for hours on end and I had no idea where it went or what it was doing while it was gone. I shudder to think.

"Come on, Mazin," I said. "Time to go."

Mazin stood up and nodded at me, that nod that was almost a bow. Davey snorted like he thought the whole bowing thing was ridiculous, but I ignored him. I had to really, considering that I completely agreed with him. About that, if probably nothing else.

I led the way out into the freezing night air, and we headed back towards the flat. We got maybe three hundred yards before it all went to shit.

"Lord Keeper!" Mazin said as six blokes turned a corner in front of us.

I looked at them, and saw that each one of them had a dark red aura.

"Oh fuck," I said.

They were Soulless, I knew that much. Their leader was fair-haired and wearing a battered leather bomber jacket, and as far as I could tell he was the one who had pissed Trixie off so much in the pub yesterday. Mikael, I remembered he said his name was. He'd had a mate with him, a more reasonable one who had given Trixie a business card. It didn't look like that one was with them tonight.

"Diabolist," Mikael said as he stepped towards me. "It is time to fight."

Oh fuck me, was it?

CHAPTER 12

I'm no good at fighting, I never have been. The Burned Man was still sulking, and Mazin might have had good shoulders but he didn't look like he could punch his way out of a wet paper bag all the same. The six Soulless advanced on us, and I saw the glint of knuckledusters on Mikael's hands. Oh joy, a steel fist in the face was just what I fucking needed after everything else I'd been through that day. I grabbed Mazin's arm and half-dragged him down an alleyway after me. I heard the sound of boots on pavement as the Soulless broke into a run and pursued us. The alley gave out into a small yard behind a row of grand terraces, the area lined with dustbins and parking spaces. It was a dead end, and there was nowhere left to go.

The Soulless followed us out of the alley and spread out, looking moody and dangerous. Mikael took a threatening step towards us, a shark's smile on his face.

Oh bugger it, what's the point of having a guardian angel if you don't let her do her job?

"Trixie!" I shouted. "I need a hand here!"

Thank God there was no one about, that's all I can say. When you call on a Sword of the Word for help you have to be prepared for what you get, you know what I mean?

A burning sword exploded out of the chest of the rearmost of the Soulless, and then Trixie was amongst them. She danced her steel ballet as though they weren't even there, the flaming blade cutting and thrusting and sending blazing corpses to the pavement almost too fast to follow.

"Angelus," Mazin whispered in awe.

This was the first time he had seen Trixie in action, after all, and I knew exactly what he meant.

She was angelic and she was terrible, a burning whirlwind of fire and steel that took the Soulless apart with joyous ease. Trixie really did love her work, I had to give her that.

Mikael was the last one standing now. He turned on her with a growl of furious hatred. His knuckledusters flared with unholy light, turning both of his fists into fizzing balls of lightning. He smashed them together and a bolt of wild electricity shot towards Trixie. Her sword came up in a blur, too fast to follow, and deflected it harmlessly into a stone wall at the back of one of the properties

"You silly little boy," she said. "You really have no idea what I am, have you?"

Mikael snarled and leaped at her, one hand high and the other low as he sought to crush her between his two crackling electric fists. Trixie pivoted like a dancer, sweeping one foot out behind her as she spun in a full circle and brought her sword around in a blazing arc. The blade took him in the side of the neck and sent his head spinning away into the side of a parked car. Mikael's body collapsed at her feet, smoke rising from the dry stump of his neck.

"*Never* call me a bitch again," she said.

"Fuck me," I muttered. "That never gets old."

Mazin bowed low to Trixie, a worshipful look on his face.

"Madam Guardian," he said.

"Never mind all that," Trixie said, "we should be going.

Their bodies will dissipate in an hour or so but I'd hate to be found with them before they do. That would be... difficult to explain to the police."

I looked at the six dead bodies on the pavement around us and found I had to agree. This wouldn't end well for anyone if the Old Bill turned up.

"Thank you," I said to her.

She gave me a small smile and twisted her hand to make her sword disappear back into whatever dimension she pulled it out of when she wanted it.

"I've probably missed the end of my television programme now," she said, "but there we are. You're welcome."

I couldn't help but smile, and also wonder what on earth a Sword of the Word liked to watch on the telly when she was on her own. We hurried back the way we had come and out into the street again, trying hard to look like three normal people just walking home from the pub.

"Eventful night," I commented.

Trixie glanced at me.

"Yes," she said. "Apparently so. I really shouldn't let you go out without me, should I?"

"I'd be fine if bloody Adam didn't keep setting his dogs on me for no good fucking reason."

"Adam is... well, I don't really know what he's doing," she said. "This seemed unnecessary, even for him."

"I'm not sure that *was* him, to be fair," I said, thinking about it. "I reckon that Mikael twat was just holding a grudge from yesterday. You showed him up, after all. Anyway, he's done and gone. Davey isn't."

"What does Davey have to do with anything?" Trixie asked me.

"He invited himself along for a drink with us," I said. "We got to talking, and he realized I, um, I had another friend with me."

I was having to be careful to phrase things in a way that she would understand and Mazin wouldn't, of course. She frowned.

"That friend we had our disagreement over, you mean?" she asked.

"Yeah, that's the one," I said, ignoring Mazin's bewildered look.

"Oh," she said. "Oh, that's not good. I didn't want anyone else finding out about your little problem until I had worked out what to do about it."

If by my "little problem" she meant the fact that I was possessed by a fucking archdemon then I'm afraid I thought she was being a bit optimistic thinking she could do *anything* about it. *I* sure as shit couldn't, and God only knew I had tried.

"I don't know who he really is," I said, "but my friend obviously takes him seriously. That's got to tell us something."

"Mmmmm," she said. "I suppose it has."

Mazin unlocked the front door to our building and we trooped up the stairs together to the apartment. I really was utterly sick of the sight of the place. Posh though it was, it wasn't home.

I sighed and went into my bedroom to be alone for a few minutes. Where the hell *was* home, these days? I supposed that home was still in London, although I didn't know what the fuck I would find waiting for me if I went back there now. It certainly wasn't in Edinburgh, that was for sure. Not bloody likely, but... what is it they say? Home is where the heart is. Well my heart belonged to Trixie, but she was right there with me so that didn't really help. I thought about Debbie for a brief, mad moment, but I knew I didn't love Debbie. I wasn't really sure I ever had, to be honest.

Oh I had *thought* I loved her at the time, sure, but until I met Trixie I don't think I even really knew what that word meant. I had treated Debbie like shit, after all, let's not pretend otherwise. I knew I would never treat Trixie the way I had Debbie. Except of course that in the last six months I sort of had.

I sank onto the bed and put my hands over my eyes. Jesus, what the fuck was I turning into? I had been bloody *awful* to Trixie, hadn't I? Yeah, I really had. I mean all right, I hadn't cheated on her like I used to run around on Debbie, but as we didn't have sex anyway I wasn't even sure if that counted.

That was the least important thing though, wasn't it? The point was that I had betrayed her trust, first over the Burned Man and then in running away and leaving her to Menhit's tender mercies. It was a wonder she was still there at all, guardian or no guardian. I had to get my fucking shit together or I would lose her, I realized.

Of course the other reason, the *main* reason I had to get my shit together was for Olivia. Trixie had asked me if I knew anything about being a father and no, of course I bloody didn't. But... well, nor does anyone until they do it, do they?

I sat up and stared at the wall, swallowing in a dry throat. Olivia was my little girl, and I was her dad. Whether Debbie liked it or not, I was her dad. I was six months late, yes, but for once that wasn't my fault.

I'd say leave it be, Trixie had told me.

Yeah, that wasn't going to happen. It was like I had told myself after Menhit healed me, I was all out of excuses now. It was time to get my life together and fix my shit. The biggest thing I had to fix, the thing I really had to atone for, was the death of Calum McRoth.

I couldn't undo what was done, of course. I couldn't bring the poor little lad back, I knew that. But I could... I didn't really know. I could look after my own child, I supposed. I could be there for her, if nothing else. I could finally try to actually be the sort of father that I had spent my whole life looking for.

The next morning I waited until Trixie was having her bath, then hustled Mazin out of the flat and down to the car.

"We're going back there," I told him once we were safely inside.

"As you say, Lord Keeper," he said as he started the engine. "Although if I may venture a comment, I had thought your visit to the lady yesterday, ah, perhaps went poorly."

I gritted my teeth. Yeah, of course he had seen Debbie slam the door on me hadn't he? He had been sitting in the car at the end of the drive waiting for me, after all. Fuck it, it was none of his sodding business. He was just a fucking flunky, just... I took a deep breath and made myself calm down. He was a decent bloke and he was only trying to be helpful, I knew that really.

Damn, but my temper was getting short these days.

"Yeah," I said after a moment. "Well, let's hope today goes better than yesterday did, shall we?"

"There is always hope, Lord Keeper," he said.

I nodded and let him drive me to Debbie's house. I could only hope he was right about that.

We only made one stop on the way and it was still fairly early when I rang the doorbell, about half nine or something like that. Debbie opened the door wearing a faded pink dressing gown and a scowl.

"What the bloody hell are you doing back here?" she demanded.

"Look, I'm sorry, all right?" I said, holding my hands up in what I hoped was a peaceful gesture. Debbie had a pretty decent right hook and I really didn't want her sticking one on me in full view of all her posh new neighbours. "I fucked this up yesterday, I know I did. I… I hoped maybe I could try again."

"Try *what* again, exactly? Turning up out of the blue and royally pissing me off? Because if so, you've just tried it again and it still works."

"Please Debs," I said. "I was hoping I could see Olivia. I, um, I brought her this."

I reached into my coat pocket and produced the fluffy toy bunny that I had stopped to buy on the way over there. I held it out towards her, suddenly feeling very, very stupid indeed. An eight quid fucking toy rabbit from the supermarket, that was supposed to buy my way through this door, was it? Oh God, that was never going to work. Only it did.

Well, sort of, anyway.

"You're such a bloody idiot," Debbie grumbled, but she stood back and held the door open for me. "Come on then, just for a minute. You're here now, you might as well give it to her yourself, I suppose."

She led me into the living room where Olivia was sitting up in a playpen surrounded by fluffy toy animals. Big, expensive looking ones. I sighed. She was chewing on some sort of rubber ring thing, and had a nice little stream of dribble hanging from the corner of her mouth.

"Oh come here," Debs said, and bent over her with a tissue in her hand.

She gave Olivia a bit of a wipe then picked her up in her arms and carried her over to me.

"There's someone here to see you, sweetie," she said.

I looked at Olivia's big, pale blue eyes, and I have to confess I sort of melted a bit.

"Um, hi," I said. "Hi, Olivia. I'm, um…"

You don't get to walk in here and be Daddy, Debbie had told me, and I had to respect that however much it hurt.

"I'm Don," I finished, a bit lamely. "I brought you a new bunny."

I held it out to her and to my amazement she reached out and fumbled it into her arms, and promptly started to chew its ear.

"Sorry," Debbie said. "She's just started teething. She'll chew anything at the moment, but at least if she's chewing she's not bawling. There's only so much of my tincture I can give her at this age so… yeah. I haven't had a lot of sleep for, well, six months…"

She tailed off, and sighed. I thought again how tired she looked, but as she was having to look after Olivia all by herself and work as well it was hardly surprising.

"Can I hold her?" I asked. "Just for a minute. Please?"

Debbie looked at me and sighed again.

"Oh, go on then," she said. "But sit down first, I don't want you dropping her. And I'd take your coat off if I were you. I only fed her twenty minutes ago and she might spit up a bit."

I shrugged out of my coat and jacket, and sat on the sofa in my shirtsleeves. I'd never held a baby before in my life, and as Debbie started to lower her into my lap I have to confess I got a bit scared. Weren't you supposed to support the head or something? I was sure I'd read that somewhere, that you were supposed to support the head. How the hell did you do that? I got my hands in a muddle and generally made an awkward twat of myself.

"Just stop flapping about for a minute," Debbie said. "You'll frighten her. She's not a newborn, she isn't made of glass. Just hold her. There, see?"

Olivia settled into the crook of my arm and looked up at me, and I felt a big soppy smile spread itself over my face. I wondered if my dad had ever held me like this when I was a baby. He couldn't always have been as bad as I remembered him being, surely? I didn't know, but I found myself really hoping that he had done. If only once.

"Yeah," I said softly. "Hello. Hello, Olivia."

She gurgled and dropped her new bunny, and Debbie put the rubber chewy ring in her hands instead.

"Her poor little cheeks are so red," she said. "I'm glad we don't remember teething, it must be bloody awful."

"I suppose so," I said, but I was only half listening.

I was looking down at my little daughter in my arms, and it was like I couldn't hear the world any more. This was it, I realized. This was my chance to redeem myself, to be a better man than I had been. I wanted to be the sort of man that I *would* be happy to have around my daughter. I wanted to be a proper father.

Debbie stifled a yawn, and I looked up and really saw just how bloody knackered she looked.

"Look," I said, "do you, um, want to grab a lie down for ten minutes or something? I'll call you if she… well, if she does *anything*, really. I don't know what I'm doing but I can sit and hold her if you want to just, you know, have a minute."

Debbie gave me a hard look.

"How do I know you won't be in that car with her and away the moment I turn my back?" she demanded.

"*What?* For fu… for pity's sake Debs, I'm scared half out of my wits just holding her. Do you really think I know how to change a nappy, or do a bottle or… or whatever else you have to do? I don't even know what I don't know how to do, you know what I mean? I'm not taking her *anywhere*, trust me."

"No," she sighed. "No, I suppose you're not, are you? Oh God, I must admit I wouldn't mind. I'll leave my door open, and you call me the *moment* she starts looking unhappy, you understand?"

"Course," I said.

Debbie shuffled off down the hall, and if you've ever

wondered what the expression "dragging your tail" actually looks like, then she was doing it right then, bless her.

I looked down at Olivia again and smiled as she dribbled around her chewy thing. I wiggled a finger at her, feeling a bit of a fool, but she reached up with one chubby little hand and curled her fingers around it. I swear to God she smiled back at me, and I must admit I got a bit of something in my eye, just then. She was just so perfect, you know? So innocent and trusting. I couldn't remember the last time anyone had trusted me that much, and I swore to myself right then that I would never let her down.

A moment later Olivia's eyes closed and she seemed to doze off, still holding my finger. I don't think I'd ever been quite so happy in my life. All the same, I knew she wasn't *mine*, not really. Oh, she was my daughter, there was no doubt about that, but she was most definitely *Debbie's* baby, and only Debbie's. I was Don, not Daddy. Not yet, anyway. Maybe not ever.

Whether I would be able to change that depended on a lot of things, I supposed, but most of all it depended on Debbie. She was letting me have this moment but I suspected that was more because she was so tired she was ready to have a breakdown than because she actually wanted me there. No fuck it, I *knew* she didn't want me there. Not really, and I didn't blame her.

Debbie knew what I had done, or some of it anyway.

She didn't know about the Burned Man, of course, and she didn't know about the heroin either. She would have called the fucking police at the first sight of my face if she had known about *that*. No, but she did know about the McRoth boy. It had been an accident and she was well aware of that, but all the same would *you* want a child-killer involved in your baby's life? No of course you wouldn't, and neither did Debbie.

I had to atone somehow, I knew that. I had to make myself worthy of being allowed to come back.

Olivia woke up again after a few minutes, and started going a bit red in the face like she was about to cry. I panicked, and did the only thing I could think of to keep her quiet. I told her a story.

It was some nonsense my own mum used to tell me when I was very little, some sort of homebrew mixture of the Three Bears and at least two different Disney movies all jumbled up together. I could only remember bits of it anyway and I'm sure I wasn't making any sense, but it was all that came to mind. I doubt Olivia understood a word of it but she seemed to like the sound of my voice, and she managed not to cry until I had finished the story.

As soon as I ran out of words her little face started to screw itself up so I told it to her again, unable to think of anything else. I supposed it didn't matter what I was saying really, so long as it made her happy. So I sat there holding my daughter and reciting nonsense while she clutched my finger in her pudgy little hand, and I knew then that I loved her. I really, really did.

I knew in those moments that I was her daddy and she was my little girl. I smiled down at her, and I silently promised her that I would do anything in my power to protect her.

Anything at all.

I told her that silly mixed-up old story four times in all before she decided she'd had enough of it and started trying to bawl the house down instead.

"Debs!" I called as I held Olivia awkwardly up to my shoulder and prayed she didn't puke on me.

I didn't have the faintest idea what I was supposed to do with her now, I had to admit. Love by itself wasn't enough to stop a screaming fit, it seemed.

"I'm coming," Debbie mumbled from the bedroom, and

a moment later she was taking Olivia from me and rocking her gently in her arms until the bawling quieted to a sort of wet sniffling.

"Twenty minutes, that's not bad actually," she said, with the ghost of a smile on her face. "I thought I'd be back within three."

"Yeah, well," I said, feeling faintly embarrassed. "Beginner's luck, I suppose."

"Mmmm," Debbie said. "Look, Don. Thanks for the toy, and for the twenty minutes, but... Well look, when you say 'beginner's luck' it makes it sound like you think you'll be back here again tomorrow, and the day after, and... No."

No, no I hadn't thought so. Not really.

All the same, I couldn't help but feel a tiny bit crushed.

"Right," I said. "Right, well. Fair enough, I suppose."

"It's just... what you do. What you've *done*. I can't have that around her, Don. You know I can't. You *do* know that, don't you?"

"Yeah." I pushed my hands back through my hair and sighed. "Yeah, I know."

"Are you seeing anyone?" Debbie asked.

"Um," I said, a bit surprised by the sudden change of subject and completely at a loss as to how to explain my relationship with Trixie. "I, um, yeah. Well, you know. Sort of. It's... I don't know. Sort of. It's complicated."

Debbie shook her head and gave me a sad smile.

"You love her, don't you?"

There must have been something in my face, I suppose. Debbie always had been able to read me like a bloody book.

"Yeah," I confessed. "I really do."

"Be better to her than you were to me," she said.

I swallowed.

Ouch.

"I... I'm trying," I said.

"Good," she said. "Now look, I don't mean to be a bitch but I need you to go now. Olivia wants changing and I have to get dressed. I think you should go now. Go back to London, I mean. Not forever, maybe, but... well. Until I can trust you again. Until you've sorted your life out, at least."

Yeah, there it was. Much as it hurt, I had a feeling I should too. I needed to be a better man, and I wasn't going to do it here with Davey and his fucking wheel looking over my shoulder, was I?

CHAPTER 13

When we got back to the flat Mazin went to make coffee. I found Trixie sitting in the living room.

"Can we go back to London?" I asked her.

She blinked at me.

"I suppose so," she said. "Although this is quite a nice flat. What's wrong with Scotland?"

"Well apart from the fucking awful weather, Davey is here," I said. "I'd quite like to be somewhere that creepy old git isn't. Anyway, I'm a London boy at heart."

"Yes, well Davey might not be in London but Menhit very much *is*, in case you had forgotten," Trixie snapped, a bit waspishly.

I remembered Trixie picking herself up off the bedroom floor where Menhit had knocked her down, and winced. All the same though...

"I don't think it really makes any difference where Menhit is, does it? If she wants us, she'll find us," I said gently. "We can't hide from a goddess, Trixie."

"No, no I suppose not," she admitted.

"Anyway," I said, "I left some stuff behind when I... left."

When I ran away, I meant. When I ran away in a fit of

chivalry, or cowardice or blind panic, or whatever the fuck it had been. I really do think I'd been having some sort of breakdown at the time, looking back on it. Whatever it had been, I had run away in the night and abandoned everything – all my books, my hexring and my precious warpstone, even a Blade of Unmaking. I had abandoned the fetish of the Burned Man for fucksake, and if I was ever going to stand a chance of getting the fucking thing out of my head I knew I would need that. It had to go *somewhere*, after all.

"Everything is still in your flat where you left it," Trixie said.

I blinked at her. She probably didn't have the faintest idea how this sort of thing worked, I realized.

"I haven't paid any rent for nearly eight months, Trixie," I said, and sighed. "Not to mention that you blew the bloody windows out. I can't imagine I've still *got* a flat."

"Of course you have," she said. "I paid Mr Chowdhury for the windows and I've been paying your rent ever since, and a little bit more on top to compensate his son for keeping an eye on the place. He's a very nice man, your Mr Chowdhury."

"Oh," I said. "Oh, right. Um, thank you."

She shrugged. "You're welcome," she said.

"So can we get out of here? Can we go back to London, I mean?"

"Yes," she said. "If you want to."

She looked a bit mournful at the prospect, and I supposed I could hardly blame her. This place was palatial, whereas my flat over Mr Chowdhury's grocers shop on the high street very much was not. Trixie would miss her private bathroom with its whirlpool bath, I was sure.

I weighed up keeping Trixie in luxury against keeping Debbie happy and the prospect of bumping into Davey again, and I'm afraid she lost. There was something about what Davey had said, about breaking people on his wheel, that had really and truly put the shits up me.

Trust me, you don't want to know, the Burned Man had told me, and that in itself was enough to fill me with dread.

I knew the Burned Man, and I knew how it thought and how fucking little it cared about, well, anything really. If the *Burned Man* said I didn't want to know, then... yeah. Fucking hell, what sort of horror show were we talking about here? It didn't bear thinking about, it really didn't.

Even leaving that to one side, Davey was quite obviously the last sort of person I should be mixing with any more. I had to get out of Scotland and that was all there was to it, whether Trixie liked it or not.

"Look," I said. "I know my place is a bit, well, shit, but... yeah. I just–"

"I don't mind," Trixie interrupted. "Really. I've lived in imperial palaces and I've lived in dirt-floored hovels. South London won't kill me. There is one thing, though."

I supposed she probably had, at that.

"What's that?" I asked.

"Your daughter is here," she said.

Yes she was, and so was Debbie, and Debbie had just told me in the nicest possible way to fuck off out of her life until I had learned to be less of a cunt.

"Yeah, she is," I said. "I... Oh fuck, I don't know, Trixie. I mean, you said yourself that she's loved and she's safe and to leave it be, and London's not all *that* far away and... well, I don't think Debs really wants me around."

"No, perhaps she doesn't," Trixie said. "All right, we'll go back to London. I'll have Mazin make the arrangements."

It sounded simple, didn't it? Needless to say it wasn't.

Moving was effortless, of course. Mazin made a phonecall and early the next morning a big truck and five blokes turned up and they packed our things for us and loaded the truck and off they went, sweet as a nut. It's amazing what money can do, isn't it? As I said before, that's the whole point of the stuff, as far as I'm concerned – not to buy piles of gaudy crap you don't need, but just to make life easier.

Mazin drove Trixie and me back down south in the comfort of the Mercedes.

No, that wasn't any bother at all, quite the opposite in fact. The bother started as soon as we actually got back.

The car pulled up at the kerb outside Mr Chowdhury's shop and I got out to see that Trixie had had my front door repainted and the sign replaced. "Don Drake, Hieromancer", that sign said, in lovely brass letters. No one had defaced it this time, and I suspected that I had Mr Chowdhury's burly eldest son to thank for that. He was a big lad and he was known around the neighbourhood, and once word had got about that he was keeping an eye on the place I knew it would have been regarded as off limits by the local scrotes. Sometimes reputation can work as much magic as money does, you know what I mean?

Trixie unlocked the door and we went up to my office. There was new glass in the windows, and she'd had the end wall fixed properly too so that the paint actually matched now and the dent where I had botched filling in a bullet hole wasn't visible any more.

Bless her, she had bought me a new desk too, to replace the one she had smashed in half. My phone and answering machine were sitting on the desk, looking old fashioned and out of place. The light on the answering machine was flashing.

I walked over and pressed the button. There was a click and rattle as the ancient machine started to play its little tape.

"You have eighteen new messages," it said.

Oh God.

Half of them were bullshit of course, wrong numbers or some tosser trying to sell me insurance, or offering to get my money back from insurance I shouldn't have bought in the first place or some other such pointless shit like that. The rest of them weren't. Three were from the Russian, getting increasingly terse as they went on. Five were from Selina, Wormwood's secretary. And the last one was from Janice.

"Don?" she said, her snuffly little voice sounding faint and muffled on the line. "Don, it's Janice. Um, the gnome? Do you remember me?"

Of course I remembered her, bless her little heart. Janice really was a gnome, an Earth Elemental from the tunnels underneath London, and she was an absolute sweetheart. She was also one of the bravest people I've ever met. She had healed Trixie after her disastrous battle with the archdemon Bianakith. She had seen me bring forth and then invoke the Burned Man, and she had kept quiet about it when it mattered. She had taken us down into the deep warrens to face a fallen Dominion, and she had guided us back out again, leading an actual living war goddess, and all without complaint. I owed Janice the mother of all fucking favours, to say the least.

"Um," she went on, "I'm sorry to bother you but I really need to talk to you. The–"

The tape ran out, and rewound itself with a noisy rattle.

Oh fucking hell! That message had been from six weeks ago. The answering machine was supposed to go back to the beginning if the tape ran out and just start recording over the oldest messages but needless to say the bloody thing didn't work properly, and when the tape got to the end it tended to get stuck. God only knew who had been trying to call me since then.

"Oh dear," Trixie said.

I stared at her. "You haven't been checking my messages?"

"No Don, I haven't," she snapped. "I've been searching high and low for you, and worrying myself sick about you, and I've been at Menhit's beck and call every hour of the day and night, and–"

"Sorry," I said, making peaceful gestures with my hands before she smashed this desk in half as well. "Sorry, I know you have. I wasn't thinking. Sorry, it's just... poor little Janice. She wouldn't have phoned if it wasn't important."

"No, no she wouldn't," Trixie agreed. She stared at the answering machine and sighed. "I'm sorry, I honestly never even thought about it."

"It's all right," I said. "I should be grateful I've still got a home to come back to, and I know that's only because of you."

Trixie shrugged and turned away, but I could see I had upset her.

Well done Don, you twat, I thought. *Way to welcome the missus home.*

Not that she *was* my missus of course, but you know what I mean.

I frowned at the answering machine. I'd got a telephone number for the gnomes out of Wormwood once before and I knew I had written it down. Somewhere.

Obviously I couldn't find the fucking thing. The scrap of paper I had written it on had probably been in the drawer of my old desk, which had no doubt gone to the tip months ago. Fuck it!

I *did* still have Wormwood's mobile number though.

I punched it into the phone and waited until he picked up.

"What?" he said.

Oh good, he was still as charming as ever then. Wormwood was another archdemon, albeit a very humanlike one. He was a child of Mammon, and he ran an illicit casino and drinking club frequented by magicians and demons alike.

He was also a businessman, in my debt, and shit scared of Trixie. For all that he was bloody horrible, Wormwood was a very useful person to know. Well, I say "person", but you know what I mean.

"All right, Wormwood," I said. "It's Don Drake."

"Fuck me," he said. "I thought you were dead."

"Yeah well, sorry to disappoint you and all that, but I'm not," I said. "And I'm back in London."

There was a pause while he nosily lit a cigarette. I could almost hear the wet phlegm on his lips.

"Am I supposed to be pleased about either of those things?" he asked.

Oh fuck you very much, you cunt.

"Spare me the charm, Wormwood," I said.

"Yeah well, Selina has been trying to get hold of you for fucking months," he said. "Them gnomes are looking for you."

"Yeah, I know," I confessed. "I didn't at the time, but I do now. I need that number you had for them. I know you gave it me before but I've lost the bastard and I need it."

"Tough," he said. "Look Drake, you–"

"Trixie is back in town too," I said. "We could come to your club tonight, if you wanted. She'd love to see you."

She wouldn't love to see him at all, obviously, but not half as much as he didn't want to see her. Wormwood really was bloody terrified of Trixie, and with good reason. He really had no business being on Earth at all. He was only here in the first place because some bloody idiot had summoned him and messed it up, and he had got loose. That was a very long time ago – if he got sent back to Hell now he'd probably never get back out again, and he knew damn well that Trixie could dispatch him without even breaking a sweat. Wormwood was a ruthless businessman but he was no one's idea of a fighter.

"Keep your panties on, I've got it somewhere," he muttered.

He fiddled with his phone for a moment then read me out a number which I scribbled down in the fresh notebook that Trixie had thoughtfully left in the drawer of the new desk for me.

"Ta," I said, and hung up on him.

I heard a horn sound from the street outside.

"The removal men have arrived with your things, Lord Keeper," Mazin said.

I waved distractedly at him. "Yeah, sort that will you?" I said. "I've got to make a call."

Fuck me, I think I was finally starting to get the hang of having "people". I must admit I rather liked it.

I called the number Wormwood had given me and waited while it rang and rang. I remembered that the last time I had tried to phone down to gnomeland it had taken forever for anyone to answer, too. I suspected they only had one phone, probably spliced into one of the backbone telecom cables that ran underneath the Tube tunnels.

Eventually someone picked up.

"Yes?"

"It's Don Drake," I said. "I'm returning a call from Janice. Can I speak to her please?"

I bloody well hoped I could. If anything nasty had happened to her in the six weeks since she had left that message I would never forgive myself.

"Oh," the voice said. "Oh, all right. Hang on."

I heard the phone being put down, and sighed with relief. It sounded like whoever that had been was on their way to find her, so at least she was still alive. I'm sorry but I do tend to assume the worst, and I really was fond of Janice.

Eventually the phone was picked up again and I heard

her snuffly little voice.

"Hi Don," she said. "It's Janice. Thanks for calling back. I was starting to think that, well, that you weren't going to."

"I am *so* sorry," I said. I put a finger in my other ear as the removal men started lugging our stuff up the stairs and into my flat, thumping and banging the way that removal men always do. "I've been, um… Sorry. I've been in Scotland. For, um, for a long time. Shit, look, are you all right?"

"Yes," she said, and I felt something in my guts unclench. Oh thank fuck for that.

"Good," I said. "So what's up?"

"I'm afraid the matriarch has passed away," she said.

I remembered the matriarch of the gnomes. Nice lady, and obviously very old even by gnome standards. I supposed it had had to happen eventually.

"Oh," I said. "I, um, I'm sorry to hear that."

"It was her time," Janice said sadly. "It's all right, we knew it was coming. What with Bianakith and all the work she had to do to heal the warrens afterwards, I think she was all used up. There's only so much root and rhyme in anyone isn't there, whoever they are?"

Is there? I had no real idea how gnome magic worked, but that was their business not mine as far as I could see.

"Right," I said. "So, um…"

"It's not that," Janice said, "it's something she said before she passed. She said it was very important that the hero should be told. That's you, Don."

The hero was Trixie as far as I was concerned, but whatever.

"What's that then?" I asked her.

"She said to tell you 'The throne is burning'. I'm sorry I don't know what that means, but it was very important to her that you be told. She was, well, raving a bit towards the end, I'm afraid. It might not even mean anything at all. I think, well, with everything that happened... Bless her. She was very old, Don. Very, very old."

I dread to think how many years was "very, very old" to a gnome. Two hundred? Three? More than that? I wondered what the poor old thing had thought when the Victorians first started digging sodding great holes on top of her warren to build the Tube. I wondered what she had made of Crossrail, for that matter. That had probably helped finish her off, poor love. Bloody technology was spoiling everything for everyone.

"Right," I said. "Well I'm afraid it doesn't mean anything to me at the moment but I suppose it might do one day so, um, thanks. Thanks, Janice."

"You're welcome," she said, and I could hear the shy smile in her voice. "I wanted you to know, that's all."

"Yeah, thanks," I said again. "So, um, do you have a new matriarch now, then?"

"Oh, well yes," Janice said. "That, um, well, that would be me."

I blinked. Shit, really?

"Well, then thank you, *Highness*," I said.

"Oh you don't have to call me that," Janice said. "It was all a bit of a surprise really, but we held the moot and I was voted for even though I didn't ask to be and, well, it's all a bit awkward at the moment. I suppose I'll get used to it in time. All the, you know, the bowing and everything."

I glanced at Mazin and I knew exactly what she meant.

"Yeah," I said. "Yeah, I can imagine. Anyway look, thanks for telling me."

We said our goodbyes and I hung up just as the removal men were bringing up the last of the boxes.

"What was that all about?" Trixie asked me. "Is everything all right?"

She was standing beside my desk smoking one of her

long black cigarettes while Mazin herded the removal guys around the flat, directing the unpacking.

I waved her a bit closer, and spoke quietly.

"Janice is fine," I said. "The gnomes' matriarch died and Janice got voted in as her replacement, apparently."

Trixie nodded. "Good for her," she said.

"Yeah," I said. "Anyway, what she wanted was to pass on a message from the old matriarch, something she said before she died. She wanted to tell me 'The throne is burning'."

Trixie seemed to pale.

"Say that again?"

"The throne is burning," I repeated. "Buggered if I know what it means, but apparently the old matriarch was insistent that someone tell us."

"It... it could be nothing," Trixie said.

"It could be the nonsense ravings of a potty old woman, to be fair," I said. "From what Janice was saying, it sounds like the old matriarch went a bit gaga before she died."

"Yes," Trixie said. "Yes, it could just be that."

She turned away and went through to the bedroom to supervise, and that was the end of it. There was something though, something about the look in her eyes and the sudden paleness of her face that made me wonder. I loved Trixie, I really did, but sometimes I was damn sure she wasn't telling me everything.

I sighed and swivelled my chair around to look out of the window. I'm not sure Trixie was *ever* telling me everything, to be fair. All this business about Adam and the Soulless, for one thing. Was he really that much of a prick, that he would set these tossers on us just to see them killed, as a way of saying hello? Actually he probably was, now that I thought about it. The Soulless were utterly dispensable, to him. Anyone who made an actual pact with the Devil had to expect it to bite them in the arse eventually, I supposed.

I thought about the Burned Man, sleeping somewhere in the back of my head, and shuddered. That wasn't exactly the same thing of course – I mean, I hadn't made any sort of deal with the bloody thing after all, I had just royally fucked up an invocation. All the same, it made my palms itch just to think about it.

Diabolists go to Hell, Don.

Yeah, thanks for that.

CHAPTER 14

The removal guys buggered off in the end, leaving me and Mazin and Trixie in a surprisingly habitable version of my flat. Obviously none of them had been allowed in my workroom, but now that we were alone I left Trixie and Mazin in the kitchen and took myself in there and shut the door behind me.

The fetish of the Burned Man hung lifeless in its chains on the altar, inanimate and thick with dust. I looked at it and felt a twinge deep inside me.

Mate, I thought. *Is there any chance…?*

Nope, the Burned Man thought back at me, waking up for the first time in hours. *Not going to happen. I hate that fucking thing and I'm not going back in there. Fucking forget it, Drake.*

I sighed. I supposed it wasn't, at that.

Yeah, all right, I conceded. *Now that you're alive again, make yourself useful. What the fuck does "the throne is burning" mean?*

I felt it mentally shrug. *Could mean all sorts of things,* it said. *The throne of where?*

Fucked if I know, I admitted.

I went to check everything was still where it should be in my cupboard. Thankfully it was. I looked at the contents of the "special" drawer, at my warpstone and the flat black case that contained the hexring, and at the curved black Blade of Unmaking that I had enchanted with the soul of the Burned Man. The Burned Man wasn't in it any more, of course, but that dagger had been forged in the depths of Hell and it was still a powerful artefact in its own right. Everything was still there, thank fuck. It really wouldn't have done for any of them to have gone walkabout while I was away. I dreaded to think what sort of mess some half-trained oik of a wannabe magician could have got themselves into with any one of those artefacts. I owed Trixie a very big thank you for keeping everything safe for me while I was off my head in Scotland.

I sighed.

I owed Trixie for all sorts of things. I owed her more than I could ever repay her, I knew that much.

The phone rang. I hurried back through to the office but Mazin had already picked up.

"Don Drake's office, how may I help you?" he said. He frowned, then put his hand over the receiver and looked at me. "Lord Keeper, there is a very angry Russian-sounding gentleman on the telephone, demanding to speak to you."

I groaned. My past just refused to leave me alone, didn't it? The Russian was a gangster like Gold Steevie had been, and no I didn't have the faintest idea what his name was. Everyone just called him "the Russian", and that was all he answered to. I had done bits of work for him in the past, for all that him and Steevie had been enemies. I had never been Steevie's bitch, you understand, no matter what he might have thought. I had always been strictly freelance. I imagined that with Steevie dead the Russian had expanded into his territory pretty quickly, and got even more obnoxious than he had already been.

"Give it here," I said, holding out a hand for the phone.

"Russian, it's Drake."

"Where the fuck you been?" he said by way of greeting. "I need a job doing."

I knew exactly what sort of job it would be, too. These pricks only ever came to me when they wanted a demon setting on someone. Now I'm sorry but I didn't do that any more. Not after Calum McRoth I didn't, and certainly not now I had Olivia to think about. I saw Trixie looking at me, her cold blue eyes watching as she waited for me to say something.

"I've retired," I said. "I'm out of the business."

"Fuck you are," the Russian said. "Gold Ponce is dead, you work for me now."

"I never worked for *him*," I pointed out. "I always just worked for whoever was paying the best, and now I've retired. Find someone else."

I didn't even know if there *was* anyone else, not in London anyway, but that was hardly my problem. This arsehole could go fuck a bear for all I cared, I was through with that life. I looked at Mazin, and thought about Menhit. I couldn't help thinking that the life I had got myself into instead was probably worse, but there we were.

"You say 'no' to me?" the Russian asked, and in that moment he sounded *exactly* like Gold Steevie. Apart from the accent, obviously.

For fucksake, I really had had it with these pricks and all their macho posturing.

"Yeah, I'm saying no," I said.

"Fuck you, Drake," the Russian growled in my ear. "I'll hurt you for this."

He hung up on me, and I shrugged. I really didn't need him as an enemy but then compared to everything else that was going on I supposed he was a drop in the ocean. I looked up and saw Trixie smiling at me.

I gave her a nod and went to put the kettle on. Which I realized was a bit pointless when I opened the kitchen cupboard and saw there was nothing in there, not even coffee. Trixie seemed to have had the place cleaned while it was empty, which I have to admit it had badly needed, but the cleaners had obviously chucked out everything in the kitchen that had been out of date. Which was everything in the kitchen, if I'm honest about it.

"Bugger," I muttered.

"I will have groceries delivered, Lord Keeper," Mazin said from the doorway behind me. "If you intend to stay here, that is."

I caught the look of slight distaste on his face and winced. He obviously didn't think much of my place. Which was hardly surprising, I supposed. What with him being the head of the Order of the Keeper and in charge of all that lovely money, I suspected that wherever he lived was a damn sight nicer than this. That put my back up at once, and I felt my stubbornness kicking in.

"Yeah I am as it happens," I said. "I live here, mate."

I was being stupid, I knew I was. I had no affection for that bloody flat at all, but Trixie had put so much effort into looking after it and cleaning it up that I didn't have the heart to just turn my back on it and get somewhere else, even assuming Mazin would have paid for better. I thought about the palatial apartment he had rented for us in Edinburgh, and decided that of course he would if I told him to.

"I… understand, Lord Keeper," he said, for all that he obviously didn't.

"Right, look," I said. "Thanks for everything Mazin, but you've had a bloody long drive and you must be knackered. Take the rest of the day off, yeah?"

To be fair it was late evening already so that wasn't particularly generous of me, but I just wanted to get rid of him. I didn't mind the bloke but he was always *there*, you know what I mean? Perhaps I *hadn't* quite got the hang of having "people" yet, after all.

Mazin bowed and went, leaving me alone in the flat with Trixie.

"You hungry?" I asked her.

I hadn't had anything to eat all day other than an alleged cheeseburger at a motorway services that I was still trying to forget about, and I was bloody starving.

"Yes," Trixie said. "I suppose so, anyway."

We had a quick wash and a brush up and headed out to the little Italian place round the corner. Everything was feeling nice and normal, like we were just a regular couple out on a date. I should have known it wouldn't last.

We were half way through our meals and on our second bottle of red when it all went pear shaped. The geezer walked up to our table wearing his long black overcoat and his sunglasses, despite the comfortably dim light in the restaurant. It was the other hunter, Mikael's mate. This was the one who had given Adam's card to Trixie in the pub in Edinburgh.

"Angelus," he said, interrupting whatever I had been in the middle of saying to her. "The Lord Adamus sends his respects."

Trixie glanced up at him, then waved him to a spare chair at our table. That surprised me a bit, I have to admit.

"Hello Heinrich," she said. "You remember Don."

I stared at the Soulless, trying to get my head around the fact that Trixie seemed to be on first name terms with him. He had been the more civilized of the two, admittedly. He had certainly been a hell of a lot better than Mikael anyway, but all the same. What the fuck was she up to?

"All right?" I muttered as he nodded to me.

"The Lord Adamus has been making enquiries, as you

asked him to," this Heinrich geezer said. "It seems your suspicions were correct, Angelus. The goddess intends to see an end to the fallen Dominion once and for all, even though it now dwells in Hell."

"I see," Trixie said.

"I bloody don't," I said, keeping my voice low. "She's a fucking *goddess*. If she wants to finish the Dominion off, why hasn't she?"

"Ah," Trixie said. "I'm afraid it's not quite that simple."

No, no, I didn't think it would be. Nothing ever bloody is, is it?

"Enlighten me," I said.

Trixie sighed. "You see, you're right," she said. "Menhit *is* a god, and that's the whole problem. A god cannot fall, Don. As such, I'm afraid a god cannot enter Hell."

"Right," I said, although that was news to me. "So?"

"So," she said, and paused. She looked at me for a moment. "There's something I've been meaning to bring up."

Uh oh.

"Oh yeah?"

"I went to see Adam in London, before we came back," she reminded me. "Well, I haven't had the chance to mention that Menhit had also been in touch with him."

"No, no you didn't mention that," I said.

I was starting to get a bit of a bad feeling about this, to put it bloody mildly.

"Yes well, there we are. Heinrich is choosing his words very carefully," Trixie said, meaning the bloke was spinning us a yarn. "Menhit and Adam have already made common cause in the matter of the Dominion."

"That's nice for them," I said.

"I'm afraid it isn't nice for *us*," Trixie said. "Adam wants the Dominion ended every bit as much as Menhit does, possibly more. He's still very concerned about the prospect of war in

Heaven, Don. The Dominion wasn't working alone. In fact, Adam fears... well, Adam fears that it may have simply been a pawn of a higher power. A Throne."

I looked up sharply at her. "The throne is burning," I said.

"Yes," she said. "Yes, that's what I was afraid of, when you told me what Janice said. If a Throne *is* behind the rebellion, then it's vitally important that it doesn't get that Dominion back. It's *far* too powerful for us to risk that happening."

"But–"

"No," she said, "I know what you're going to say and I'm afraid it doesn't work like that. A Throne is... oh I have no idea how to explain it to you. It isn't like a Dominion but bigger, if that's what you were thinking. A Throne is a different thing altogether, more pure intellect than physical power. It won't fight by itself, that's what it has Dominions for. And angels, for that matter. It needs *weapons*, Don. That's why it wanted Menhit in the first place."

I drained my glass of wine and poured another. Heavenly politics were a bit beyond me, I have to admit, and their power structure seemed to be arcane beyond belief. I didn't think I'd ever get my head all the way around it.

"Is this our problem?" I asked her.

"Yes, I'm afraid it is," Trixie said. "Adam is a duke, in Hell, and it seems he can come and go as he pleases. All that show he made about having escaped again after the Dominion cast him down into Hell was, well, more of his theatre I suppose you'd say. You know what he's like."

Don't I fucking just? He's like a prick, is what he's like.

"Right," I said again. "So he's got the keys to the back door, has he?"

"Effectively, yes," Trixie said.

That explained something that had been bothering me for a while, actually. As I've said before, you can't summon something that's already on Earth. It's flat out impossible, but last year I had summoned Adam. I'd been so fucking surprised that it had worked at all that I hadn't given a thought to *how* it had worked, at the time. All the same it had been on my mind off and on ever since. If he could return to Hell on a whim though, then maybe he *hadn't* been on Earth when I forced him to come to me against his will. That was an interesting thought in itself.

"He used his way out then," Trixie went on, "for all that he came to us burned and ragged and pretending to have fought his way out. No, I'm afraid he just slipped out, and he can slip back in the same way. And we're supposed to go with him this time."

I choked on my wine. Fucking *what?*

"That's not funny, Trixie."

"No, it isn't," Trixie said, "but it's where we are."

Oh fucking is it? I glared at her as she went on.

"Adam isn't strong enough to end the Dominion all by himself, even in its fallen state, and Menhit cannot enter Hell. But Adam can get us in. Between him and me and… and *you*," she said pointedly, and I knew she meant the Burned Man, "we should be able to finish it off once and for all."

"And why exactly the fuck would we want to do that?" I said.

Diabolists go to Hell, Don.

I'm sorry but I had absolutely no desire to go to Hell. Aside from the obvious, Hell was the Burned Man's home turf. Hell was the one place where the Burned Man wasn't even bound, for fucksake. If I walked in there with the bound version of the Burned Man inside me I had no idea what would happen, but I couldn't see that it would be anything good. And then there was Trixie herself, of course. She wasn't a fallen angel, not quite anyway, but by her own admission she had most definitely slipped a bit. A trip to

Hell might just be enough to shove her over the edge and into Adam's open arms. And I'd have bet good money the smarmy bastard knew that.

"We haven't got any choice," Trixie said. "We swore to serve Menhit."

Well we'd have to fucking see about that. However scared I was of Menhit, this was worse. Much, much worse.

"I'm not doing it," I said.

Trixie gave me a level look.

"We have to," she said.

"No, we fucking don't."

Trixie's mouth tightened in a furious line for a moment and I suddenly realized that Adam's henchman, this Heinrich geezer, was quietly sitting there listening to us argue. She glanced at him.

"Thank you Heinrich," she said. "You may go."

If he took any offence at being so offhandedly dismissed he gave no sign of it. This bloke was obviously a fair bit cleverer than Mikael had been, that was for sure. He knew who and what Trixie was, all right, and he knew that what she said went.

"I bid you a good evening, Angelus," he said as he rose. "Don."

I nodded at him as he turned on his heel and left the restaurant.

"We must not argue in front of the Soulless," Trixie hissed. "Every word they hear is a word Adam hears, don't you understand that?"

I shrugged. "I suppose so," I said, "but that's neither here nor there. I'm not going to fucking *Hell*, Trixie."

"Menhit will *make* us," she said, and there was a hint of a tremor in her voice.

I looked at her, and I remembered Menhit knocking her to the floor back in Edinburgh. It suddenly dawned on me that she was every bit as scared of Menhit as I was. I mean of *course* I was scared of Menhit, but then I'm scared of a lot of things. Trixie wasn't.

"How?" I asked. "How can she make us?"

Trixie's eyes flashed with frustration. "You said it yourself Don, she is a *goddess*. She can do anything."

"Well she obviously *can't*, can she?" I countered. "Otherwise she'd be doing *this*, not plotting with the likes of Adam and having to bully us into doing it for her."

Trixie blinked at me. It looked like she hadn't thought of it quite like that.

"Well not *anything*, perhaps," she said. "But you know what I mean."

I did, but all the same something was nagging at me. Something Davey had said… no, it was no good, it was gone. I knew there was something though, something I was missing.

"We'll see," I said. "For now I'm saying 'no', and unless she puts a fucking gun to my head it's staying 'no'. Besides which, she hasn't even fucking asked."

"Ah," Trixie said. "I'm afraid that's another thing I've been meaning to bring up."

I stared at her.

"Fucking *really*?"

Trixie at least had the good grace to blush.

"There was never really a good time," she said.

"We've been in the back of a car together for eight sodding hours today, bored out of our skulls," I said. "That might have been a *great* time, Trixie."

She cleared her throat and took a long swallow of wine. Her hand was trembling as she put the glass down, I noticed.

"I don't want to go to Hell, Don," she said quietly.

Oh dear God, bless her. Of *course* she didn't. Trixie knew all too damn well how close she had come to falling before, and she of all people should know how close she *still* was. She was terrified of Hell, I realized. Of course she was, but she was apparently terrified of Menhit too. Jesus, what sort of fucking corner had we painted ourselves into when we took up with her? I reached out and put my hand over Trixie's.

"It'll be all right," I said. "I know it will. There's something in my mind that I can't quite catch, but I know it's important. Look, let me talk it out with Papa Armand, I'm sure we can figure it out between us."

Trixie swallowed and nodded.

"I hope you can," she said.

I fucking well hoped so too.

CHAPTER 15

I phoned Papa Armand the next morning.

"Don-boy Drake," he said, and I could hear his warm smile down the phone. "I startin' think you dead!"

I grimaced, but I knew Papa meant well.

"No, not quite Papa," I said. "Almost, perhaps, but not quite. Look, can I come and see you? I need some advice."

"Of course, Don-boy," he said. "You always welcome come Papa. That what I here for."

Papa Armand was there for himself of course, I knew that damn well. All the same the old Houngan *had* taken me under his wing of his own accord, and I respected him immensely. He was such a cool old guy for one thing, and I couldn't help but feel like he was almost the dad I'd always wished I'd had. Not quite, perhaps, but almost. He would have been a damn sight better than the dad that I *had* had, that was for sure.

I took a taxi to his building in Knightsbridge and stood self-consciously in the private elevator as it wafted me up to his penthouse apartment. Papa Armand was seriously rich. He opened the door wearing black linen slacks and a big, baggy white shirt, untucked so that the long tails hung

193

almost to his knees. His big black feet were bare on the thick white carpet in his hall.

"Don boy, come in," he said with a wide grin.

He led me inside and I kicked my shoes off and followed him into his enormous living room. I padded across an acre of pristine white carpet towards the huge smoked glass windows that stood open to lead out onto the balcony. The view from up here was breathtaking, a multimillion pound vista of Kensington Gardens and across to Hyde Park and the Serpentine. Papa led me outside and waved me into an antique wrought-iron chair between heavy planters full of mature shrubs. There was already a glass of eyewateringly expensive single-malt whisky on the table waiting for me, the bottle standing invitingly beside it.

Papa sat down opposite me and picked up his own drink, a dark rum that I could smell even from where I was sitting. He raised it in salute.

"Your health," he said.

We drank together, and he lit a cigar with a slim gold lighter.

"God but it's good to see you, Papa," I admitted.

He smiled and nodded, letting me take my time. That was one of the things I loved about Papa Armand. He always seemed to know when I had something on my mind, and he knew I would tell him at my own pace so long as he didn't interrupt. I stared out at the view for a moment, listening to the muted noise of the traffic far below.

I started to talk, and I told him everything.

The whole business with the Blade of Unmaking had been Papa's idea in the first place, of making a talisman to carry the Burned Man down to the warrens to face Bianakith. An Ouanga, he had called that. I had never told him just how badly wrong that had gone. He knew what I had done, but not that I had managed to get myself possessed by the

Burned Man in the process. I still wondered if he might have at least suspected it, but he hadn't known for sure. Until now.

"Heroin," he said when I was done. His voice was uncharacteristically hard. "Perhaps it a good thing Menhit found you before I did."

I looked at him, and realized he was completely serious.

"I'm sorry, Papa," I said.

"You know what that *shit* has done to my country?"

I didn't, but I doubted it was anything good. I hung my head in shame.

"I just…" I said. "Oh fuck Papa, I'm *sorry*, you know? I just… I didn't know how else to hide."

"Bondye's balls, Don-boy," he said, and now his expression was one of pity.

Pity. I think that was worse than his anger had been. I could cope with his anger. I could stand there and take my bollocking like a man, but his pity? No, I couldn't live with that. I felt six inches tall all of a sudden, and I felt a desperate need to try and excuse myself.

"Yeah," I said. "I mean, I… I can't explain it really. Sometimes I'm not even myself. This thing inside me, the–"

"Shhhhh!" Papa interrupted me urgently. "It quiet now, yes? Don' disturb it. You think I don' know about spirits in the head? I'm a Houngan, Don-boy. I'm a Horse of the Barons. I know *all* the fuck about wild spirits in the head."

I supposed that he did, thinking about it. He was a Vodou priest, after all, and the invocation of the loa was a big part of his religious practice. All the same, that was a different relationship to the one I had with the Burned Man, I knew that much. Even Baron La Croix went away again eventually. The Burned Man didn't.

"Of course, Papa," I said. "Look, now you're up to date I need to ask you about something."

Papa refilled our drinks from the bottles on the table and tapped ash from his cigar.

"You can ask me anything," he said. "I your Papa, that how this works."

"Yeah well, thanks and all that," I said, "but this might be a bit, um, delicate. I need to ask you about Menhit."

Papa snorted.

"Very strong lady," he said, which considering she was a goddess was probably a bit of a fucking understatement as far as I could see.

"Yeah," I said.

"Too strong for me," he said, and laughed. "Two months she stay here, two months she fuck me raw and spend my money. She nearly get me banned from Wormwood's place. Then, her people come and they say 'your house is ready, Mother' and off she fucked, with never a look behind her."

I gave him a wry smile. I had a feeling he wasn't exactly telling me the whole story, based on what Trixie had said.

Even Armand was at the end of his tether before she left him, she had told me, or something like that anyway.

He obviously wasn't going to bring up the little matter of that poor bloody waiter Menhit had torn in half with her bare hands. God, I wished Trixie hadn't told me about that. That was the last thing I wanted on my mind while I was working my way around to saying "no" to her about this proposed fucking mission to Hell. There had to be a way to get out of it without having my *own* spine ripped out. Could the Burned Man really stand up to her, if it came to it?

"I'm sure," I said. "Look, Papa, how powerful *is* she? Really, I mean."

"Really? Not so powerful as she pretend, I'm thinking," he said. "Not any more. Oh, when she first arrive she was terrible, make no mistake. You could feel the power coming off her like lightning."

He was right, I knew. I remembered how she had been after she had fought the Dominion, how I had knelt at her feet and accepted the mantle of Keeper with never a second thought. Her power had been overwhelming, how you might *expect* a living goddess to be. I had honestly feared for the world, with her walking the Earth in physical form. But… nothing had happened. Nothing at all.

"Yeah, I remember," I said.

"That her old power, brought through with her from her endless sands," Papa said. "Here though… I dunno Don-boy, truth be told. She has… diminished, the Mère de la guerre. No one worship Menhit, these days."

That was it, that was what I had been grasping for in the restaurant last night. That thing Davey had said – *There are computer game characters with more worshipers than Menhit these days*. Ridiculous as it sounded he was probably right, at that.

"And that makes a difference to a god, does it?" I asked him. "Worshipers, I mean?"

Papa shrugged. "It seem to," he said. "Oh she still a god, don't forget that, and only a god can create energy from nothing. How *much* energy though, well, that seem to depend."

I felt a slow smile cross my face.

I knew it!

Menhit fucking well *couldn't* do anything she wanted, could she? Not these days she couldn't, not when only Egyptologists and occultists had even bloody heard of her and only a handful of headcases actually still worshipped her.

I grinned at Papa Armand.

"Papa, you've made my fucking day," I said.

"I don' want you to get carried away, Don-boy," he said. "You serve her, diminished or not, and she won't forget that. You can't disrespect a goddess."

"Maybe not, but I can fucking well refuse to walk into Hell for her," I shot back.

Papa blinked at me.

"To do what now?" he said.

So I told him about that, too. I told him about the Dominion, and about how Adam and Menhit had made common cause together to see it destroyed once and for all. Papa Armand nodded slowly.

"No, no that sound like the mother of all bad fucking ideas," he agreed. "That thing you carry in your head, you don' want to be carrying that back home. And Madam Zanj Bèl... no, Don-boy. Hell is not a good place for her to be going, I don't think."

I didn't think it was a good place for *anyone* to be going, but I knew what he meant. Trixie, Madam Zanj Bèl as he called her, was particularly vulnerable in that aspect.

"Quite," I said, "so I'm not fucking doing it. Sorry Papa, but bugger Menhit. She can whistle for this one, goddess or not."

He nodded slowly. "That your choice to make, Don-boy," he said, "and I can't say I blame you. Remember though, every decision have its consequences."

I swallowed my whisky and stared out across the park.

Didn't it just.

I got home sometime in the early afternoon, and found Trixie had gone out. I shrugged and went through to the kitchen, biting back irritation when I saw Mazin in there watching two lads unloading groceries. I mean don't get me wrong, it was nice not to have to do shopping and all that shit but this was my home, you know what I mean? I didn't like finding it full of strangers.

"Hi Mazin," I said.

He turned and bowed to me.

"Lord Keeper," he said.

The other two dropped to their knees without a word.

Oh for fucksake... These had to be Mazin's boys then, members of the Order of the Keeper. These were my "people". They did grocery shopping, apparently.

"Get up, lads," I said. "I'm not, um, as formal as Rashid was. Go on, you're all right."

They got slowly back to their feet, giving Mazin nervous looks. He nodded and they went back to filling my kitchen cupboards with no end of shit I hadn't asked for and didn't really want. I could see half of it going in the bin in a few months once it had grown arms and legs and started trying to escape. I'm really not much of a cook, to be honest with you, and as far as I knew nor was Trixie.

I pinched the bridge of my nose between my fingers and sighed.

"Any idea where Trixie is?" I asked Mazin.

"The Madam Guardian had business to attend to," he said.

Oh joy. That was never good.

"Right," I said. "Look, Mazin, no offence but get your boys here to finish up and clear off will you?"

He bowed again, and I'm sorry if he looked a bit hurt but for fucksake. I really wasn't cut out for the whole "having servants" thing and I valued my privacy too much to be putting up with this in such a small flat.

Why the fuck, the Burned Man demanded suddenly, *are we still here?*

That made me jump. It had been quiet for so long I had almost managed to forget about the bloody thing.

What? I thought.

Seven hundred and however the fuck many million fucking dollars, Drake, it said. *Maybe he won't give you the actual money but make him buy you a fucking house! Make him buy a* big *fucking house, you stupid twat.*

It's not my money, I thought back at it. *Besides…*

Besides fucking what?

Oh God, this was where I was going to look stupid again, wasn't it? Why not? Because Trixie had looked after this place so faithfully for me, that's why. Because this was where I had first met her. Because… oh for fucksake I didn't even *know* why, really. Because I'm a stupid sentimental sap who was hopelessly in love with her. Most of all it was because everyone seemed to want me to be somewhere else and I'm a stubborn bastard. That was the essence of it, I supposed.

Shut up, I told it, for want of a more eloquent argument. *Actually no, if you want to talk then tell me this – how much power does a god with no worshipers have?*

The Burned Man was quiet for a moment, and I like to think I had nonplussed it a bit with that one.

Less, it said, after a pause. *Less than it would have done, but certainly not none. Are we talking about our beloved goddess of slaughter here?*

I let Mazin and his boys out and locked the door firmly behind them.

Yeah, we are, I said as I put the kettle on. At least there was fresh coffee now, that was something.

The Burned Man pondered for a bit.

Hmmm, it said at last. *That's a fucking good question actually. I mean, she came through her Veil like a thunderbolt and knocked that Dominion into the middle of next week, but she's done fuck all since.*

Exactly, I thought. *Which makes me wonder…*

You're not as fucking stupid as you look, Drake, it thought, and I found myself glad it had apparently slept through my chat with Papa Armand.

I liked the little bastard to have *some* respect for me, after all.

Right, I thought. *So if she used up most of her stored power on the Dominion, and recreating that power isn't going too well due to no one having a clue who she even fucking is anymore, then… she probably isn't so tough right now, is she?*

The Burned Man's laugh was horrible.

No, no she probably ain't, it said. *Oh what a fucking shame. Want to go round to her place and let me kick her arse?*

Oh for fucksake, no of course I didn't. She had defeated the Dominion for us, and however that had ended I owed her that much if nothing else. That and I *had* sworn to serve her. I still put some importance on that promise, I just didn't agree that it extended to walking into Hell for her.

No way, I said. *I just want to be sure that I can say "no" to her when I have to without getting my head torn off.*

Yeah, I reckon you can, the Burned Man said. *She won't fucking like it, though.*

No, no I had never expected that she would.

Trixie came back a couple of hours later, while I was finishing the sandwiches I had made myself. She had a face like thunder and a black eye.

"Oh bloody hell, Trixie!" I said when she came in. "You've been to see Menhit, haven't you?"

Trixie glared at me. She took her coat off and threw it on the sofa. She was wearing a short-sleeved blouse, and her arms were covered in bruises.

"What do you think?" she said.

I pushed my hands back through my hair and stared at her. I couldn't fucking believe it.

"And?"

"And I told her we wouldn't do it," Trixie said. "And she hit me. She beat me like a dog, Don, and she told me that I was the most worthless guardian she had ever heard of and that you are the most faithless Keeper she had ever encountered, and she commanded – *commanded*, mind you – that you be at her house at seven o'clock this evening to explain yourself in person."

I looked at her and I felt about six inches tall. I had felt the same way every time my dad had battered Mum and there hadn't been anything I could do about it. There hadn't been anything *she* could have done about it either other than run away and leave him, and of course as a good Catholic wife she'd never have done that. There was *plenty* Trixie could have done about this, though, and I just didn't understand why she was putting up with it.

"Oh God, Trixie," I said, "I never… I didn't mean you had to go and say 'no' to her yourself."

"I know," she said, "but I'm your Guardian, Don. It's my job to do this sort of thing for you. If you say 'no' to Menhit then it falls to me to deliver the message."

"Shit," I said. "Oh shit I'm sorry, I never even thought…"

"No," she said. "You didn't."

She went into the bathroom and closed and bolted the door behind her.

I sank onto the sofa with a weary sigh. I just couldn't stop fucking things up with her, could I?

I had to go, of course. Whether Menhit still had the power of a god or not was a bit of a moot point just then, as far as I could see. She had hundreds of millions of pounds, and these days that virtually came to the same fucking thing. She had also, if the two big lads she'd had with her in Edinburgh were anything to go by, been recruiting some pretty serious muscle. Yeah, I had to go, or I would be brought.

Mazin drove us out to Surrey late that afternoon, me in a good suit and Trixie sulking in the seat beside me in black jeans and a long-sleeved black silk blouse that hid the bruises on her arms. Her eye was looking a lot better but it wasn't healed yet. I looked at her beside me in the car and sighed. I had to ask. I had to try to understand, if only for Mum's sake.

"Didn't you try and stop her?" I asked quietly, not wanting Mazin to hear.

Trixie looked at me.

"She is our Mother, Don," she said. "If she feels the need to discipline us then so be it."

Now I'm sorry but I'd had enough parental "discipline" growing up to see *that* for the pile of steaming horseshit that it was. My dad had been more than happy to batter me when my poor mum couldn't get in the way quick enough, and I wasn't fucking having it any more. I simply wasn't. I wasn't going to be made to feel nine fucking years old and helpless again, not by her or anyone fucking else. Never again. Besides, Menhit might insist on being called Mother but that was all it was, a form of address. No, I wasn't having this at *all*.

"Look," I said, "I went to see Papa this morning. He backed up what I was trying to tell you the other night. She *isn't* all that powerful any more, whatever she might say. If she tries to hit you again, for God's sake don't let her."

"I…" she said. "Don, I'm a soldier. I can't be insubordinate to my commanding officer."

"Well I fucking well can," I snapped. "I'm no more a soldier than I am an angel, and I'm *not* having it. Not again."

I wasn't scared of her now, I was too fucking angry for that. This was going to stop, right now.

Good, the Burned Man thought in the back of my head.

Trixie winced.

"Well," she said, after a moment. "This is going to be an interesting meeting, then."

Yeah, I had a feeling it would be too.

We didn't talk any more after that, and I just sat and watched the motorway roll past us. After a while Mazin took an exit onto a big junction and turned off onto a dual carriageway, and then a few miles later onto a country lane. Eventually the big Mercedes nosed between high wrought iron gates and onto a sweeping gravel drive that led up to a Georgian mansion. For fucksake, Menhit didn't do things by halves did she?

Mazin parked outside the enormous house and a huge black geezer in a suit came out to meet us. He nodded to Mazin as he opened the car doors for us.

"Lord Keeper, Madam Guardian," the bloke said. "The Mother will receive you in the blue drawing room."

Oh fuck me how posh does a house have to be to even have *a* "drawing room", never mind a choice of them so you have to give them names? We followed this goliath in a suit up lichen-covered steps and into a grand hall, where he showed us down a dimly lit corridor and through to a room done out in pale blue and white like an old Wedgwood plate. Menhit was reclining on a chaise longue in front of a fireplace, a tall glass of red wine in her hand. She arched her eyebrows at us as we entered.

"Good evening, Mother," I said.

I mustered a respectful bow but I was buggered if I was kneeling to her. Trixie followed my lead and did the same.

"Ah, my rebellious children," Menhit said, setting her wine down on a side table. "Explain yourself, Lord Keeper."

Right, so we weren't being offered a drink then. Or even a seat, it seemed. The big bloke had followed us in, I noticed, and he'd brought a mate with him. They closed the double doors behind them and stood in front of them like they were giants carved out of Armani and obsidian.

"I don't see what you want me to explain," I said. "I'm not going to Hell for you and nor is Trixie. That's it pretty much explained, as far as I'm concerned. Mother."

Menhit was on her feet too fast to follow, six foot five of

lean, hard muscle and barely contained murder. Her elegant evening dress swirled around her ankles as she took a step towards me.

"You disobey me, Keeper?"

"I do in this, yes," I said. "I'm not doing it."

I looked into her eyes and I saw the lion in her, glaring back at me in fury.

She's going to go for you, the Burned Man said. *Get out of my fucking way, Drake.*

Lots of things happened at once.

Menhit roared and her hand flashed towards my head, her fingers hooked into claws that would probably have ripped my face clean off.

The Burned Man barged past me and took over just in time. My arm shot up to meet hers, lent an unnatural strength and speed by the Burned Man's rage. The back of my wrist hit the inside of Menhit's forearm with a crack like a tree hit by lightning, stopping her blow a foot from my face.

"No," I said.

Menhit roared at me again, her eyes flashing brilliant amber in the dim light. I took a half step backwards and my outstretched hands burst into flames. The two mercenaries were moving away from the door now, startled into action by the sudden violence, but I knew Trixie would have my back. Sure enough I heard the familiar *whummf* as her sword appeared in her hands, the blade already burning.

I stood my ground and faced down She Who Massacres.

I'm sorry but not any more she didn't, not if Davey and Papa Armand were right. And from the look on her face I was pretty damn sure that they were.

"*No*, Mother," I said, the fires streaming up from my hands as I held her gaze.

I wasn't backing down, not now. It was time to put my

life in order, I had told myself, and getting out from under Menhit was a big part of that. I knew some of that was the Burned Man's thinking, pushing back against any sort of authority but its own, and I didn't care. I wasn't going to be bullied any more.

"Lord of the Below," she whispered.

I nodded. She knew that of course, she had known that from the start. She had recognized the presence of the Burned Man inside me the first moment she had seen me. That had been most of the reason I had had this bloody job inflicted on me in the first place, I was sure. All the same, she obviously hadn't realized at the time just how much that might be liable to bite her on the arse eventually.

"I respect you, Mother," I said, "but there are things I will not do. Not even for you."

"Stay *back*," I heard Trixie say behind me. "Draw those guns and I will kill you both before you can use them."

I knew she meant it. Trixie didn't kill humans if it could be helped, but that in no way meant that she wouldn't. I think Menhit's bodyguards knew that. They backed off, and no one got shot.

"I..." Menhit said, and for the first time since I had met her she sounded unsure of herself. "Keeper, this must be done."

"Not by us," I said. "If you have made common cause with Adam then so be it, Mother, although that's something I would advise against. But if you have, then look to him to find a way to do it. I'm not going into Hell, and I won't see Trixie sent there either."

"I see," Menhit said. She sat down on the chaise, and waved at her bodyguards. "Go away, both of you."

They backed slowly out of the room, their wary eyes never leaving Trixie and her burning sword. When they had gone Trixie closed the doors behind them and stood in front of them with her sword in her hands. The flames went out, I noticed, but she kept the blade erect in front of her like some sort of carving of a medieval knight.

God, but she was magnificent.

Now that I was sure Menhit was calm, I let my own fires die away and sat down in an armchair across from her. Perhaps now we could talk like grownups instead of posturing at each other.

"I mean you no disrespect, Mother," I said again. "Truly I don't."

Menhit sighed and picked up her drink. She took a long swallow of her wine and regarded me over the rim of the glass.

"Tell me, Keeper," she said, "what is the purpose of a war goddess in a time of peace?"

This was a time of peace, really? Had she *seen* the fucking news recently? The question threw me a bit, I have to admit.

"Um," I said.

"I have no land, no people, no worshipers," she went on, and I had to admit that was pretty much where I had been coming from. "I have grown soft and indolent, decadent and diminished at the end of my time."

I looked at her, once again taking in the sheer, murderous ferocity of her. If this was Menhit grown soft then I dread to think what she must have been like back in her day.

And I just fronted her out, I thought. *Fuck me, that's a turnup for the books.*

Sometimes the Burned Man was almost worth putting up with, I had to admit.

All the same though, Menhit's day was a fucking long time ago now, wasn't it?

"This world has no need of me, Keeper," she went on. "Oh, there is war enough for everyone but it is a modern war, fought by machines and weapons that kill from a mile distant and more. Who burns sacrifices to Menhit in this day and age? *No one.*"

No, no I supposed they didn't. Odd though it may sound, I couldn't help but feel a little bit sorry for her.

"The world moves on, Mother," I said, for want of anything better to say.

She nodded, her thin black braids swinging around her leonine face.

"It does, Keeper," she said. "Once this thing is done, when this last revenge is taken, I shall retreat behind my Veil once more. One day this world will lose its technology, and man will fight man face to face once more upon the bloody sands. *Then* they will call out to Menhit, and I shall return in fire and blood. But that day is… far away."

I blinked at her. *Right…* Yeah. That was a fucking cheerful thought, wasn't it?

Post-apocalyptic visions aside, I was all in favour of her buggering off back behind her Veil. Well, behind *a* Veil anyway. Hers was dead, if Rashid had been telling the truth, but I was sure there were ways and means. Either way, it sounded like a bloody good plan to me.

"Well," I said, "it would be my honour to keep your Veil, Mother."

She nodded.

"And this other thing, this thing you will *not* do," she said. "I understand, my Keeper."

There, that didn't go too badly, did it?

CHAPTER 16

There were those famous last words again.

Menhit let us go after that, and Mazin drove us back into London in the comfort of the Mercedes. It was maybe ten at night by then and I was feeling pretty damn good. I had faced down Menhit, and proved Papa Armand right. If she really *had* still been as powerful as all that then she would have just bloody well made me do as I was told. But she hadn't, had she? No, we had called her bluff, me and the Burned Man, and she'd backed down.

I reckoned that was us winning then. At the time I did, anyway. Trixie was very quiet though, sitting beside me in the darkened interior of the car.

"You all right?" I asked her.

"Mmmm," she said. "I'm not sure."

"What is it?"

"Well you stood up to her, you and… yes. And she backed down, but… well *think*, Don. She said she would go once this thing is done and this last revenge is taken. So she still means to do it."

"So what?" I said. "I don't see that we care one way or the other, do we? Not so long as we aren't expected to do it for her, anyway."

"Yes, I suppose so," Trixie said, but she didn't sound convinced.

I sighed and stared out of the window, watching West London flow past as Mazin guided the big car effortlessly through the traffic.

Something was bothering her, I could tell, but I didn't know what and she obviously didn't want to talk about it right now. I knew better than to press Trixie when she wasn't in a talkative mood.

Still, like I said, our visit to Menhit hadn't gone too badly, all in all.

I spent most of the next day at my desk, reading Mazin's famous book at long last. I still wanted to understand what this Order of the Keeper of his was actually *for*.

It is all in the book, he had told Trixie when we first met him, but as far as I could see it really wasn't. The book, a slim black volume filled with cramped handwriting and columns and columns of figures, didn't really tell me all that much. Trixie had told me I should read it, but to be fair she hadn't actually said it would be helpful.

There was some preamble dedicated to the glory of Menhit's bountiful wisdom that had obviously been written a very long time ago by someone who had never actually bloody met her. After that it was all business shit and the histories of companies they had bought and sold, merchant ships and banks and accounts and investments and credits and debits and things that made my eyes sting just trying to follow them. I wondered if Trixie had actually understood any of it, because I knew damn well that I didn't. All the same, some of it didn't look quite right to me, but then I'm afraid I was no one's idea of a businessman. But I knew someone who was.

I picked up the phone and called Wormwood's office.

The phone was answered by Selina, his secretary. I know I had his personal number but I didn't want to abuse that too much, and anyway it seemed to me that if I wanted to set up an actual business meeting the least I could do was go through the proper channels.

"Mr Wormwood's office," she said when she picked up. "May I help you?"

"Hi Selina, it's Don Drake," I said.

"How nice," she said, in a tone that meant the complete opposite.

Damn, I had forgotten just how much she seemed to dislike me. I had never even met the woman, after all.

"I was wondering if I could get some time with his nibs this afternoon?" I asked her.

"No," she said. "He's a very busy man, Mr Drake. The best I can do is…" There was a pause as she checked his diary, the clicking of her fingers on a keyboard clearly audible down the phone. "This evening at eleven pm. At the club. You are still a member, Mr Drake."

Well I must admit I had bloody well *assumed* I was still a member, for all that she sounded surprised to be reading that particular fact from her screen. That was just charming, that was. Wormwood owed me, after all. That and I still had a good couple of grand in winnings sitting on my account at his club. If he had cancelled my membership in my absence I would have wanted a pretty stiff word with him about it. Obviously by that I mean I would have set Trixie on him. He knew that.

"Right," I said. "OK, that'll do. Tell him I'll see him then."

Now, Trixie had been through this book of course, and I didn't want her to think I was doubting her. Not that I was, exactly, but… Well, I don't know how much she knew about business accounting but I was willing to bet it probably wasn't a hell of a lot. No more than I did, anyway.

We had a bit of dinner together before I got round to bringing it up. Well sort of, anyway.

"I thought I'd pop over to Wormwood's tonight," I said. "You know, show my face and all that. It doesn't hurt to keep the relationship going, does it?"

"No," Trixie said. "No, that's a good idea. You do that."

She still seemed distracted, but after the previous day's confrontation with Menhit I supposed that was only to be expected. I had been rather counting on it, in fact.

"Want to come with me?" I asked casually as I forked another heap of takeaway Vietnamese noodles into my face. Damn they were good.

"Not particularly," she said. "Anyway, I think it would probably please Wormwood if I stayed away, don't you?"

Of course it would. The last thing on God's green Earth Wormwood wanted to see was Trixie walking into his club again. Every time she had been to the place there had been violence, or the very heavy threat of it. No, Wormwood was going to be more than happy for Trixie to avoid him for the foreseeable future. Which suited me just fine, of course.

"I suppose so," I said, as though I hadn't given it a moment's thought.

I know, I know, but… well look. Trixie was as fragile as a glass vase at the moment, and the very last bloody thing she needed was to be mixing with demons. She didn't need to see me second guessing her about Mazin either. I need to have a word with myself sometimes, I know I do, but I really was trying my best to look out for her.

"You go," she said. "I don't mind. There's a programme I wanted to watch on the television later, anyway."

I nodded. That suited me fine, although I still found it a bit hard to get my head around an angel watching the bloody telly. I only *had* a telly so I had something to watch old films on, you know what I mean?

Once we had eaten I cleared away the takeaway containers and left her to smoke and drink coffee in peace. I had a bit of a wash and brush up before I went out. Wormwood's place is fairly formal, and I had to iron a shirt and shine my shoes and all that shit before I was ready to get suited and booted. It was about half ten by then so I called a cab and headed off, leaving Trixie with her feet up on the sofa in front of the TV. How domesticated, I thought with a wry smile.

The cabbie dropped me at the end of a dark alley a few miles away, and I paid and waited for him to bugger off before I headed down there. Walls of damp, graffiti-covered brickwork loomed on either side of me, and somewhere in the darkness I could hear a siren wailing as a police car hurtled through the city night. Ah, London. Home sweet home.

I could see the glamour that covered the front door of the club, of course, and it gave way as I muttered the words of entry under my breath and walked into the wall. The illusion parted like cold, sticky cobwebs and I stepped through into the snug little downstairs bar. This was where patrons who weren't actually members of the club itself were allowed to hang out and drink and generally brown-nose for an invitation upstairs.

There was no one in there that I knew except Connie, Wormwood's faithful minder. He was standing at the bottom of the stairs and looming like a good bouncer should, easily nine foot-tall in his ridiculously huge tuxedo. His horns were almost brushing the ceiling.

He turned and stared at me as I walked in.

"Don!" he exclaimed, his big, ugly face breaking into a wide grin. "I thought you were dead!"

I really did like Connie. I could have got the hump at yet another person writing me off for dead but he was so affable

I just couldn't hold it against him.

"All right Con," I said, giving him a smile in return.

I got myself a beer from the bar and went over to talk to him.

"How's it going?"

"I can't complain, Don," he said. "I look after Mr Wormwood and he sees me all right, you know how it is."

He coughed and wiped his left hand slowly and conspicuously over his mouth to make very sure I could see the thick gold band on his ring finger. Bless him, no one had ever accused Connie of being subtle.

"Did you get married, big lad?" I asked him.

"Me and Tasha," he said, and I swear to God the great lunk was blushing. "We tied the knot a couple of months ago."

Tasha was a pretty little demon with a cute tail who waited tables upstairs in the club. I knew her and Connie had been seeing each other but this was a bit of a surprise, I had to admit. I hadn't even realized demons *did* get married. I assumed it hadn't been a church ceremony.

"Nice one," I said, and reached up to give him a friendly clap on the shoulder. "Good for you, mate."

"Yeah, thanks," he said. "What about you, Don? Are you and the Lady still, you know, friends?"

I could hear the capital letter in his voice, and I knew he meant Trixie. I nodded.

"Yeah, we're still friends," I said. "Not really any more than that, I'm afraid."

Connie nodded with the sage wisdom of a man who has been married for two whole months.

"You will be," he said. "Give her time, Don. I gave Tasha time until she said yes."

If only it was that simple. I gave him another pat on the shoulder and headed up the stairs in search of Wormwood.

It was eleven by then and the club was starting to fill up. It was dim and smoky up there, the way a proper club should be, and 1940s jazz was playing from nowhere in particular. I could hear the clatter of the roulette wheel, and the rattle of dice on the craps tables. I breathed in the scent of whisky and rum and cigar smoke as I finished my beer, looking around for Papa Armand.

For once he didn't seem to be there, but Wormwood was. He was sitting at a card table by himself reading the *Financial Times* and smoking a cigarette, the two decks of cards on the table in front of him set out ready for Fates. There was a bottle of single malt and two glasses there too, waiting for someone to come and play him. I wondered if Selina had "forgotten" to tell him that he was supposed to be meeting me.

I snagged a glass of champagne from a passing waiter and wandered over there.

"Evening Wormwood," I said.

"You're late," he said. "Three minutes."

For fucksake…

"I was congratulating Connie on his recent wedding," I said, sitting down opposite him.

Wormwood snorted.

"Fucking ridiculous, that is," he said. "Stupid bleedin' human custom."

He folded the huge salmon pink expanse of his newspaper and set it down on the table, and grinned at me. Wormwood had a truly repulsive grin. It was every bit as bad as Davey's, but where Davey didn't have enough teeth Wormwood had far too many, and they all looked very rotten but very sharp. His long, greasy hair was limp and lank, and there was a strand of it stuck to the stubble on his sallow cheek. He stank of cigarettes and other people's misery. You'd never think he was amongst the hundred richest men in London, to look at him. Well not officially he wasn't, of course, on account of being an archdemon and therefore not officially even existing. That didn't seem to stop him living in Mayfair and being chauffeured around in a bloody great Rolls Royce though. He was truly and utterly horrible, but he was a child of Mammon and if anyone knew business it was him.

"What do you want, anyway?" he demanded. "If you've come to ask me to let your fucking psychotic goddess back in here you can fuck right off. Bleedin' bad for business, that was, and good waiters don't grow on trees. I ain't having it."

"No, it's not that. I want your opinion on something," I said, and took Mazin's book out of the inside pocket of my suit.

"Oh yeah?" he said. "It'll cost you."

I sighed. Of course it would cost me. Getting Wormwood to say more than "hello" always cost you something, I knew that all too well.

"There's money on my account," I said with another sigh. "Take a grand out of it for business consultancy services."

It hurt, but any less than that would have insulted him. Wormwood didn't talk in hundreds, if you know what I mean. He grinned again and took the book from my hand.

"Deal," he said.

He lit another cigarette and looked at me.

"You've changed, Drake," he said thoughtfully. "You'd never have come to me with this a year ago. Finally starting to realize which side your bread's buttered on, are you?"

Fuck me, was I?

"Something like that," I muttered.

Wormwood snorted and started to read.

I finished my champagne and helped myself to a scotch from Wormwood's bottle. Champagne is the most overrated stuff on Earth, if you ask me. All it tastes of is bloody bubbles. I swallowed a mouthful of very old, very expensive whisky, and smiled. That was more like it. That was a proper drink, right there. I looked at Wormwood and saw his brow was furrowed in concentration as he ran a nicotine-stained finger down one column of figures after another, starting from around 1740 when the accounts began. Fuck knows what had happened before then. His mouth worked silently as he mumbled numbers to himself under his breath, factoring inflation and historical currency conversion ratios in his head as he went. There are supercomputers that aren't as good at this shit as Wormwood is, I tell you.

He leafed through the pages of cramped figures with alarming speed, his frown deepening as his finger kept tracking down the lines. At last he looked up at me with a scowl.

"These numbers don't work," he said.

No, no I didn't think they did.

"I guessed as much," I said. "How badly is it out?"

His mouth twisted with distaste. "By now? About three hundred million fucking quid, all in," he said. "Whose fucking money *is* this, anyway?"

Ah, now this was where me and the truth were going to have to part company, I realized. It would never do for Wormwood to know I had even a tangential connection to that sort of wealth.

"A client of mine," I said. "Highly confidential, sorry. Any idea where it's been going?"

He shrugged. "From this? No. But I'd suggest you ask whoever's been cooking these fucking books."

I coughed and had another swallow of whisky. Yeah, that might be tricky. Those numbers went back hundreds of years, after all. Sometimes Wormwood seemed to forget that not everyone was immortal. Still, it went to show though, didn't it? Whoever you are, however powerful you think you are, there's always someone who will betray you, cheat you, steal from you. Even if you're a goddess. Money is the dark heart of… well, everything really. You only had to look at Wormwood to see that.

"Right," I said, taking the book off him and slipping it carefully back into my pocket. "Thanks for that, Wormwood."

He nodded, but I could see he looked tense. The very thought of embezzlement made him itch, I could tell. Unless it was him doing the embezzling, no doubt. He was a grotty, avaricious little bugger at the best of times, and… That made me think of something. Grotty old Davey had reminded me a bit of Wormwood, I remembered.

"One other thing," I said, offhandedly. "You're good at Fates – what would you make of a man who drew the Hermit as his trump?"

"Just the once, or repeatedly?" Wormwood asked.

"Can't really say," I said. "I only played him the one hand."

"Hmmm," Wormwood said. "Then it might not mean anything. It might just be the luck of the cards, a quirk of fate, whatever. But if he kept drawing it, well, that might mean all sorts of things. The Hermit means achievement and accomplishment, a spiritual pinnacle and maybe a teacher for those willing to undergo hardship to earn his wisdom."

I nodded. That was pretty much my understanding of the card too.

"But I can't tell, based on just one hand?"

"If you think you can tell much of *anything* based on one hand, you've drawn the Fool," Wormwood said. "It takes time, and patience, and a lot of hands to really get the measure of a man from Fates. Now piss off, I've got a club to run."

I nodded and left him to it. He had a point, I supposed.

Still, as these things went my visit to Wormwood's club hadn't gone too badly either.

Maybe things were looking up at last.

•••

Things kept on not going too badly for the next few days, in fact, and then everything went to shit in the most horrendous way possible.

It was about nine in the morning when the phone rang.

"Don Drake," I said as I picked up.

"It's Debbie," she said. I blinked in surprise. "You've still got the same phone number."

I had, but only because I had refused Mazin's offer to move to somewhere better than my flat. There was some benefit to resisting temptation after all, I thought. Sometimes, anyway.

All the same, that struck me as a bit of an odd thing to say.

"Yeah," I said. "Yeah, I have. How are you?"

"Very heavily sedated," she said, and that made me sit up in surprise.

Alchemist or not, Debs had never been one to sample her own wares. Now that she mentioned it I noticed how flat and hollow her voice sounded.

"Um, why's that then?" I asked cautiously.

There was a pause, and I heard her talking to someone in the background.

"Olivia has been taken," she said.

I felt my heart drop through the floor.

"*What?*"

"You heard me. In the night. At gunpoint."

"Fucking hell, Debs! Have you gone to the police?"

"Of course I've gone to the police you fucking *cretin!*" she screamed at me, and I couldn't help thinking that whatever sedative they had given her might not have been quite strong enough. "That's what people *do* when their only child is kidnapped! I've got the police here with me right *now.*"

She got a bit incoherent after that, which wasn't really surprising to be fair. I was feeling a bit incoherent myself. My little girl, my beautiful Olivia, had been… *taken?*

A moment later a different voice came on the line, another woman.

"Mr Drake? This is PC Newland, Inverleith Police family liaison. I understand you're the father?"

"Yeah," I said, conscious of how my voice was trembling. "What the bloody hell happened?"

Of course she wasn't going to tell me, was she? As the estranged father I was probably the fucking prime suspect. I'm sorry, but there might not be time to cock about with alibis and proof of who was where and when and with who and all of that shit. I concentrated, forming an image of PC Newland in my mind.

I only had her voice to go on but I'm pretty good at this, if I do say so myself. She's older than me, I thought. Late forties. Blonde hair pulled back under her uniform cap. An old scar on her forehead, a strong chin. The scar's from before she was a copper, maybe when she was in her early teens. She's lived a bit, definitely.

That was a good start. Keep going, go deeper than the image. Who *is* she?

First name is Sarah. She's been twenty years on the force and she's seen it all before. Tried for sergeant twice and failed the exam. Stopped trying. She still cares, though. A good copper, doing her best.

I didn't have to be right, of course, or at least not accurate anyway. I just had to convince *myself* that I was right. That's how this kind of magic works – once you've got a connection to someone you can fill in whatever details feel right to you, whatever it takes to flesh them out in your mind until you can see that someone as a real actual person. I just had to convince myself that this was really *her* long enough to form an astral link with the disembodied voice on the end of the phone.

Go deeper. *Why* is she?

She's been married for eighteen years. He drives a lorry for a living. Name's Dave. He doesn't really like her being a copper but they rub along all right, and they need the money. They still love each other. They've got two kids, both boys. One plays football, the other one's badly disabled. Brain damage at birth. She still blames herself. Her overtime helps to pay for his special school.

Yes. There. There she is. That's Sarah Newland, right there.

Got you.

I focused down the phone and gave her an almighty stab of my Will.

"Tell me," I said.

Yeah I know, I *know*, all right? I try not to do this to people, I really do – it's hardly bloody healthy, is it? All the same, added to the long list of other things I had done what did it fucking matter?

Do not ask, command. *That is the true way to power.*

I remembered Adam saying that once, and I shuddered. Adam was hardly a fucking role model, after all. That and poor PC Newland was probably going to get suspended for this if her guv'nor found out about it. Which he wouldn't from me, admittedly. Whatever, I had done it now and this was far too important to fuck around with worrying about karma.

"Three masked IC1 males came to the house in the early hours of this morning armed with unspecified handguns, and demanded the child be handed over," she said. "They left in a black van, index unknown. One was heard to address another as 'Dimitri'. No witnesses apart from the mother."

"That's it? That all you've got?"

"So far sir, yes," she said.

"Right," I said. "Thanks. Look after Debbie."

I hung up, breaking the mental connection and no doubt

leaving poor PC Newland of the Inverleith Police wondering
what the bloody hell she had just done. Still, so long as she
had the sense to keep quiet about it there was no real harm
done, as far as I could see.

I stared out of the window and thought about it in the
moment of icy calm before the rage hit me. "IC1 male" was
police-speak for "white bloke", I knew that much. And one
of them was called "Dimitri". The Russian had a Dimitri on
his crew, a big ugly bugger who liked to hurt people.

I'll hurt you for this, I remembered the Russian telling me.

I couldn't fucking believe it.

My sweet little Olivia had been taken away from her
home by these animals? Away from her bunny rabbit? With
guns?

No.

Hurting me was one thing but this was fucking *way* out
of line.

We might all basically be criminals but there are certain
unwritten codes of acceptable practice, you know what I
mean? You didn't go after people's families. Not over the
small shit, anyway. You certainly didn't take their kids, not
ever.

You didn't *do* this!

No!

I was on my feet, I realized, breathing hard and fast
through clenched teeth. I don't think I'd ever been so fucking
furious in my life. A strangled scream of rage escaped me,
and brought Trixie running from the kitchen.

"Don, what is it?"

I forced in a shuddering breath and I told her, all the while
fighting the burning heat in my hands that threatened to
explode into flames at any moment. Trixie's mouth set in a
hard line, and she nodded.

"Where do we find this Russian?" she asked.

That, of course, was a bloody good question.

"All I've got is a phone number," I admitted.

Trixie nodded and went over to the sofa to get her handbag. She reached inside and pulled out a cheap plastic mobile phone, the sort you can get for twenty quid from the supermarket that come with a prepaid phone card and look like they're from 1998.

I gave her the Russian's number and she dialled, holding up a hand to tell me to be quiet.

"Put him on," she said, in a thick accent I'd never heard her use before.

A moment later she started speaking fluently in what I could only assume was Russian. She paused, nodded.

"Da," she said, and hung up.

She tossed the phone onto the sofa and smiled at me.

"Remind me to throw that away when we go," she said.

I stared at her. Trixie constantly amazed me, she really did. Not only did she apparently speak Russian and understand the concept of burner phones, but she actually had one. Wonders never ceased.

"Right," I said. "Where and when?"

I had calmed down a bit now, which was probably for the best. Trixie had a sort of soothing effect on me like that. When we weren't yelling at each other, anyway.

"Stockwell Park estate," she said, "and as soon as we can get there. He has a car dealership there, apparently"

I winced. *Oh joy.*

The Stockwell Park, in case you didn't know, isn't exactly what you'd call one of the more desirable parts of London to live in.

"How the fuck did you get him to agree to see us, anyway?" I asked as I put my coat on.

Trixie gave me a disarming smile and completely ignored the question.

"Me, not us," she said.

"You what?"

"For heaven's sake Don, you're not thinking straight. These people know you by sight. If they see you, they could hurt the child."

I sighed. She was right, I knew she was.

"And if she's not there? If they've got her somewhere else?"

"Then you can come in and discuss it with them," she said. "But we need to do this carefully. You'll have to wait in the car."

All right, I'd give her that one. The Burned Man wasn't exactly what you'd call careful, I had to admit. I called Mazin and had him come and pick us up. Trixie tossed her burner phone in the dustbin outside Mr Chowdhury's shop without breaking stride, and got into the car. She had obviously done that before.

I got in beside her and let Mazin drive us to the delights of Stockwell. It wasn't really the sort of place you went in a limousine, and I wasn't sure how safe we'd be parked up round the corner without Trixie there. I told him so, but he just nodded.

"All will be well, Lord Keeper," he said. "I am armed."

Fuck me, are you?

I'd never figured Mazin for the type to carry a gun, but I supposed I shouldn't really be surprised. He was the head of an organisation that served a sodding war goddess, after all. I shut my eyes and just tried to stay calm.

That didn't go very well, I have to admit.

Mazin and I stayed in the car like we had been told while Trixie went to speak to the Russian on whatever pretext she had given him. She had her hair up and was wearing her long black leather coat over smart black slacks and a white blouse, and she had produced a pair of big black sunglasses from somewhere. I have to admit she actually *looked* Russian, in some way I couldn't quite put my finger on. She really was a woman of many talents.

I watched her cross the street and stroll across a thoroughly unwelcoming looking garage forecourt. The place was littered with fifteen-year old motors with optimistic prices on the stickers in their windscreens. There was a shabby prefab building at the end of the lot, one of those things that are halfway between a trailer and a static caravan. The badly illuminated sign over the door said "Grigoryev Quality Cars". I'm sure they were quality, too. Low quality, to be precise. This place was so obviously a front for something else it was ridiculous. Whatever other businesses the Russian might be involved in, he wasn't here to sell cars.

I drummed my fingers nervously on the armrest. I knew Trixie was more than capable of looking after herself, but I couldn't help fretting all the same. If they had Olivia in there, could she get her out safely and fight the Russian's gorillas at the same time?

Ten minutes passed in uneasy silence, and nothing happened. I nearly jumped out of my seat when a great spray of blood suddenly exploded across the inside of one of the prefab's windows.

Mazin's mobile rang.

"Yes, Madam Guardian," he said a moment later, and hung up.

He turned around in his seat and looked at me.

"She says to go in," he said. "There is no child there. I will watch the car."

I got out and hurried after Trixie, weaving between the shabby cars on the forecourt. I couldn't help staring at that window, at the blood slowly running down the inside of the plastic pane. I shoved the door open and walked in.

A dead man lay on the floor in front of me, face down in a spreading pool of red. I stepped carefully over him and coughed to announce myself. The last thing I wanted was a foot of burning steel through my guts.

"In here, Don," Trixie said from the office at the end of the corridor.

I followed her voice, and stood frozen in the doorway. There was blood splattered up the walls and across the window and even on the ceiling, and three more dead bodies on the floor. One of them was missing his head, which I suppose explained why there was claret everywhere. Trixie had been busy.

The Russian himself was on his knees in front of an overturned desk, his eyes wide with terror and sweat glistening on his unshaven face. There was blood all over his face and suit, but it didn't look like any of it was his. Trixie was standing over him with her sword held loosely in one hand, more blood dripping from the blade.

God but I loved that woman.

"I want a fucking word," I said.

He stared up at me, shaking his head and blathering something in Russian. Trixie cuffed him across the face with the back of her free hand and barked something back at him in the same language. I caught the word for "English", one of the few Russian words I recognized.

"Drake, whatever I do to offend you, I–"

I lost my shit all at once.

Whatever he had done to fucking *offend* me? I crossed the space between us in two long strides, my right hand bursting into flames of pure rage as the Burned Man caught my mood. I grabbed the front of the Russian's bloody shirt with my left hand and yanked him up, holding my burning fist in front of him.

"Where's my daughter?" I bellowed in his face.

"What daughter?" he said.

I belted him, knocking him off his knees and into the overturned desk in a shower of loose papers. He screamed and beat at his face, swiping at stray flames that were trying to catch in his greasy hair.

"You kidnapped my little baby daughter!" I roared at him.

"I didn't know you *had* fucking baby daughter!" the Russian wailed, spittle flecking the corners of his mouth.

He looked from my burning hand to Trixie's glistening red blade and back again, and he wet himself.

I was so surprised, the rage went out of me at once. He just sprawled there on the filthy floor, the crotch of his grey suit turning darkly wet. The Russian was a hard, evil bastard, but there was no way he was that good an actor. He was scared out of his mind, and he quite obviously had no idea what I was talking about.

Fuck.

"Fuck!" I threw back my head and bellowed with helpless, impotent rage. "Where's my fucking daughter?"

"I don't know!" the Russian blubbered.

"Where's Dimitri?"

"Dimitri is gone," he said. "He look at my woman, I fire his dirty arse. Four, five weeks ago."

He stared up at me and lapsed back into Russian again.

I had no idea what he was saying now but it sounded like he was praying. Trixie didn't seem to be taking any notice of whatever it was, anyway.

I stepped back and took a long, shuddering breath. It was like an abattoir in there. Four men were dead for no good reason, and I was no nearer finding Olivia. I looked at Trixie, and winced. She met my eyes with a cold blue stare, and said nothing.

Oh God, what have I done?

I had jumped to an almighty conclusion, that was what I

had done, and these poor bastards had died for it. Trixie had killed for it, for that matter. I swallowed. She had just taken my word for everything, and look what had happened. Not that I had asked her to paint the place with blood, admittedly. All the same, I should have known that was going to happen once she got involved.

We really ought to be leaving. Someone was bound to notice the state of that window soon, and whatever sort of reputation the Russian had around here I knew it was only a matter of time before someone got nosey and called the Old Bill.

"We should go," Trixie said, as though reading my mind.

I nodded. She made her sword disappear and I followed her silently out of the prefab. We left the Russian behind us, sobbing and praying on his knees in a puddle of piss.

Mazin opened the car door for Trixie without a word, as though he couldn't see the blood splatters all over her white blouse. Nothing seemed to surprise Mazin, you had to give him that I suppose. I got in the other side of the motor and slammed the heavy door behind me.

"Home," I said. "Now."

The late morning traffic was terrible. We sat in hostile silence for a very long time.

CHAPTER 17

I couldn't get rid of Mazin quick enough once we got back to my place. Trixie stalked into the bathroom and closed the door, and I sagged onto the sofa with a defeated sigh. That couldn't have been more of a clusterfuck if it had tried.

Oh fucking hell, whatever was Trixie going to say when she finally started talking to me again? More to the point, where was Dimitri? Where the *hell* was Olivia?

I put my head in my hands. How long was it going to be until the Old Bill turned up, wasting my time and theirs satisfying themselves that I hadn't arranged to have her snatched myself? I would hardly have been the first estranged father to do something like that, after all. I could only pray that Debbie had managed to convince them that was the last thing I was likely to do.

I turned around to see Trixie standing in the doorway, staring at me. She had changed out of her blood-splattered clothes into clean jeans and a brown jumper, I noticed. Her face was unreadable.

"Look, Trixie..." I started.

I had no idea what to say to her. She had killed four innocent men for me this morning. Well not exactly *innocent* men, granted, but they hadn't been guilty of this particular thing at least.

"Yes?"

"About those blokes... I'm so sorry."

"It doesn't matter," she said. "Finding Olivia is the important thing. The steps we have to take along the way don't matter, as long as the objective is met. We have eliminated one line of enquiry, and narrowed the search. The morning hasn't been a complete waste."

I stared at her.

The ends justify the means, don't they Trixie? Every bloody time.

Some of her means were getting to be pretty fucking questionable these days, I had to admit. I spared a glance for her glowing white lie of an aura, and wondered what state she was in underneath it. I knew if I asked her to show me we'd only end up having another fight. She would stop hiding when she was ready to, I supposed, but definitely not before.

She seemed rational enough at the moment, I'll give her that. Too rational, if anything, almost cold. Six months of being bullied and beaten by Menhit probably hadn't done her a power of good, after all, and now there was this.

Yeah Don, there's this, I told myself. *This was* your *fucking doing more than hers. Don't you feel anything?*

I didn't though, not really. They had been scumbags and even if they *hadn't* taken Olivia I was pretty damn sure they had done more than enough other things over the years to... to what? Deserve to die? Really, Don?

Fucking really?

Jesus wept, what am I turning into?

I wondered just how much of my soul the Burned Man had eaten by then. What the fuck *was* I turning into? I put my head in my hands and sighed. I was not the man I wanted Olivia's father to be, that was for fucking sure.

I decided to worry about that later, and forced myself to stop thinking about it.

"I still have to find Dimitri," I said.

Diabolists go to Hell, Don.

Shut the fuck up.

Trixie nodded. "Yes. And now that we know one place where he is not, there are fewer places to look."

Well there was that, I supposed. If you really squinted at it, anyway. I shook my head. It was no good, I couldn't be worrying about her as well. Not now, not with everything else that was going on.

She has her own path to follow.

Adam had told me that once, too, what felt like a long time ago now. Of course, the lying bastard had been deliberately trying to engineer her fall back then as well. The last thing I needed was to be remembering *his* words right now. Any of them.

For fucksake, shut up Adam. Just shut up about everything and let me find Olivia. I'll worry about everything else later.

I got on the phone and started making enquiries. I know a lot of fucking insalubrious people, I have to admit. If Dimitri had been fired by the Russian then he had to be working for someone else by now – the bloke was hard as nails but he was far too stupid to have set up his own firm. Sure enough it wasn't long before one of my pet scrotes informed me he was now working as a minder for Mickey Two Hats.

Mickey was a grotty old wanker who ran a snooker hall about a mile away from my flat. Well, what he *actually* did was launder money for armed robbers and drug dealers, but the snooker hall was his front. He must have been doing quite well for himself too, if he could afford to take Dimitri on. Muscle like that didn't come cheap.

I put the phone down and looked at Trixie. She was

sitting on the sofa smoking a cigarette, and staring vacantly into space.

"Trixie?"

"Mmmm? Oh, sorry I was miles away," she said. She smiled at me but it really did look a bit forced. "Any luck?"

"Yeah," I said. "Mickey's snooker hall down by the station. Can we do it without Mazin this time? I can get away with going in there, but not with turning up in a sodding limo. Mickey's no detective but even he might think that was a bit fucking odd."

Trixie shrugged. "If you like," she said.

It was only about a mile away as I said, so we walked. I'm not a big fan of walking as a rule but it was actually quite a nice afternoon for once and I felt like stretching my legs to work off some of the tension. We turned the corner at the end of a parade of tatty shops and crossed the car park behind the station, and there next to the cash and carry was Mickey's place. The faded green sign just said "Snooker", with an unimaginative picture of a pint of lager and a triangle of red balls underneath it.

Mickey wasn't exactly a marketing expert, but then he didn't need to be. People who knew what he really did came to him, if you know what I mean. I had been to the place a few times myself to be fair, but only to play a couple of frames when I was bored. I'm not that great at snooker and I'd never had enough money to need to launder it so it wasn't one of my regular haunts.

I pushed the front door open and stepped inside with Trixie behind me. It was gloomy in there, with most of the table lights switched off that early in the day. There were a couple of lads I didn't recognize knocking balls about on a table at the back, but one look was enough to tell me they were just killing time rather than playing properly. They were staff, then, which meant they were crooks.

Mickey himself inhabited a cramped little office at the back of the club and seldom came out of it. I nodded to the boys at the table and walked that way. As I had been rather hoping, Dimitri appeared from somewhere and got in my face before I reached the office door.

"You want something, Drake?" he asked me.

I could feel Trixie slide away from me and get between me and the snooker players, covering my back as always. I took a slow, cold breath and felt the Burned Man rear up inside me.

"Yeah, I do as it happens," I said. I looked at Dimitri's flat, ugly face and went hot and cold all over, all at once. "I want my *fucking daughter!*"

I went for him in a rush of rage so violent it even surprised me. Dimitri was six foot four and must have been half again my weight, but when the Burned Man got the bit between its teeth there was no stopping it. My left hand shot out and closed around Dimitri's throat, squeezing mercilessly as I rammed him backwards into the wall. His eyes bulged in his ugly, scarred face and I hit him in the guts. Hard.

Again, the Burned Man encouraged me. *Burn him!*

My right fist burst into flames and I pulled it back ready to break Dimitri's head open, and never mind that that wouldn't have got me any answers at all. When the Burned Man got fired up so did I, these days.

A deafening roar made my ears ring. It's amazing how loud a shotgun is in a confined space.

My head whipped round and I saw Mickey Two Hats standing in his office doorway with a smoking double-barrelled sawnoff in his hands. He was a fat bloke in his mid sixties, with a dodgy combover and a crumpled and dandruff-encrusted suit that looked like it had last been drycleaned sometime in the Nineties. All the same, he was the one with the shooter. He had fired the first one into the ceiling, thank fuck, but there was another shot left in that bloody thing and now he was pointing it right at my head.

This was a bit ticklish, to put it mildly.

Trixie was balanced on the balls of her feet, keeping one eye on the two blokes at the snooker table whilst obviously figuring how quickly she could reach Mickey and whether or not she could get that gun out of his hands before he blew my head off. Just the fact that she was thinking about it rather than simply doing it made me realize how thin her chances were. I still had Dimitri pinned to the wall in front of me, and my hand was still very conspicuously on fire.

"You'd better have a fucking good excuse for this, Drake," Mickey said. "And that's a smart trick, but however you're doing it you'll run out of paraffin in a minute. I can wait."

I stared down the barrels of his shooter and slowly let the fire gutter out. It was easier to let Mickey believe what he wanted, and if he needed hurting I'd rather let Trixie take him from the side than run the risk of a face full of lead.

"All right, Mickey," I said. "I've got no problem with you, it's this fucking animal I'm here for."

Dimitri was standing very still, taking shallow, laboured breaths with my hand all but crushing his windpipe. Not for the first time I wondered where the Burned Man was getting the physical strength it was feeding to me. It's horribly powerful but only a god can create energy from nothing, and it's not a god. I risked a glance to my left and saw one of the snooker players sway unsteadily on his feet. He was white as a sheet and his face was shiny with sick sweat, as though he was about to pass out.

Right, well I supposed that answered that question then.

"He ain't done nothing to you," Mickey said. "He works for me now, not that Russian cunt."

"So who wanted my little baby daughter taking then, Mickey? You?"

"Your what? Nah. For fucksake, geezer. I don't do that sort of thing."

No, no I knew he didn't. Mickey Two Hats was as dodgy as they come but he was old school, you know what I mean? He'd no more hurt someone's kid than he would their mum. People just didn't *do* that sort of thing, as I said. The right sort of people didn't, anyway. The gang kids these days, well maybe they were different, but not the sort of geezers I knew. No one in the life would do that.

Only someone bloody well had, hadn't they?

"He was called Dimitri," I said. "I only know one Dimitri, and I'm about to break his *fucking* neck."

"Don," Trixie said quietly. I turned and looked at her. "Don, do you really suppose there's only one man in London called Dimitri?"

I stared at her, and I started to feel a bit cold.

Well I mean no, obviously not, but I had been so sure. So *fucking* sure it was him. Of course it was someone I knew, it had to have been. It always fucking is, isn't it? Why would anyone else…

"I've got problems with the Serbians," Mickey said, interrupting my train of thought. "Big problems. That's why I'm all tooled up and shit – I need the protection. Whatever you think he's done, Dimitri ain't left my side in three fucking weeks."

Oh for fucksake.

I'd been a complete fucking idiot about this, hadn't I? Thinking about it, I had no idea *why* Olivia had been taken, which meant it could have been *anyone*. Absolutely fucking anyone at all. I let go of Dimitri's thick neck and took a cautious step backwards, keeping an eye on Mickey's shooter as I went.

"I think…" I started, and all of a sudden I felt ill. "I think I might have been a bit of a prick."

"I think you fucking have," Mickey said. "It's a good job I know you, Drake."

I nodded. He didn't of course, not really, but he probably knew *of* me if nothing else. We had a lot of iffy acquaintances in common, after all. He knew I was part of his world, at least. That was basically why he hadn't shot me yet.

I looked at Dimitri, and sighed.

"Sorry," I said.

He rubbed his neck and glared at me, but said nothing. He'd probably never been choked that hard in his life, and certainly not by a bloke my size. I reckoned that had probably surprised the crap out of him.

"We should probably go," Trixie said.

I looked at Mickey Two Hats and his sawnoff shotgun, and nodded.

"Yeah," I said. "Look, Mickey..."

"Fuck off," Mickey said. "Fuck off, and don't ever come back."

We went.

It was a bit of an uncomfortable walk back to my flat. That was twice today I had dragged Trixie into a pointless confrontation with people who were nothing to fucking do with anything. Four men were dead and I couldn't even make myself care. Fuck me, I had changed recently. Not for the better, I'm ashamed to say. What exactly was I becoming?

A man who has to get his daughter back, I told myself.

You really are a thick cunt, the Burned Man helpfully informed me as we trudged back down the high street.

Even the nice weather had deserted me, and it was bloody cold out there now.

Yeah, thanks pal, I thought at it. *You got any better ideas?*

You're fixated on these worthless fucking gangsters, it said. *Think bigger. For fucksake Drake, you work for a fucking goddess.*

Think outside the neighbourhood for once.

It went quiet after that, but I supposed it had a point.

I still had no idea where Olivia was and now I didn't even know who had taken her. *Think, Drake,* I told myself. White blokes. Masks. Guns. Dimitri. A black van. It certainly still *sounded* like gangsters' handiwork, but as the Burned Man said maybe I should be thinking bigger than that. I had to do something.

Fuck what I was becoming, it didn't matter. Not now. I *had* to find Olivia.

Anything in my power to protect you, I had promised her, and I had promised myself I wouldn't let her down, too.

It was time to fucking prove it.

When we got home I got back on the phone. It was about three o'clock by then and I was starving, so I sat nibbling at a bloody horrible sandwich from the newsagents while I called every scumbag I knew. That was a lot of phonecalls, to be fair. Trixie sat on the sofa, looking at me with a tight-lipped expression that I didn't even want to think about. She really, *really* wasn't best pleased, and I honestly couldn't blame her. I tried my best to shut her out as I made call after call.

I even reached out to Wormwood for fucksake, that's how desperate I was now. No one knew anything, or if they did they weren't talking. Eventually I worked my way all the way down my mental list of useful people, and there right at the bottom was Harry the Weasel.

The Weasel, in case you don't remember, was an unfortunate little bloke who wanted to be my apprentice. He was thoroughly horrible, and last year he had betrayed me for a paltry amount of money and almost got me killed. I wasn't really on speaking terms with Harry the Weasel any more, but needs must when the devil drives and all that.

"Mr Drake," he said in obvious surprise when he realized

it was me on the phone. "I thought you were dead, like."

I was getting heartily sick of hearing that by now, and I had never had a lot of patience with the Weasel at the best of times. All the same, he knew damn near everyone and he was fucking good at sniffing out information. I looked at what was left of my grotty sandwich and chucked it in the bin under my desk.

"Well I'm not dead, and I need to see you," I said. "Meet me at Big Dave's and I'll buy you a late lunch."

I hung up on him and looked at Trixie. "Right," I said. "I'm meeting Weasel for a bite to eat down at Dave's. I want to see what he can ferret out for me. Want to come?"

"No thank you," she said, and stalked into the kitchen.

Right, that was me told then wasn't it? I sighed and went out.

Big Dave's café was on the high street next door to Mr Chowdhury's grocers shop. It was a proper old fashioned greasy spoon too, not one of these poncy hipster places where they want to serve your chips in a Wellington boot and your drink in an old jam jar or some such stupid fuckery like that. I pushed the door open and grinned at Big Dave.

"All right?" I greeted him.

"Rosie!" he exclaimed, his fat face lighting up like the sun. "Fucking hell, I thought you were dead!"

He always called me Rosie. It's because I don't like tea, you see. No, of course you don't. "Rosie Lee" is cockney for "cup of tea", and I can't bloody stand the stuff. I'm strictly a coffee drinker, so Big Dave calls me Rosie. That's about the standard of the local banter around these parts. You get used to it.

I went up to his greasy counter and shook his big greasy hand.

"Do us a coffee will you, mate?" I asked him. "I'm meeting

the usual grotty article here for lunch in a bit. You'll have to excuse him, I'm afraid."

Dave just shrugged.

"As long as someone's paying for him, he's welcome," he said.

"Yeah, I'll sort him out," I said.

Dave nodded and handed me a chipped mug full of thick, burned black coffee, and I gave him a pound. You can keep your five quid crapachinos, thank you very much. This is what a cup of coffee should look like. I headed to a table in the corner and sat leafing through someone's abandoned newspaper. I was just finishing my coffee when Weasel appeared.

He was a sorry sight, as usual. He was no more than five foot six, and already half bald despite only being in his early thirties, with a droopy lower lip and a lazy eye that made him look thick. He wasn't thick, though. He could be stupid sometimes maybe, but he wasn't thick. He was wearing a nasty cheap tracksuit and a pair of prison-style white trainers, and that big naff gold ring he had bought with the money he had earned by selling me out last year. Little git.

"All right, Weasel?" I said.

"Hello Mr Drake," he muttered as he wriggled into the seat opposite me.

I waved Big Dave over and ordered us both a coffee and a fry up. It really was the safest thing on the menu. Dave's not exactly what you'd call a culinary adventurer, if you know what I mean.

"Where you *been*, Mr Drake?" Weasel asked me once Dave had set our drinks down in front of us and retreated to his frying pans.

"Away," I said, I and that was going to be the end of it as far as he was concerned. It was hardly his fucking business, after all. "You keeping your nose clean, Weasel?"

He had just got out of prison last time I saw him, after all. I needed him out on the streets listening and watching, not banged up in the Scrubs where he was neither use nor ornament.

"I have, Mr Drake," he said proudly. "I've been studying, too. I'm getting good at my Goetia these days."

Oh joy.

The Goetia, in case you didn't know, is one of the great classical grimoires. It's the first book of *The Lesser Key of Solomon the King* and it's basically a manual of how to summon demons.

If there was one thing Harry the Weasel shouldn't be allowed anywhere near, it was magic.

Dave came back with our lunches before I could say anything about that. He put a big plate of fried sausage, fried bacon, fried eggs, fried bread and baked beans down in front of each of us, and mercifully went away again. I think he would have fried the beans too if he could have worked out how to do it.

"Listen to me, Weasel," I said. "I need some information. Someone kidnapped a little baby girl in Edinburgh last night. *My* little girl."

Weasel gaped at me, a forkful of dripping, greasy bacon halfway to his mouth.

"Have you *got* a little girl, Mr Drake?"

"Yes Weasel, I have," I said. "I have, and I. Want. Her. Back. Do you understand me?"

"Yes, Mr Drake," he whispered, and it looked like he had lost his appetite all of a sudden. "Do we know anything?"

I told him what the copper had told me. I also told him to forget about the Russian. I was more than satisfied that *that* line of enquiry was a dead end.

"I know a Dimitri," he said, after a moment. "Not the Russian's monster, another one. I had a look at him once, in this pub we was both in. A *proper* look, as you might say. He's got a red aura, Mr Drake. I think he's... you know. Not human, like, if you know what I mean."

Oh, I knew all right. Hard though it might be to believe, Harry the Weasel was already a magician for all that he shouldn't have been. Not a very good one, to be fair, but good enough that he could see auras if he really worked at it. He might not know what a red aura meant when he saw one, but I fucking did.

"Soulless," I muttered around a mouthful of eggs.

"You what, Mr Drake?"

"Nothing," I said. "Cheers Weasel. I might forgive you yet."

"I hope so, Mr Drake," he said. "I really do still want to learn off you, you know."

I nodded.

"I know you do, Weasel," I said. "I know."

And I want a fucking Bentley, mate. Looks like we're both out of luck, doesn't it?

CHAPTER 18

I paid up after we had eaten, and chased Weasel off down the road. He still wanted to learn off me, did he? Well the first thing he needed to learn was not to fucking sell me out again. After that little lesson had well and truly sunk in maybe we'd see, but that was a long way off yet as far as I was concerned.

I opened the front door and went back up to my office, where Trixie was sitting waiting for me.

"How was the Weasel?" she asked me.

I shrugged. At least she was talking to me again, that was something.

"Interesting," I said. "As grotty as ever, but the little bugger does know things."

"See?" Trixie said. "I told you the day hadn't been a complete waste. Anything that narrows the search is progress, however it may be achieved."

"Yeah, you're right," I said with a sigh. "And you were right about that, too – we've narrowed the search quite a bit now, actually."

I know, I was taking the easy way out as usual. It was just... it was just fucking *easier*, you know? If she wanted to overlook certain things, like four dead geezers in a car lot, then that was her business and not mine.

I told her what Weasel had told me, and her eyebrows lifted in surprise.

"I don't know a Soulless called Dimitri," she said, "but Heinrich might."

"Right, good," I said. "Can you get hold of this Heinrich? By the throat, ideally."

Trixie gave me a smile. There was no warmth in that smile, none at all. It looked reptilian, almost shark-like, and I have to admit that frightened me a bit. Her blinding white aura was taunting me with how much *utter* bullshit it was. I tried to ignore it, tried to stop thinking about what she might be hiding underneath that brilliant white lie. I couldn't help but wonder just how badly rotted her real aura was by now.

Oh my poor love, you're getting so close to the edge aren't you?

She was, but I had no fucking idea what I could do about it. Trixie was strong and fiercely independent, and I dread to think what would have happened if I had started trying to lecture her on morality. Not that I was exactly in a position to do that, not any more I wasn't, but you know what I mean. What she really needed was a shrink but that was hardly going to happen, was it? Half an hour's conversation with Trixie would probably have sent a psychiatrist running to his symbolic mother.

She has her own path to follow.

I wished I could stop hearing the memories of Adam's voice in the back of my head. The bloody Burned Man was quite bad enough, ta very much. The last thing I needed was that smug wanker's deceitful platitudes wafting through my brain as well.

"Of course I can," Trixie said, and I must admit I almost wished she had said no.

I mean sure, that was handy but... well, it raised some

questions of its own, didn't it? I mean like *how*, for one thing? All the same, she produced another burner phone from her handbag and punched a number from memory.

She spoke for a moment in German, listened, and hung up. She looked up at me and smiled. At least it was a proper smile this time, a *Trixie* smile. That was the face of the woman I loved, not that cold, reptilian killer's grin.

"He'll be here in five minutes," she said.

I swallowed. *She gets to order Heinrich about now, does she? That's new, and not in a good way.*

"Right," I said. "Right, good. Thanks, Trixie."

She lit a long black cigarette and blew smoke at the ceiling.

"I have… reached an understanding, with the Soulless," she said.

"Oh? How does that work then?"

"They do as I say, and I don't kill any more of them."

I have to admit that was pretty much exactly the same deal I had made with the local night creatures when I first moved into this part of South London, so I supposed I couldn't really fault her for that. All the same though, there was a matter of scale. The Soulless were a sight scarier than night creatures, for one thing. Still, I supposed I had to admit that Trixie was a whole order of magnitude scarier than *me* so it probably worked out much the same in the end.

They're not much to worry about unless there are an awful lot of them, she had told me, or something like that anyway. I supposed that made sense. There was only one of Trixie, but a Sword of the Word had to be worth thirty of those arseholes any day. At least.

The doorbell rang.

Trixie answered the buzzer and a moment later Heinrich was standing in my office in his overcoat and sunglasses. Now I've had Lucifer himself round my flat so I suppose I shouldn't really have been fazed by this geezer, but all the same the sight of him there was enough to raise goosebumps on the backs of my arms. I think it was because he had been the reasonable one, you know what I mean? Pricks like Mikael I knew how to deal with. They were just thugs at the end of the day. Supernatural thugs maybe, but they were still basically just oiks like the Russian's minders had been. This one though, he was connected. He was the one who had given us Adam's card, after all. He was the one who got to make the decisions, and talk with the grownups.

"Take your shades off," I told him.

I don't even know why, really, but he did as I asked and I stared into his glowing red eyes.

Talk to me, I told the Burned Man. *What are we dealing with here?*

Soulless, it said at once, *but you know that. Him in particular? He's a cut above the rest of them, I'll give you that. I don't know who he was before he died but he must have had some serious bollocks on him. His pact isn't like most of them, I can see that much. He's got clout, this one has. Even Adam listens to him, I reckon.*

Yeah, I had thought so. Heinrich was just a little bit too sure of himself, a little bit too together, to be like the other Soulless. I reckoned he must have been a pretty serious magician in his Earthly life, whenever that had been. He may even have been a magus of some sort, for all I knew. He'd still been greedy and stupid enough to make a pact in the first place though, hadn't he?

"Good evening," he said.

"All right," I said. "I want a word."

"I assumed that you did," he said. "The Lord Adamus has told me about you, Don Drake. When the Angelus telephoned me, I–"

"Yeah that's nice," I interrupted him. "Where's my daughter?"

He held me with his red gaze for a long moment, then

put his sunglasses back on as though to make the point that actually no, I *didn't* get to order him about. Well we'd soon see about that.

"Do you *have* a daughter?" he asked me.

"You know fucking well that I have," I snapped. "Your Dimitri took her, him and two other of your clowns. Are you really going to try and tell me they're *not* yours?"

"I know a Dimitri," he said with a shrug. "It may not be a common name in this country perhaps, but it's hardly unheard of. What makes you think that–"

"Don't, Heinrich," Trixie said, cutting him off. "If you know something, now would be the time to say."

Heinrich turned and looked at Trixie, and he suddenly seemed to lose his bottle. Funny that.

He sighed.

"You refused the request of your goddess," he said.

I felt cold all over.

"You mean *Menhit* arranged this?" I said. "To blackmail me?"

I couldn't believe that, somehow. Oh, I was sure she was extremely fucked off with me at the moment, but this just didn't seem like her style. Blackmail wasn't how a war goddess went about getting things done, was it?

"Great lord, no," Heinrich said. His lip twitched with an amused smirk that made me want to hit him. "The Lord Adamus set this in motion, to persuade you to his point of view."

Menhit and Adam have made common cause, I remembered Trixie saying.

Mazin knew I had a daughter, which meant Menhit knew, and she had told Adam. Common cause indeed. Menhit wanted me to go to Hell and end the fallen Dominion once and for all. Adam wanted the fallen Dominion ended, and he needed help to do it. I had, funnily fucking enough, not much fancied the idea of going to Hell. And now my daughter had been kidnapped by Adam's buttmonkeys. Yeah, it made sense. It also made me want to smash Heinrich's head open.

I felt the Burned Man growl in the back of my head, low and menacing. It was getting very attuned to my emotions, I had noticed. That or I was getting very good at rousing it when I wanted it, one or the other. I wasn't too sure which way around it was, these days.

Either way, my right hand suddenly burst into flame and I was at Heinrich's throat before I even really knew what I was doing. I felt the rush of power as the Burned Man took over, but this time I was still sort of there too, still at the front of my mind instead of elbowed into the background like I usually was. Come to think of it, it had been like that in Mickey Two Hats' snooker hall earlier, too. I'd been so bloody angry that I hadn't really taken it in at the time, but it was true all the same. That was new.

Whatever, one way or another Heinrich was suddenly bent backwards over my desk with my left hand around his throat and my right raised over his face, flames streaming up from my extended fingers.

"Those pretty glasses won't stop me shoving my fingers through your eye sockets and nailing your fucking head to the desk," the Burned Man growled at him with my voice. "Who's Dimitri, and where's my fucking daughter?"

I felt Trixie take a step towards us. I wasn't sure if she was intending to intervene or if she just wanted to be certain I had the situation under control. Either way, she stopped short of us and stood there, watching as I held Heinrich pinned over the desk. I'm sorry but if she was about to get in the middle of us then we were going to have a fucking row, right here and now.

I had promised Olivia that I would do anything in my power to protect her, and this arsehole was about to find out exactly how far that power could reach.

"Dimitri is one of us," he said, "and your child is safe. For now."

"For now?" I shouted at him. "What the fuck does *for now* mean, you cunt? You might have been a big shit in your day but I'm the man with his hand round your fucking throat. A pact doesn't look too fucking clever when it comes time to pay up, does it?"

He smiled up at me, and there was no fear in his face. None at all.

"Can you end me, Burned Man?" he asked. "Can you? Then *end* me. I would welcome it."

Fuck.

Fuck, yeah, perhaps he would at that. It suddenly dawned on me that threatening what was effectively a shade bound to eternal damnation might not be that much of a threat after all. Oh sure, the Soulless had a bit of power and a sort of pseudo-life, but I dreaded to think what they went home to at the end of each little job they did for their infernal masters. Heinrich, I was pretty sure, was enslaved to Adam himself. That probably wasn't a lot of fun, all things considered.

Also, I suddenly realized, he knew he was talking to the Burned Man and not me. That little secret seemed to be getting less secret by the day and I didn't like that one little bit, but the point was that he *still* wasn't scared. No, fuck it, this wasn't going to work, was it? That meant I was going to have to change tactics and do what I do best.

Cheat.

I yanked him back up to his feet and grinned at him.

"Nah, that'd be far too easy mate," I said. "Tell you what, I'll make a deal with you."

Heinrich arched an eyebrow behind his thick black sunglasses.

"Oh?"

"You help me," I said, "and I won't *tell* Adam you helped me. Refuse me and I'll fucking get there in the end somehow, and when I do I'll tell him all about how you rolled over for me and told me everything."

Heinrich went white, and I knew I had won.

Of course he was scared of me – well of the Burned Man anyway – and I knew damned well he was scared of Trixie too. He might have said he wanted to be ended but I was sure he didn't, not really. The human spirit clings to any sort of life it can get, and eternal death holds a terror for us all, but he was obviously much *more* scared of Adam. The thought of Adam's rage, of Adam thinking he had betrayed him, of Adam's *punishment*... Oh yeah, *that* broke him in a way that violence never could have.

I have to admit to feeling a bit irritated that this geezer was more scared of Adam than he was of Trixie and me but I supposed it was hardly surprising really. Still, what the fuck did it matter? The ends justified the means, as Trixie was forever telling me. *Whatever* those means might be.

"All right," Heinrich said. "All right, you win."

I let him go and took a step backwards to let him straighten himself up. Trixie lit a cigarette and stood watching us.

"So?" I said, after a moment. "Start fucking talking."

"You'll never get her back, you know," Heinrich said. "The Lord Adamus has her now. He holds the child as collateral to *force* you to go along with his and Menhit's plan."

"Where is he?" I demanded. "I'll find him and I will take Olivia back with all the power I can muster. A Sword of the Word stands beside me. I will storm any fortress he has built, and I will tear down his walls and bring her out. I can raise devourers from the very depths of the pit, if I have to, and I *will not be denied!*"

Fuck me, can I? That was the Burned Man talking again,

I knew. I also knew that summoning a devourer required human sacrifice. I sincerely hoped the Burned Man was bluffing, as there was no way on earth I was doing that. Unless it knew something that it hadn't been telling me, of course. This would hardly be the first time that had happened.

Heinrich smirked.

"I wish you well with that," he said. "The Lord Adamus has taken the child to Purgatory."

He started to laugh, and to weep, and once he had started he didn't seem to be able to stop.

We obviously weren't going to get any more sense out of him after that, so I let Trixie kick him out. I wanted to kill the fucker, personally, but I had a word with myself about that until I calmed down a bit. He might come in handy again later, after all. Maybe, anyway.

"Purgatory," I said to Trixie once he was gone. "Fuck, my mythology is all over the place. I've got too many pantheons going on. What exactly is he talking about in this context?"

"Mmmm," Trixie said as she lit another cigarette. "That rather depends."

I gritted my teeth. I loved her dearly but fuck me she could be hard work sometimes.

"Depends on *what*, exactly?"

"Well," she said. "Purgatory can mean a lot of different things to different people. As far as *I'm* concerned, it's where I would have to go before I... before I could go home, I suppose. A place of purification, prior to entering Heaven. To others it's a sort of limbo. Hades, the land of the dead between Heaven and Hell. A place to await judgment. Others might just call it the 'spirit world'. It's sort of, well, I don't really know how you'd phrase it in English, I'm afraid. We have a word for the idea but... oh I don't know, Don. I suppose it's whatever you *think* it is."

Fucking hell, that's helpful, I thought. *Not.* I gave the Burned Man a mental kick up the arse.

Where the fuck is Purgatory? I asked it. *And more to the point, how do I get there without dying?*

The Burned Man snorted in the back of my head.

Purgatory? it said. *That's Hell with training wheels. Fucksake Drake, why do you want to know about that all of a sudden?*

That threw me, I have to admit. Had it been asleep while I was having my little discussion with Heinrich? No, of course it hadn't – it had been right there with me, setting my hand on fire for me when I wanted it to, and threatening Heinrich with my voice. I had heard it growl and everything, and threaten to nail his head to the desk with my fingers. I had heard it talk of summoning *devourers*, for fucksake. I mean, that *had* been the Burned Man, hadn't it? That hadn't been me.

Had it? Jesus Christ, I had a sudden awful realization that perhaps it had. I couldn't be so far gone that the lines between us were blurred that much, could I?

I only fucking wished I knew. I knew I had changed, though, I knew *that* much. I had changed very fast and very much for the worse. I hated it. I hated the thought of this man who threatened to nail heads to desks and set people on fire being anything to do with me or my daughter, but he was, wasn't he? He was, and there just wasn't fucking time to worry about it now.

Anything in my power to protect her. Anything at all.

And I meant it, too.

Anything.

Humour me, I thought at the Burned Man. *Purgatory. How do I go there?*

By dying? the Burned Man suggested. *I don't fucking know, dickhead. I've been owned by about two hundred different magicians since Oisin first bound me and I don't think I've ever been asked* that *before. Why the fuck would anyone in their right mind want to go to Purgatory?*

I shut it out of my head and turned and stared out of my office window. Why? Because Olivia was there, according to Heinrich anyway. He might have been lying, of course, but I didn't think so.

How do I get to Purgatory without dying? I had no fucking idea, but I had a feeling I might just know a man who did.

CHAPTER 19

Davey wasn't an easy bloke to track down. I know we were in London and he was supposedly somewhere in Scotland, but the more I thought about Davey the more I figured that a lot of people down here ought to know who he was. I was right, too. They did, but they didn't want to talk about him. I spent the evening working my way back though my telephone list of scumbags, and this time I got a lot more cold shoulder than I had before. Davey, it seemed, was a bit of a taboo subject. Thinking about how badly he had made my skin crawl, I supposed that shouldn't really have surprised me.

It was nearly midnight by the time I gave it up for a bad job and just phoned the Weasel again. Now as I might have said, Harry the Weasel was bloody horrible but he knew pretty much everyone else who was horrible too, and in our circles that was a fucking lot of people. Weasel knew Davey all right, or at least he knew who he was.

Now Harry the Weasel, don't forget, was still trying to get back into my good books even after our lunch date today. So the little shit should be, after he had betrayed me last year. He probably didn't want to talk about Davey any more than anyone else did, but he was clever enough to know when he could work something to his advantage. He spilled his guts.

"Yeah I know about Davey, Mr Drake," he told me over the phone. "A lot of people know about Davey, for all they might not exactly want to say so."

"Good," I said. "Well done, Weasel. Good for you. I know him too. What I actually asked was how do I fucking get *hold* of Davey? The bloke's bleedin' invisible."

"Ah," said the Weasel. "Ah, yeah. Right, I've got you, Mr Drake."

Oh well that was fucking all right then. Harry the Weasel had fucking *got* me. Wonderful. I felt so much better for that, knowing I was in such safe hands. For fucksake…

"How do I contact him?" I asked, slowly and clearly.

Honestly, Weasel wasn't thick but he did a bloody good impression of it sometimes, you know what I mean?

"Well," he said, "I might be able to get you a phone number."

The unspoken "but it'll cost you" hung in the air between us for a moment.

"You fucking owe me, Weasel," I reminded him, "and not just for lunch. You sold me out to the peacock woman, remember? You nearly got me killed. If you fucking *ever* want to learn anything from me again you'd better start being bastard well helpful, you understand me?"

"Yes, Mr Drake," he muttered. "Leave it with me."

It was the middle of the next morning before Weasel finally called me back, by which time I had practically worn a groove in my office floor from pacing up and down. He gave me a mobile phone number.

I hung up on him and dialled.

"Aye?" Davey asked, after a few rings.

"It's Don Drake," I said.

He laughed.

"Fuck me, it's Danny's bane so it is," he said, sounding Irish today. I wished the horrible old bugger would just pick an accent and stick to it, I really did. "And what can I do for you, Don Drake?"

Now this might be a bit tricky, I thought.

"I don't suppose there's any chance you're in London?" I asked him.

"Almighty God, no," he said. "Why would any right thinking man be in London?"

I had to admit he had a point there.

"Shit," I said. "It's just... look, I really want to talk to you, and it's not a conversation for over the phone, if you know what I mean."

He laughed. "I can be in London in an hour or so," he said. "Where?"

I suppose I shouldn't have been surprised by that, but I still sort of was. I mean, as far as I knew he was in Glasgow. It's only about an hour's actual *flight* from Glasgow to London, but with all the fannying about that's involved in airports these days that still meant a good three or four hours' travelling time at least. Still, I wasn't going to argue about it. I gave him the address of the Rose and Crown. A lunchtime pint it was, then.

"Aye, I'll see you there," he said, and hung up.

I put the phone down and pushed my hands back through my hair with a sigh. Was this really what it had come to? Going to *Davey* for advice? Grotty old Davey of the eight brown teeth and the mysterious and inexplicably horrifying wheel? I had to admit that it really had. I knew I could have asked Papa Armand but this was well outside of his pantheon and I didn't want to accidentally end up in the wrong fucking dimension, you know what I mean? Davey though... Oh fuck it, I don't know. I didn't know a lot about him but there was just something about the bloke that I was struggling to articulate, even to myself.

He was obviously very, very powerful, whoever he was. The Burned Man had called him famous, for all that I had no fucking idea who he was supposed to be, and it obviously took him seriously. I didn't even really know what *sort* of magician he was but... oh I didn't fucking know, did I?

Call it a hunch. Call it a gut feeling, whatever. If there's one thing you have to learn as a magician, it's to listen to your gut. To listen to your intuition. And mine was telling me to talk to Davey, however much I didn't want to.

Trixie was in the kitchen, drinking coffee and smoking.

"I'm going down the pub," I said. "Want to come?"

"Not particularly," she said, which I must admit I had been sort of banking on.

I had a feeling it might be best to keep Trixie and Davey apart, at least for now. I didn't really know why, but... yeah. Listening to my gut, I suppose. Davey was so abrasive I just had a feeling it wouldn't go well.

"Fair enough," I said. "See you later, then."

"Yes," she said.

I shrugged and went to find my coat and wallet and keys and all the other shit you need when you're going out. Trixie was in a funny mood in general at the moment, but after yesterday's encounters with the Russian and Mickey Two Hats and then Heinrich I supposed it was hardly surprising. I was worried about what all this was doing to her, I have to admit. She was hard as iron of course, but she was also so brittle these days I was starting to think she could just shatter at any moment, like a pane of glass dropped from a height. I had to keep that from happening, whatever the cost. If that meant keeping certain things from her then so be it.

Of course, I really should have been worrying about what

all this was doing to *me*, but by then I was too fixated on finding Olivia to think about that.

The ends justify the means, I could almost hear Trixie saying.

Yeah, right now they really did. At the moment the only end that mattered was getting Olivia back, and that fucking justified *anything*.

I put my coat on and went out.

The Rose and Crown was my local, or sort of anyway. Whatever you've seen on the telly there really *isn't* a pub on every street corner in London, and it was a good fifteen minutes' walk there from my flat. Even so, when I finally got to the pub I felt like I was home. I ducked under the hanging baskets and pushed the door open, and stepped into a long, dim burrow of beery warmth and comfort and people who knew how shit was supposed to work.

The Rose and Crown was one of those places where everyone knew everyone, and pretty much everyone was dodgy in some way, shape or form. It was full of what the people around these parts call "characters", which is a sort of friendly euphemism for "hardened criminals". All the same, these were my people. This was family.

I weaved my way through the lunchtime crowd, exchanging nods and handshakes and pats on the back as I went. Shirley was behind the bar as usual, all peroxide blonde hair and shiny satin blouse. She was sixty if she was a day and she was an absolute sweetheart, but in here her word was law. Shirley was the unquestioned monarch of the Rose and Crown, and you behaved yourself in there if you knew what was good for you. It's funny really, but the sort of trendy bars that normal people go to usually have bouncers on the door at night and coppers outside at the weekends, waiting to mop up the trouble. In the Rose and Crown there just *wasn't* any trouble, and on the rare occasions someone tried to make some it was very quickly taken care of by either the regulars or Alfie, Shirley's son. There's a lot to be said for a self-policing society, I tell you.

Anyway, that aside I was fucking glad to be home at last.

"Don, how are you, duck?" Shirley said, treating me to a wide smile as I made my way to the bar. "I ain't seen you for so long I was starting to think you were dead!"

It's a good job I love Shirley. I really was getting heartily sick of people thinking I was dead, although looking back on how I had spent the last six months I might as well have been.

"Nah, I'm all right thanks, Duchess," I said. "I've been away, that's all. Do me a pint and a chaser will you? And one for yourself, of course."

Shirley gave me a sympathetic nod. In these circles, "away" was shorthand for "in prison", and I was perfectly happy for everyone to think that. It was nothing remarkable and it would save any awkward explanations. Being banged up was a lot more respectable than being a junkie was, that was for damn sure.

I put a twenty quid note down on the bar. I was still spending Trixie's money and she didn't mind and always seemed to have plenty of it, but now that I thought about it I couldn't help wondering why I should have to. I mean, surely Mazin should have put me on a retainer by now if nothing else? I frowned as I watched Shirley sort herself a large vodka and tonic before she pulled my pint. I mean, seven hundred and however many million dollars and he couldn't give me some pocket money?

Mazin was all right, don't get me wrong, but I couldn't help remembering what Wormwood had told me about the books. An awful lot of Menhit's money had gone missing over the years. An *awful* lot. I knew Mazin couldn't have had anything to do with that – he was human after all, and at his age I guessed he couldn't have worked for the Order of the Keeper for more than twenty years tops. All the same, it made me wonder. He seemed like a clever bloke; maybe he had figured out what had been going on. Maybe that explained why he was being so bloody tight with the funds.

Oh fuck it, it was Menhit's money not mine at the end of the day, what did I care? I only hoped Mazin had enough of a lid on it that Menhit herself wasn't going to find out. I dread to think what she would have done to anyone she caught stealing from her. Shirley gave me my drinks and I retreated to a blissfully empty corner table by the fireplace to wait for Davey.

He didn't keep me long, to be fair. It can't have been much more than an hour since we spoke on the phone before he walked into the pub, so I supposed I had to give him that. He still looked like shit, like some grotty old tramp who'd spent the night passed out in a gutter somewhere, wrapped up in his rancid old tramp's coat. Even so, people got out of Davey's way and made room for him as he shuffled across the pub to the bar.

I watched with narrowed eyes, examining his aura as he went. It was still a normal human blue to a casual glance but yeah, there was that nagging feeling again. That sensation of running your hand over smooth wood and feeling a tiny splinter you couldn't see. There was definitely something very *wrong* about Davey, something I couldn't quite put my finger on.

Looking at him was making me feel a bit ill. Not just that itchy, skin-crawling feeling that I had got from him before but something worse than that. He was giving me the same sort of sick knot in the guts that you get the moment you realize that you're actually the butt of the cruel joke you've been laughing along with for the last however long. That feeling that told you someone had well and truly taken you for a cunt.

No one else in the pub had an ounce of magical sensibility as far as I knew, but all the same this was like the time I had brought Papa Armand here. People just got out of his way, and they looked at him with respect even though I could tell they didn't even really know why. Oh yeah, grotty old Davey was a lot more than he seemed, all right.

But what, though?

That was the fucking question, wasn't it? I waved at him across the bar and he came and sat down at my table with a pint and a whisky in his hands.

"Donny boy," he said. "How's the world treating you this fine day?"

"Like fucking shit," I said, meeting his twinkling, fatherly eyes with a hard stare of my own. "I'm not in the mood for the jolly old Scottish-Irish-Welsh-fucking-made-up-shit Daddy routine, Davey."

All the twinkle went out of his eyes at once, and he necked his whisky in a single swallow.

"Oh is that right?" he asked me.

"Yeah it fucking is, as it happens," I said. "Can we just cut through all the bullshit this time and talk like grownups?"

"We can do that," he said. "If I'm talking to you, we can. Don Drake, that's who I came to this miserable den of sin you call London to talk to. The Burned Man, I wouldn't give the steam off my piss."

"You know I'm fucking here, you syphilitic old whoremonger," the Burned Man said with my voice. "I'm sitting right here in front of you wearing this pathetic excuse for a magician but you remember *me*, don't you? You remember me, right *Davey?*"

Davey cleared his throat and looked at me.

"Aye," he said. "We fought once before, Burned Man. You beat me then, aye, I'll give you that. But that was a *fucking* long time ago, and it wasn't *me* who got himself bound in a wee fucking toy doll, now was it?"

"Oh go and stick it up your arse," I said, before I got a hold of myself and remembered that it was actually me who had invited him here, because I needed his help. "Look, shit. Look, sorry about that. I, um, I'm not always myself these days."

That was a fucking understatement if ever I had uttered one. I hadn't been myself for quite some time now and I bloody well knew it.

"No you're not, Donny boy," he said, and grinned at me. Fuck but I wished he wouldn't do that, it really wasn't a pretty sight. "You're the Burned Man half the time, aren't you? Even when you're not you still sort of are, these days. It's changing you, isn't it, having that filthy wee shite living in your head? It's changing you, and not for the better."

I had to admit he was all too right about that. Having your soul slowly eaten could only lead in one direction, as far as I could see. Straight down to Hell in the end, whether I liked it or not. But not now, not for Menhit and most fucking *definitely* not for Adam.

Diabolists go to Hell, Don.

I pinched the inside of my wrist until it hurt to shut myself up. That wasn't a conversation I was having with fucking Davey of all people.

"Yeah, well," I said. "You know how it is."

"Thank fuck I *don't* know how it is," he said, "but you've my sympathy all the same. Well, some of it anyway. What do you actually want, Donny boy? London's no better than I remember it and I'll not spend any longer here than I fucking have to, if you know what I mean."

Of course I knew what he meant. That said though, he was here wasn't he? He was here because I had asked him to be, and he had come for all that he obviously hadn't really wanted to. That had to mean something. Him and the Burned Man obviously had history together, which must make him very old indeed. Oh yes, there really was something about grotty old Davey that I hadn't quite got my head around yet.

"What are you?" I asked him. "Really, I mean?"

Now that was downright rude of me, I have to admit. You just didn't ask people about who and what they were, you know what I mean? That wasn't done, in our circles.

You're a fucking rude prick, I remembered Davey telling me in Glasgow.

Oh screw it, yes I was. But then so was he, by his own admission. I reckoned that made us about even in the rude prick stakes, and I had far more important things to worry about at that moment than fucking etiquette.

"Now what sort of question is that to be asking?" he said.

"Oh come off it," I said. "Your aura looks human but I fucking *know* there's something wrong with it, and if you know the Burned Man from before it was bound then you sodding well *can't* be human, can you? Even Methuselah didn't live *that* long."

"My mother was human, God rest her soul," he said. "My father... aye well, I suppose I had one somewhere along the line. Do ye know what a cambion is, Donny boy?"

That felt like an exam question, all of a sudden. I racked my brains, trying to remember what I had read in the stack of dusty old books I kept in my workroom. I did a bit of mental cross-referencing and the little bit of my brain that will be forever an undergraduate kicked into action.

"An impossible half-breed demon," I said, starting to lecture like I tend to on the rare occasions when I'm asked an interesting question that I actually know the answer to. "Well sort of, anyway. I don't think the term itself was used until the nineteenth century, in De Plancy's Dictionnaire Infernal, *but there's* something in the *Malleus Maleficarum* about the idea. About how demons can't breed with humans, but if a succubus fucks a geezer and passes his sperm on to an incubus who then has his way with a human woman using the mortal seed then she's guaranteed to get up the stick and the offspring isn't quite human, and… bloody hell! Is *that* what you are? Cambions are rare as all *fuck*. Sorry, but should I have heard of you?"

"Aye, that you should, although you might know me by another name," Davey said, grinning to make sure I could see every one of his spit-slick brown teeth. "You might know me as Merlin."

I almost choked, and the look on my face at that moment was probably somewhere between goldfish and simpleton. This grotty, smug, foul-mouthed old git was *Merlin*? Seriously?

Nah, I couldn't believe that. All the same I couldn't help remembering that first game of Fates I had played with Davey, back in Glasgow, and how he had drawn the Hermit as his trump. The Hermit, as Wormwood had pretty much said, is the card in the major arcana representing wisdom, power and authority, a great teacher and respected elder. A father, by any other name.

Is he taking the piss? I thought at the Burned Man.

Nope, it replied, and I could feel the horrible little thing sniggering in the back of my mind. *I did tell you, Drake.*

Did you fuck as like, I snapped at it.

"Oh fucking come on," Davey said. "You've got the Burned Man living in your head, Donny boy. You cannae tell me that my name never came up in conversation."

You knew? I thought furiously at the Burned Man. *You bloody well knew and you didn't think to say anything? You didn't think to tell me he was cunting* Merlin, *for fucksake?*

Course I knew, it sniggered. *And I did tell you, you just weren't paying attention at the time.*

Fucking hell, had it?

Actually now that I thought hard about it I *did* remember the Burned Man asking me "what do you make of old Merlin here", the night I first met Davey. Of course I had thought that was just a turn of phrase, on account of his bushy beard and wild hair. I had never dreamed for a moment that it was being bloody serious.

I gritted my teeth in frustration. The Burned Man never said anything it didn't mean, I knew that, but sometimes the things you think don't really mean anything turn out to be vitally important. All the same, this was just taking the piss. It was usually so free and easy with the vernacular, after all. How the fuck was I supposed to have picked up on that? The bloody thing really wasn't on my side half the time, I was sure it wasn't.

Right, I thought at it through the mental equivalent of gritted teeth. *So grotty old Davey is really Merlin. Oh that's fucking wonderful that is. I don't suppose there's* any *chance he's on our side?*

Hard to say, the Burned Man said. *He hates me, but he seems to like you well enough. Anyway, Merlin is always on* Merlin's *side, if you know what I mean. That's how he's lived so fucking long.*

I supposed it probably was, at that.

"Anyway," Davey went on, "now you've finished being rude to me, and you *have* fucking finished with that, what do you actually want?"

"Oh Jesus," I said, and put my head in my hands.

I mean, now that I knew who he was did I even want to tell him? I supposed having dragged him all the way down here for nothing would have been even worse than asking him for a favour but... but he was fucking *Merlin!* To a magician like me, this was like meeting Jesus, Elvis and the Easter sodding Bunny all at the same time.

"Go on, I'll no bite you," he said, grinning his awful grin again.

I sighed.

"Right," I said. "All right look, it's like this. I've got... oh shit a brick. Come here, I don't want to say this loud enough for anyone to overhear me. I've got a big fucking problem. Someone's kidnapped my little baby daughter, and taken her to Purgatory to... to use her to threaten me, and to make me do something that I don't want to do. I mean that I *really* don't want to do. I need to get to Purgatory so I can rescue my daughter, and I have no sodding idea how to do it."

"Your wee bairn has been taken by someone who can just stroll into Purgatory when he feels like it?" Davey asked. "I don't like the thought of people walking in and out of *there* at will. I think you'd better tell me the rest of this, Donny boy."

I looked at him, and met his twinkling blue eyes. Could I trust him, really? I shouldn't bloody think so, but as far as I could see I didn't have a lot of choice. From what little I knew about him he wasn't likely to be a friend of Adam's, so I supposed there was that if nothing else.

So I started to tell him.

I'd just got to the bit about the ghostly child or whatever the fuck had been tormenting me when he started to laugh.

"It's not fucking funny," I snapped.

"Aye well, it was at the time," he said, wiping a tear of glee from under his eye with one grubby finger.

"You what?" I said, and the penny dropped with a rusty clang. "Are you trying to tell me that *you* sent that bloody thing after me?"

I stared at him across the table, sorely tempted to punch him in his horrible toothless face whoever he fucking was.

"Aye, that I did," he said.

"What the fuck *for*?"

"To put the shits up you of course," he said. "That and because you deserved it for being a gobby wee shite to your elders and betters, and because it was *funny*. Until it saw what you were in bed with, anyway. Then it fucked off on me and refused to go anywhere near you again."

I remembered how scared the apparition had looked of Trixie. I supposed the sight of a Sword of the Word lying there beside me would have given virtually any demon a minor nervous breakdown, whoever it was working for.

"That's why I came to see you after that, to get my truth out of you," he went on. "I knew she had been looking for you, aye, but I'd never have guessed why until I saw that. There's no way a simple gobshite like you was going to be in bed with the likes of *her*."

Oh fuck, yes. The very next night after the apparition had seen Trixie in bed with me and I had banished it for good, Davey had shown up in that bar when I was out with Mazin, and that was when he had figured out that I had the Burned Man inside me. I felt like telling him that actually it *was* me she was in bed with, and she fucking hated the Burned Man being inside me and would have much preferred it if it was *just* me, actually, but I simply couldn't muster the energy. I didn't really care *what* he thought about that.

"What was it, anyway?" I asked him. "That fucking horror show you were plaguing me with."

"A talonwraith," he said, "with a bit of my special sauce on it, if you know what I mean."

I glared at him but I couldn't help wondering exactly what his "special sauce" might be. I remembered telling Trixie how it was just about possible that a strong enough magician could have hidden a talonwraith's true nature with something stronger than a glamour, and how they might have been able to skim the memory of the child out of my head and imprint it into a summoned wraith to torment me.

That was how you manifested someone's own nightmares on them, theoretically at least. I knew that, but I had never really believed that was what had actually happened. An actual real ghost would have been more likely than someone being powerful enough to do that, and I don't even believe in ghosts. *That's proper fucking magus stuff,* I remembered telling her. Well if there was ever a proper fucking magus it was Merlin, wasn't it?

"Cocking hell," I muttered. "You horrible old git."

He laughed at that.

"Aye, I've been called that and worse," he said. "Tell me the rest of it."

"In a minute," I said. "I need another bloody drink first. You almost drove me mad with that fucking thing."

I supposed I had to buy him one as well. When I got back to the table with two pints and two whiskies he was still looking pleased with himself, and it took some effort not to just chuck the lot at the smug old bastard.

I need his help, I had to remind myself. I remembered the card he had drawn, back in Glasgow. The Hermit, the great sage and wise teacher. The father. Maybe...

Jesus, I was never going to stop looking for that father figure, was I? It was fucking pathetic and I knew it was. Davey could never be a father to me, Merlin or not, no more than Professor Davidson or Papa Armand or even the bastard Burned Man could. That wheel had turned full circle and the only father in my life now was *me*, I suddenly realized. I was *Olivia's* father whether Debbie liked it or not, and that was the important thing. The *only* important thing. I had responsibilities now. It was finally time to stop worrying about myself for once and sort this out.

I sat down opposite him again and had a quick gulp of my lager, then I told him the rest of it. By the time I was done he had stopped smiling.

"A Dominion, is it?" he said. "And the Fallen One, *and* this mad fucking imported war goddess of yours? I have to hand it to you Donny boy, when you fuck up you do it in style."

I had to give him that one, I must admit.

"Yeah well, there we are," I said. "Shit Davey, I just want my little girl back."

"Of course you do," he said. "I understand that. I'll help you."

I blinked at him. I mean that was great, that was what I had wanted after all, but all the same it was a bit of a surprise.

"Thank you," I said, and I meant it. "Um, do you mind if I ask why?"

"Let's just say we've got something in common," he said.

"Oh yeah? What would that be, then?"

"You're like me, Donny boy," he said, showing me his repulsive grin.

I was *nothing* like him, as far as I could see.

"Like you how?"

"Your parentage, you fool. We came into this world the same way, you and me, and you're right – that *is* a rare thing. That makes us almost brothers. Why do you think I gave you the time of day in the first place?" He paused for a moment and looked at me, no doubt taking in the expression on my face. "Did ye really not know?

I gaped at him. Was he saying I was... *I* was a cambion, like him? My father... I thought about my dad, dead since I was ten. I remembered him coming home stinking drunk and bearing some grudge or another, taking it out on my poor mum or me or both of us. I remembered him stumbling into the kitchen, bouncing off the sink and ripping the cupboard open looking for more booze. I remembered how he would lash out at us when there wasn't any, knocking my mum to the floor with a bloody mouth. I thought about him, and I slowly let it sink in that he *wasn't* my father after all.

Oh dear God.

I took a long, shuddering breath as I let that really sink in. It wouldn't make the memories go away, of course. It couldn't erase what had happened, or take away all those childhood years of pain and guilt and feeling worthless, but it meant one very important thing.

I wasn't that man's son after all.

Oh dear God, thank fuck for that.

All the same though, that meant I had been sired by an incubus. Well sort of, anyway. I must have *had* a biological human father I supposed, some bloke who had been visited by a succubus somewhere along the line, but he could have been literally anyone on Earth. Bloody hell. I wondered if Mum had the faintest idea, and decided that she almost certainly hadn't. They came in dreams, from what I had read. Oh bless her, she might have woken up a bit sore and confused one morning but no, she wouldn't have had a clue, would she?

Bloody hell…

I suddenly remembered something Trixie had said to me, shortly after we had first met.

The more I saw of you the more I realized you were a little bit different from most other mortals.

Yeah, apparently I fucking was.

I mean, I was sure she didn't have the faintest idea either and now I had the bloody Burned Man living in my head it was a bit of a moot point anyway. All the same, I supposed she had probably felt *something*. That same little auric snag that I had seen in Davey? Perhaps she had felt that, I really didn't know.

I remembered summoning Adam all by myself too, wherever he had been at the time, and wondering where the hell I had found the power to do that. Had that been

my demon blood at work? No, no that wasn't right, it
didn't work like that. I didn't actually *have* demon blood,
did I? Demons can't breed with mortals, after all, but the
whole horrible process of transference from human man to
succubus to incubus to human woman had to do *something*,
didn't it?

The offspring isn't quite human.

I mean, just look at Davey. I stared at his aura with that
faint snag in it, that slight but hard to define *difference* from a
human aura that made my skin crawl so badly.

"No," I said to Davey, after a conspicuously long pause.
"No, I can't say that I did."

He raised his glass in salute, and I rather halfheartedly
clinked mine against it.

"Wee brother," he said, and laughed at me. "Why do
you think I bothered to go to all the trouble of tracking you
down in Edinburgh? To please your lovely lady angel? For
the reward money? Dinnae make me laugh. Because we're
family, after a fashion, and I couldn't leave you in that state
forever. You were making me look bad."

"Are we… immortal?" I whispered.

He snorted. "I could shoot you dead right now, and you'd
stay dead," he said. "Don't go getting your fucking hopes up,
Donny boy. I'm old, aye, very old, but I'm no immortal. I'm
still alive because I'm very clever and I'm very cruel and I'm
the greatest fucking magus most people have ever heard of.
You, sonny lad, are not."

No, I supposed he had a point there, but at that moment
I realized something.

I don't know what happened, it was like something just
clicked inside me as I sat there looking at Davey's ugly gap-
toothed grin. It almost felt like it did when the Burned Man
took me over, but that wasn't it. Not this time. This was
something different, something that felt like I had finally

woken up at long fucking last.

I wasn't the greatest fucking magus in history, no.

But I *was* half the Burned Man, and apparently I was demon-born too, and all that mattered in the world, the *only* thing that mattered, was that my little girl had been taken away from me.

How *dare* they?

Those dead Russians? Mickey Two Hats and Dimitri? Heinrich, even? Fuck them. They were just collateral damage, and they didn't matter. *Nothing* mattered except Olivia. Nothing at all.

Yes I had changed, I accepted that now. No, it wasn't for the better. And that didn't fucking matter either, not now.

Diabolists go to Hell?

So *fucking* what.

If that's what it took then I'd gladly sell whatever was left of my soul to get Olivia back. Anything in my power, I had promised her, and I meant it.

Anything.

I was going to man the fuck up and I was going to take responsibility, and I was going to bring Adam down *whatever* it took. If that meant war, if that meant raising devourers from the pit, then so be it.

ANYTHING!

And that's when I knew.

That's when I knew I had lost my battle, and it simply didn't matter any more.

"Right," I said, and I couldn't help biting back just a little bit. "So why are you living like a grotty old tramp, then? It seems to me that a great and ancient magus ought to be a bit fucking better off than you are."

"Oh, I do very well for myself, thank you," he said. "I don't live in these parts, you understand. When I come here, I like to be invisible. I like to mix with lowlifes, with people like you. The man at the top of a high tower sees only ants below him, after all. But when you're in the gutter looking up, then you can see everything."

There might be something to that, I supposed. It would be nice to have the fucking option though, wouldn't it? One day, I promised myself, when this was sorted, I was going to have that option. If I was the Keeper of the Veil then I was going to take what was due to me, and bugger Mazin and his purse strings and his cooked books. He'd just have to cook them a bit more, wouldn't he? I'd had enough of grubbing around in poverty.

The Burned Man was right about this. It had *always* been right, about everything. I deserved better. I was going to *have* better, but first I was going to get Olivia back.

"Right," I said again. "So are you going to help me or not?"

"Aye, I said I would," Davey said. "Do you have somewhere we can work?"

I nodded. "Yeah," I said.

Trixie was going to just love this, wasn't she?

CHAPTER 20

Needless to say she didn't. I got back to the flat in the middle of the afternoon, smelling of booze and with grotty old Davey in tow. Trixie gave me one of those very special, very *Trixie* looks that she reserved for the occasions when I have truly and exceptionally pissed her off.

"Hi," I said. "This is Davey."

Trixie was sitting on the sofa in my office with a cup of coffee in one hand and a long black cigarette in the other, her legs crossed and an ashtray balanced on the knee of her black jeans.

"Yes," she said. "We met, in Glasgow."

"So we did," Davey said, treating her to his horrible grin. "You paid me all that lovely reward money for finding yon fool here."

"And now you're here," Trixie said.

Her voice had that flat tone to it that meant someone was likely to get hurt soon, and badly. I only hoped it wasn't going to be me.

"It's all right, Trixie," I said. "Me and Davey, we've sorted it out. He's going to help us. Help us to find Olivia, I mean."

"Oh is he?" Trixie asked archly. "You can open a portal to

Purgatory, can you Davey?"

"That I can," he said.

That took the thunder out of her sails a bit, I had to admit.

"I believe him," I said. "We've been talking and... yeah. Davey is...well, um..."

"You may know me as Merlin, Angelus," Davey said, and to my utter fucking astonishment he bowed to her.

"Ah," Trixie said. "Oh Thrones, how did I miss that?"

Davey smirked. "It's easy to miss the things you least expect to see, Angelus," he said.

He gave me a bit of a sideways look when he said it, too, but I didn't think Trixie noticed that. I bloody well *hoped* she didn't, anyway. Having the Burned Man inside me was quite bad enough without her discovering I had apparently been sired by an incubus as well. None of these things was exactly doing any good for my standing as boyfriend material, if you know what I mean.

"I suppose it is," Trixie said. She stubbed her cigarette out and got to her feet, looking businesslike all of a sudden. "Right, how do we do this?"

"Ah, well now," Davey said, and I got a sinking feeling in my guts.

He wasn't just going to wave a magic wand, then.

Bugger.

"Yes?" she prompted.

"Now for me, Angelus, I come and go as I please," he said. "Purgatory is where I've made my home, after all, and the Veil is like a lover to me after all this time. But if I'm taking Donny boy here, and especially if I'm taking *you* along with us, this isn't going to be that simple."

I sighed. Nothing ever bloody is, is it?

"What do we need?" I asked him.

"You've an alchemist, of course?" he asked. I thought sourly of Wormwood, and nodded. "Of course you have.

Well I'll be needing a goat, two pounds of iron filings, five ounces of quicksilver, and this is the bit that'll hurt your pocket and test your alchemist to the limit, Donny boy – I'll need a warpstone."

My sigh of relief made his bushy eyebrows lift.

"I've already got a warpstone," I said.

"Have you now?" he said, and for the briefest of moments he almost looked impressed with me. Almost. "Well, that's good. Run along and rustle up the other bits, there's a good laddie."

Patronizing old git. I picked up the phone and called Wormwood.

I put in an order for the goat and the mercury, and was assured they would be delivered by the evening. Conversations only diabolists have, if you know what I mean. That done, I went into the workroom and retrieved my warpstone from the drawer while no one was looking. There was a sack of iron filings sitting on the floor in there already so that was taken care of, but I didn't want Davey seeing what else was in that drawer. I *really* didn't want him seeing that I had a Blade of Unmaking in there, that was for sure. That was strictly on a need-to-know basis, and he didn't need to know at all.

The warpstone was a flat black disk about the size of the palm of my hand, inscribed all over with sinuous spiral lines that seemed to move if you looked at them for too long. It was strangely similar to the hexring I also had tucked away in that drawer, but it served a completely different purpose. Warpstones, in case you didn't know, are the keys to the Veils. With a warpstone, a magician who knows what they're doing can open portals to other dimensions and even speak with the recently dead. I'd spoken to a dead man once before and I hadn't bloody liked it, but that was beside the point. It was a portal we wanted now, and apparently Davey knew how to make one all the way down to Purgatory.

So he said, anyway. If he wasn't lying to me. If he really *was* Merlin it was quite believable, but of course I only had his word for that, didn't I? Still, I supposed he probably was. It was such an outrageous claim that I doubted anyone would dare to make it unless it was actually true, and the Burned Man certainly seemed to believe it. So did Trixie, for that matter. I sighed. Even supposing he *was* Merlin, did that mean I could trust him? Depending which version of the stories you read, Merlin wasn't necessarily a very nice bloke. To put it bloody mildly.

I didn't really have a lot of fucking choice, did I? Come hell or high water I was getting Olivia back, and this was how we were doing it. If that meant trusting Davey, then so be it. I spared the dust-encrusted fetish of the Burned Man a sour look, then slipped the warpstone into my pocket and went back into the office.

The fuck are you doing with that? the Burned Man suddenly piped up in the back of my head.

Have you been asleep on me again? I asked it. *We're going to Purgatory, to get my daughter back.*

We are?

Yeah we are, and you're going to do what you're fucking told for once. And oi. You remember those ten truths you told me once, and only reminded me of five of them? I think I've figured out what one of the missing ones was, you little git.

Ah, it said. *You and Davey been talking family history, have you?*

You might fucking say that, I said. *I'm a fucking* cambion, *seriously?*

Yeah, it admitted. *You are. I took up with you for a reason, Drake, after all.*

It went quiet on me again after that, thankfully.

It was about five o'clock by then and Wormwood's boys

wouldn't be bringing the goat and mercury for hours yet. I looked at Trixie and Davey, who were eyeing each other in hostile silence like two strange cats in a closed room. Oh fucking hell, this was going to be a barrel of laughs, wasn't it? Thankfully Davey seemed to be thinking the same thing.

"Well I'll leave you two sweethearts to it until tonight," he said. "I'll be back about ten."

With that he got up and left, and I heard the front door bang closed behind him. On impulse I hurried over to the window to see if he was actually outside, but of course he wasn't. It seemed he could just disappear into thin air the same way Trixie did sometimes. Oh what a joyous thought that wasn't.

"Do you trust him?" Trixie asked me.

"Not particularly," I said, "but I can't see that we've got a lot of choice."

"No, we haven't," she said. "I was just making sure your eyes are still open, that's all."

I sighed and turned to look at her, sitting on the sofa with a cigarette smouldering between her fingers. My eyes were open all right. They were now, for the first time in a very long while. I felt... different. Determined. Strong. I had just told the Burned Man to do what it was told, for fucksake, and it hadn't even argued about it.

Do not ask, command. *That is the true way to power.*

"Yeah, my eyes are open all right," I said. "What do you know about him?"

"No more than you do, I shouldn't think," she said. "When he was supposedly making legends here in England I was chasing the Furies across Persia, I'm afraid."

"Oh," I said. "Oh, right. Ah well."

I realized I hadn't eaten anything since breakfast, and I was bloody starving. I rustled us up some sandwiches and we sat and ate together in silence. Trixie never bothered to eat unless

I actually put food in front of her, I had noticed. It didn't seem to make any difference to her either way, in the same way that booze didn't seem to have the slightest effect on her. I suspected she only ate at all in an attempt to be sociable.

"What are we going to find when we get there?" I asked her, after a while.

"I have no idea," she said. "Nothing good, I suspect."

No, I didn't suppose we would. What had the Burned Man called it, "Hell with training wheels" or something equally fucking encouraging like that. Oh joy. I slipped a hand into my pocket and stroked the warpstone, running my fingers reflexively over the cool surface. I'd had it for years but I must confess I'd never actually used it before. The only time it might have come in handy, when we had needed to speak with Lavender's corpse, I had temporarily lost it in a game of cards with Wormwood. This would be its first proper outing and I have to admit the thought was making me a bit nervous.

I didn't even really know what it was. It seemed to be made from the same stuff as the hexring, but of course I didn't really know what that was either. I was fairly sure it wasn't of Earthly origin, at least. I sighed. I had been a magician for twenty years and there were still far too many things I didn't know anything about. Davey was right – I was a very long way from being a magus. That was something else that was going to change, once this was over. It was time the Burned Man starting earning its fucking keep around here.

The doorbell rang about half nine, and I went down to find one of Wormwood's creepy croupiers on my doorstep. There was a black van pulled up to the kerb outside with the engine running.

"Good evening," the man said. "I have a delivery for Don Drake."

"That's me," I said. "I hope it's still bleating."

"Mmmm," the man said, and went to open the back of the van.

He had a quick look up and down the street to make sure there was no one too close before he led a live goat out of the van and herded it quickly through my front door. It's a good job goats can climb stairs, that's all I can say. He passed me a small briefcase as well that I assumed had the mercury in it.

"Payment on account, right?" I said.

He shrugged. "That is between you and Mr Wormwood."

He got into the van and drove off without another word, leaving a cloud of disapproval in the air behind him. Tosser. He wasn't even human and he worked for an archdemon for fucksake, what right did he have to be looking down his nose at me for needing a goat?

I shooed the thing up the stairs into my office, where it promptly crapped on the floor. Lovely. I hoped Davey wasn't going to be much longer – the last thing I wanted in my flat was a live goat. Not that a dead one was going to be much better, of course. There are aspects of the sort of magic I do that I really don't like.

For fucksake get over yourself, the Burned Man said. *You eat the fucking things, what's the difference?*

I sighed. I knew it was right. There was a Jamaican place down the road that did a bloody marvellous curried goat, after all. I supposed I could always let them have the carcass afterwards. At least that way it wouldn't go to waste.

Oh what did it matter? It was only a fucking goat. I was ready to burn the world to get my daughter back, what the hell difference did a goat make?

Davey arrived ten minutes later, while I was on my hands and knees cleaning up goat shit. I have a way of looking impressive like that, you know what I mean?

"Ah, the glamorous realities of the magician's life," he smirked.

"Yeah, innit," I said, deliberately not mentioning the fact that he had strolled through my locked front door without so much as a by your leave.

I supposed he got to do things like that, being who he was. Not to mention that he was doing me the mother of all favours here. Trixie came out of the kitchen where she had been brewing coffee, and gave him a look.

"Evening, Angelus," he said.

"Yes, it is," she said. "How long will this take?"

She looked tense, I realized. She had changed her clothes while I wasn't looking too, and now she had her hair tied back and was wearing bulky army boots with black combat trousers and the same sort of articulated matt-black body armour that she had worn to face Wellington Phoenix and his devourers. Oh fuck, she hadn't even bothered with that for Bianakith for fuck's sake. She really wasn't expecting this to be easy, was she?

"Not too long," Davey said. "We cast a circle, do the goat, mix the blood with the quicksilver, feed the warpstone and we're all done."

That was pretty much what I had been expecting. That was the same way the Burned Man and I had powered the hexring the one time I had used it, after all, although we had only needed a couple of toads for that. Like I said, they seemed to be made of the same stuff so I supposed that made sense.

"Right," I said.

"Then I'll need your blood," Davey said. "Both of yours, if you're coming too, Angelus."

You fucking what now?

"Um," I said. "Really?"

"Aye, fucking really," he said. "The Veil has to taste you,

boyo, or it won't let you through. Me it knows, aye, but not you. And most *definitely* not her."

I thought about the Veils, and about how some people said they were alive. I had to admit that prospect was getting even more unpleasant now that I was seriously planning to cross one. Passing through Veils just wasn't something humans *did,* if you understand me. Although, as I had recently found out, I might not be quite as human as all that after all.

"Right," I said, casting a nervous sideways glance at Trixie.

I wasn't expecting her to like this idea one little bit. I could see in her face that she didn't, but she was a soldier, and soldiers do what they have to do.

"If you need to then so be it," she said with a short nod.

Davey took the goat into my workroom, and I trailed behind him. He smirked when he saw the inanimate fetish of the Burned Man slumped in its chains on my altar, thick with dust. Trixie obviously hadn't been able to let the cleaners into this room when she had had the flat done for me, and unsurprisingly she hadn't felt the urge to clean the bloody thing herself. I couldn't say I blamed her, really.

"Oh Donny boy," he said. "Oh fuck me silly, I never thought I'd see that."

"Yeah, well," I said, feeling a bit tongue-tied.

This was *Merlin* for fucksake. What the hell do you say to Merlin when he's about to do magic for you? I felt as close to starstruck as I'd ever been in my life.

"Close your mouth and give me that warpstone," he said, still smirking. "Then get the circle piped out with the iron filings, there's a good lad."

I passed him my precious warpstone and busied myself pouring iron filings carefully into the outline of the grand summoning circle that was carved into the wooden floor of my workroom. I watched with some trepidation as Davey tossed the warpstone carelessly onto the floor in the middle of the circle. I mean sure, I'd won it years ago in a game of cards and I'd never actually used it, but I knew how much that thing was worth. A modicum of respect might have been nice. Still, to him I supposed it was nothing special.

Davey reached inside his shabby old coat and produced an alarming looking ritual dagger. He made as clean a job of the goat as a kosher butcher would have done, I must admit. He held it easily in one hand to bleed out over the warpstone, which gave me a bit of a nervous twitch about how strong he must be. Now you'd think that would have made an almighty mess but the stone drank every drop, even greedier than the hexring had been. Even the splatters of blood that had inevitably gone all over the floor slowly flowed towards the warpstone like iron filings drawn to a magnet, until every drop had gone. He crouched down beside the dead goat and very carefully poured the mercury over the stone, and I watched in astonishment as the thick liquid metal flowed perfectly into the swirling lines that covered the stone until the whole thing was gleaming.

That done, Davey stood up and tossed the drained goat carcass into a corner. He met my eyes and showed me his gap-toothed grin.

"Your turn," he said.

I swallowed. "You're not planning on slitting my throat I hope," I said. "The whole point of this exercise is to get there *without* having to die, remember?"

"Don't be such a fucking baby," he said. "A wee slice of your hand will do it."

I reluctantly held out my left hand to him, suppressing a wince before he'd even started. I've never been all that fond of the sight of my own blood, I have to admit. He slashed the blade across the meat beneath my thumb and held my hand over the stone, squeezing it to let the blood flow. The blade was so sharp I had barely felt the cut itself, but now that he was squeezing it burned like a bastard. I hissed through clenched teeth until he let me go a moment later.

"Put some pressure on that and it'll be fine," he said. "I'll need Madam herself, too."

"I'm here," Trixie said from behind me, making me jump.

"So y'are," he grinned.

Trixie held out her hand the same as I had and he cut her in the same place, squeezing until her own blood splattered on top of mine and the stone absorbed it all. If she even felt it she gave no sign.

"Now," Trixie said, "are we ready?"

I was holding a rapidly darkening towel to my bleeding hand, but Trixie seemed to have healed over already. I gave her a bit of a look.

"Oh, I'm sorry," she said.

She came and touched a fingertip to the gash in my palm, and I sighed with relief as it closed up and healed. She really was good at that, bless her.

"Thanks," I said.

"Aye, we're ready," Davey said.

"Let's do it then," I said.

He looked at me.

"You might want a coat, laddie."

I might?

I went and got one all the same, and stuffed a pair of gloves into the pockets while I was at it. I mean I'm sorry but I'd never been to another dimension before. I wasn't too sure what the fucking dress code was.

When I came back Davey and Trixie were standing in the middle of the circle with the warpstone on the floor between them, blood-slick and glistening black in the low-wattage glow of the overhead light. It was crowded but I joined them there, feeling too warm with my heavy winter overcoat on over my suit.

All the same, it was good to be prepared... shit! I could be a damn sight more prepared than I actually was, I suddenly realized. I quickly turned away again and opened the cupboard drawer, keeping my back to them so Davey couldn't see what I was doing.

"Are you no done fannying about yet, laddie?" he asked tersely.

I snatched the Blade of Unmaking out of the drawer and pushed it through my belt, covering it with my jacket and coat. Adam himself had given that dagger to Aleto the Unresting, the leader of the Furies. Even without the soul of an archdemon inside it any more it was still a weapon of unholy power that had originally been forged in the depths of Hell. It might help or it might not, and I didn't even really know how to use it. All the same, as I had no fucking idea what I was about to walk into it certainly couldn't hurt to have it with me.

"Yeah, sorry," I said, smoothing my coat as I turned back to them. "I'm done."

"Join hands," Davey said, so we did.

Trixie's hand was warm in mine, her calloused palm like a piece of polished hardwood from God only knew how many centuries of sword fighting. Davey's hand was rough and grubby and I really didn't want to touch him, but I clutched it all the same as he muttered under his breath.

You'd better be fucking awake in there, I thought at the Burned Man. *You're coming too.*

Oh, I wouldn't miss this for the world, it replied.

I should have known, shouldn't I?

CHAPTER 21

Davey started to chant in some language I didn't recognize, and a moment later the air tore open in front of us and projected a thin pillar of swirling matter. The column of whatever-the-fuck-it-was shot up out of the warpstone where it lay in the centre of the circle and went into the ceiling overhead. It gradually began to widen, with the three of us making a ring a ring o' roses around it.

"Keep still," Davey said. "Let it take us in its own good time."

I swallowed as the column gradually resolved into something that looked horribly like flesh. If this was a Veil, and if Veils really were alive, I wasn't sure I liked the thought of being *taken*, as such. I could only hope he knew what he was fucking doing. I squeezed Trixie's hand and she smiled at me.

"We'll be fine," she reassured me.

A moment later the pillar of spinning fleshy energy was almost touching my face, then it swelled all at once and seemed to split open as though swallowing me whole. I gasped, feeling a curtain of moist heat sweep over my body. Everything went pitch dark for a moment and I clamped my hand down on Trixie's in sheer terror.

When the light came back we were standing in a stone hall, all still holding hands. I looked around, taking in the high vaulted ceiling and a huge, cold fireplace stacked with coals. It was bloody freezing in there.

There were old rushes on the flagstones underfoot, dry and grey with age. High narrow windows lined one wall, letting in thin shafts of dim grey light. Davey let go of my hand and took a step back. He gestured absently at the fireplace as he moved. Flames roared up in the grate, making me jump.

"Welcome to my keep," he said. "This is Kelmeth, that stands in the shadow of the La'hah. This is my castle."

Fuck me, we were in Merlin's castle? Seriously?

There was a long wooden table running down the middle of the room, with chairs along either side and a great carved wooden throne at its head on a raised platform. There was no round table here, that was for sure. This was Davey's place and it was obvious he wanted whoever came here to know it.

"My thanks, magus," Trixie said, inclining her head.

A door opened and several young serving boys filed in, carrying platters of bread and meat and a great flagon of red wine. The lads laid out the food and drink on the table, never speaking. It took me a moment to realize that none of them had a mouth.

I blinked in revulsion and looked again. They looked like normal boys otherwise, maybe ten to twelve years old and dressed in old fashioned page's outfits, but beneath the nose each one was just smooth skin down to his beardless chin. I swallowed. That was beyond nasty, in ways I was struggling to even think about.

Even Trixie looked slightly queasy at the sight of the boys, but she managed to ignore them.

"Sit," Davey said, waving us to the table as he settled

himself down into his throne.

I took the chair at his right hand and Trixie sat across from me at his left. She averted her eyes as one of the awful boys poured wine for her into a plain silver goblet. I could tell they were creeping her out and I really didn't care for them either, but I couldn't be worrying about the likes of them now.

Davey noticed her reaction and smiled.

"Children should be seen and not heard, Angelus," he said.

Oh wasn't he just a fucking delight? Trixie's eyes flashed with anger, and I interrupted before she picked a fight with him over it.

"How do I find Adam?" I asked him.

"My guess is he'll be waiting for you at the mouth of Hell," Davey said. "At his postern gate, as you called it. Where the La'hah strikes."

"The what?"

He kept using that word, and I hadn't got a fucking clue what it meant.

"It translates roughly as Guardian Lightning," Trixie said.

"Aye, it does, although that's an old tongue indeed," Davey said. "The La'hah is a living thing, so it is, not so very different to the Veils. It's supposed to keep the abyss closed, so nothing can crawl up out of Hell and into this plane. It seems that the Fallen One has tamed it."

Oh wasn't *that* a joyous thought.

I sipped my wine and looked at him.

"This won't keep, Davey," I said. "Thanks for the drink and all that, but we need to get after Olivia as soon as we can."

He shrugged.

"I'm not stopping you, Donny boy."

"So when are we going?"

"You can go when you like," he said. "Me, I'm going nowhere."

Trixie looked up sharply at that.

"The matter of the abducted child is–" she started.

"Aye," Davey interrupted her. He chased the boys away with a wave of his hand. "That's your affair, Angelus, not mine. The way out is that way."

He waved at the far wall and a pair of huge oak double doors swung silently open, showing us a long stone corridor lit with smoking torches.

"I..." I started, "I, um..."

Fuck, that really hadn't been the answer I was looking for.

Davey poured himself a cup of wine from the flagon and sat back with a contented sigh.

"Off you jolly well fuck, then," he said. "I've done my bit, the rest is up to you. Head towards the lightning. Towards the La'hah, where angels fear to tread."

"Oh, I assure you there's *nowhere* I fear to tread," Trixie snapped. She got up and strode into the corridor without a backward glance. "Come on, Don."

I swallowed. Right. Right, that was fucking marvellous that was. Davey had brought us to Purgatory but it seemed that was all the help we were going to get out of him. Miserable old git. I followed in Trixie's wake, unable to keep from wincing as the doors to Davey's hall swung shut behind us with a dull thud. The corridor ended in another pair of heavy doors which opened at our approach. We stepped outside into a courtyard under a threatening grey sky. The great stone mass of the keep loomed behind us and a moss-covered curtain wall extended around the castle yard. The gatehouse was before us, the way barred by a mighty portcullis.

In the yard stood Davey's wheel.

I've dealt with ruder pricks than you over the years, and broken them on my wheel, he had said.

It was fully twelve feet high, a great construction of ancient, weathered wood like the paddle wheel of a watermill but rimmed with ridged iron that looked designed to break bones and rend flesh. There were old, dark stains on the wood, and more on the stone flags of the courtyard beneath it. I felt sick just looking at it.

He's not kidding about his wheel, I remembered the Burned Man telling me. No, no it didn't look like he had been. Fucking hell, *this* was Merlin?

Really?

I supposed by then it shouldn't have surprised me. If there's one thing in life that you can rely on, it's disappointment.

I looked around me with a shudder. The sky overhead was the thick, textured grey of overlapping cloudbanks, and the light was dim and utterly without warmth. I was bloody glad of my coat, I had to admit. Thunder rumbled in the distance.

"Come on," Trixie said again, walking towards the portcullis. "I don't like this place."

I had to agree with her on that one. Kelmeth castle was a fucking shithole, as far as I was concerned. The huge iron portcullis rumbled up into the gatehouse as we approached, and we passed through a wall so thick it almost made a tunnel over our heads. As soon as we were outside, the portcullis slammed down behind us with an awful finality that made the ground shake underfoot. I swallowed. It didn't look like we were going to be welcomed back any time soon.

We were in a country of low, rolling hills, covered in dead looking greyish grass. The few trees were leafless and bent, as though twisted by a wind that I couldn't feel. There was no castle town, no road or farms or villages as far as the eye could see, and no indication of where the food or the wine or the ghastly mute boys had come from. There was nothing at all, in fact, but the endless deadlands. It seemed that Kelmeth ran on pure magic.

I looked at the parched, lifeless ground and wondered where that magic had come from. Again I thought about the Hermit, the card that Davey had drawn as his trump when we had played Fates together. In some interpretations of the card, the Hermit stands not on the mountain peak of knowledge but at the edge of a vast wasteland. Like this one. Lightning flashed in the distance, colourless and painfully bright against the brooding sky. Thunder rolled in its wake. No, I had to admit I really didn't like this place either.

Not even a little bit.

"Head towards the lightning," Trixie said, and set off marching in that direction.

I followed her, sparing a brief glance behind me at the forbidding walls of Merlin's castle. The battlements were topped with iron spikes, I noticed, the sort of spikes that might have had severed heads stuck on them. There were no heads today, but old rusty stains on the stone told me that there might have been once. I swallowed bile and turned my back on the place.

We walked in silence for maybe a mile, towards the growing fury of the storm. At last I plucked up the courage to ask.

"Trixie," I said, "how are we going to get back home?"

She gave me a bleak look.

"I have been trying to get back home for two thousand years," she said. "I have no idea."

CHAPTER 22

I pushed my hands back through my hair and sighed. That wasn't quite what I had meant but... yeah, I supposed I could see her point.

Davey had brought us here through a portal, and once we had rescued Olivia I had no idea how to open another one to get us all back to London. My warpstone was still on the floor of my workroom, after all. I turned and looked back the way we had come once more, and saw that Kelmeth castle looked much further away than it should have done. It was little more than a shadow on the horizon now, for all that we had only been walking for twenty minutes or so. Was Davey likely to let us back in, or help us to get home again? I thought about that portcullis crashing down behind us and had to admit that he probably wasn't.

It took me a moment to realize that Trixie was crying.

I reached out and took her hand. She turned to face me with tears glistening on her cheeks. She looked utterly lost.

"I'm never going home, am I?" she said.

"You don't know that."

"This is *Purgatory!*" she screamed at me, suddenly furious. "It's supposed to be a place of cleansing and purification prior to entry to Heaven. *Look* at it, Don!"

I winced. I had to admit I could see her point. If this had once been the beautiful Summerland she had been thinking of then Davey had leached every drop of life out of it over the millennia to feed his magic, hadn't he?

Fuck.

Of course he had, I realized. All that "I'm still alive because I'm clever and I'm cruel" bullshit had been just that – bullshit. Davey, Merlin, was still alive because he had eaten the life force of a whole other fucking dimension to keep himself that way, the horrible old bastard.

There was no way I could tell Trixie that, though. That would break her completely, I knew it would. The only thing that kept her going was the thought that one day, somehow, she might be able to go home.

"You told me yourself that Purgatory is whatever you think it is," I reminded her. "I mean, I didn't know *what* to think it was but maybe… I dunno. You're not at peace with yourself, Trixie. Maybe this is just what you were expecting to see?"

She sighed and sank into a crouch, her head in her hands.

"Maybe it's what I deserve," she said. "Maybe I knew that, all along. I have… slipped, after all."

Slipped, yeah.

She had done that all right. Not fallen, not quite anyway, but she had most definitely slipped a bit. To put it fucking mildly.

But then so had I, hadn't I?

"Yeah but you can always get back on your feet after a slip, can't you?" I said, trying to sound encouraging when I felt anything but. "Come on, come here. It'll be all right. Trust me."

Trust you? the Burned Man sniggered. *I wouldn't trust you to–*

Shut the fuck up, I snapped at it. *Not now, all right?*

I held out my hand and she got to her feet and let me give her an awkward hug. The only way to hug someone wearing armour is awkwardly, I'm afraid. Still, she mustered a weak smile after that.

"Come on," she said. "We've got a job to do. We can worry about afterwards, well, afterwards."

I nodded and followed her towards the lightning.

Distances were deceptive in that awful place. It seemed to be getting colder and colder as we drew nearer to the storm, and the hills were getting steeper. We hadn't seen a tree for what seemed like hours, although with no visible source of light there was no real way to measure the passing of time. I don't wear a watch, and even if I had done I suspected it would have stopped the moment we went through the Veil. The grass underfoot now was as grey and dead as the rushes on the floor of Davey's hall had been, and it crunched under our feet as we walked. It was as though all the life had simply been sucked out of the ground. Which I was pretty sure was exactly what *had* happened.

Eventually we crested a hill and stopped dead in our tracks. There was an army below us.

"Oh cocking fuck," I said.

There must have been the best part of two hundred of them, spread out around a standard planted in the ground. Behind them the plain dropped away into a great abyss that seemed to be full of boiling fog. The fog glowed with a flickering ruddy light, as though lit from below by terrible fires somewhere in the deep. The lightning raged overhead, stabbing down into that abyss again and again. The thunder was still impossibly distant, as though miles away. The standard showed a complicated sigil that I recognized from my books.

That was Lucifer's sigil. The mark of the Fallen One.

That was Adam's banner, and these were his soldiers. They were Soulless, every one of them. I could see their auras quite clearly in the unearthly light, making the entire mob seem to glow with a dull reddish light.

"Bloody hell, what do we do now?" I asked her.

Trixie turned and gave me a fierce look.

"The only thing we *can* do," she said. "We go on."

We walked down the hill together, to the plain where the army of Soulless awaited us. The thunder was constant now, rumbling in the distance even as the lightning flashed like a strobe lamp overhead and the glowing fog heaved and boiled in the depths.

The Soulless moved apart and a tall, handsome man walked through them with his hands held out beside him like Moses parting the Red Sea in some awful ancient film. He was wearing a black overcoat over a very expensive looking suit.

This was Adam, at last. This was Lucifer himself.

"Donald Drake, Meselandrarasatrixiel, I bid you welcome," Adam said. "Welcome to the postern gate of Hell."

Trixie had been right, I realized. The smug bastard *did* have a back door he could sneak in and out of. I glared at him.

"Where's my fucking daughter?" I demanded.

"She is safe, for now," he said. "Do this one small task for me and she will be returned to you, Don. All I ask is for the Burned Man to fight at my side."

"How about you just fucking give her back right now, you smarmy wanker?" I snarled at him. "I'm not your fucking errand boy, and I can take you down if I have to."

I realized that the Burned Man and I were speaking with one voice now, one set of thoughts, one purpose. The hairs on my arms rose in cold chills even as my hands grew hot with the need to release the flames of my anger.

Adam ignored me, and turned his attention on Trixie instead.

"Come to me, Meselandrarasatrixiel," he said.

"Answer his question," Trixie said. "Where is the child?"

"She is safe, as I said. Come aid me in this battle. A battle you were *born* to fight. Do you not want revenge on the Dominion who betrayed you? Do you not wish to end it every bit as much as I do? As much as Menhit does?"

I saw confusion cross Trixie's face. She had been utterly betrayed by the Dominion who had been her father and her king, and quite possibly her lover too. Of course she wanted revenge, I realized that. All the same, I also knew she didn't like being manipulated and ordered around by Adam one little bit.

"Don't tell me what to do," she said. "I'm not one of your soldiers, Adam."

"But you *are* a soldier," he countered. "A soldier without a general, without a purpose. You have nothing in your life now but a forgotten goddess and this one stubborn human man."

"I serve Menhit now," she said. "And I stand with Don."

He snorted.

"I'm tired of playing these stupid games with you," Adam said. "Once Menhit has her revenge she will grow bored of her Earthly posturing and return home, and then where will you be? Adrift without a patron. Heaven will never have you back now, but I will. I will welcome you at my right hand, as the sword of *my* word. I will welcome you, but if Don Drake will not also stand with me then you must choose between us."

He fixed me with a smug sneer that said he knew damn well she would choose him. I hated to admit it but I knew she would, too.

But she didn't.

"I'm sorry, Adam," she said. "I choose Don."

She came and stood beside me, and slipped her hard, calloused hand into mine.

I almost fainted.

"How dare you?" he demanded.

"Adam, I..." she said.

"I *command* you, Meselandrarasatrixiel!" he snarled.

Oh fuck.

Do not ask, command. *That is the true way to power.*

Oh dear me no, not with Trixie it isn't, mate.

"No!" she shouted at him, her grip on my hand tightening until it was almost painful. "No Adam, you do *not* command me! Not any more. Not *ever* again!"

I don't think I had ever loved her as much as I did at that moment.

All the same, her rage was cataclysmic. If she could have torn Adam limb from limb right then, she would have done. She let go of me and then her sword was in her hands, blazing with heavenly fury. She was a hair's breadth from charging the lot of them, I realized.

Everything changed with a dull shimmer of reality that made my head hurt.

We were suddenly closer, and Adam was standing almost near enough to touch. His army of Soulless were behind us now, spread out in a crescent that stretched from the edge of the abyss at either end and encircled us completely, with that terrible drop the only way clear. Adam turned to face the great open gulf of boiling fog, and an inferno of flames roared up out of it to touch the clouds above like a blast furnace of curiously cold fire. This was his postern gate. This was the mouth of Hell itself, yawning open in front of me.

This was where I had been headed for a long time now.

He turned to us once more, a mocking smile on his thin lips.

He had Olivia in his arms.

She was wrapped in the same pink blanket with the bunnies on it that I had seen her in that first time at Debbie's house. She seemed to be asleep. Adam took a step backwards until he stood smiling on the very edge of the abyss, the flames racing up behind him and the baby in his arms.

My baby. My little daughter.

I will do anything in my power to protect you, I had promised her. *Anything at all.*

There were almost two hundred of the Soulless massed around us, all of them armed and dangerous looking.

Soldiers of the Fallen, they call themselves, Trixie had told me. *They're not much to worry about unless there are an awful lot of them.*

There were an awful fucking lot of them right now, as far as I could see.

"I will not be denied, Donald Drake," Adam said. "Not by you and most definitely not by her. You are coming with me. The Throne is burning, and your destiny lies below. You and the Burned Man *will* fight for me whether you like it or not. *My* kingdom come, *my* Will be done, on Earth as it is in Hell."

He took another step backwards and plummeted into the mouth of Hell with Olivia in his arms.

"*No!*" I screamed

I reached for the Blade of Unmaking at my hip, but it was too late. He was gone, and so was Olivia.

I looked from Trixie and the advancing ranks of the Soulless to the edge of the cliff, helpless with indecision.

There are so many of them, I thought. *Too many, even for her.*

Heinrich stepped out of the massed ranks of the Soulless with a long blade in his hands.

"Now, Angelus," he said, "we shall have our reckoning."

Your choice, the Burned Man said.

Every decision have its consequences, Papa Armand had told me.

Wasn't that the fucking truth. The Burned Man could make all the difference in this fight, I knew. Between the two of us we might stand a chance, but I knew I had to go after Olivia.

I *had* to.

Anything in my power to protect you. Anything at all.

Diabolists go to Hell, Don.

I'm sorry, but yes.

It looked like they did.

The flames from Trixie's sword underlit her face, making her look every inch the Angel of Death.

She raised the burning blade to me in salute.

"Go," she said. "I'll hold them here as long as I can."

She has her own path to follow.

It was no choice at all.

I took a run up and followed Adam into the abyss.

ACKNOWLEDGMENTS

You'd think writing a series gets easier the more of them you write, wouldn't you? You'd be wrong, and so was I.

I owe enormous thanks to my editor, Phil Jourdan, who really did have to make me bleed for this one, and to Paul Simpson for saving me from my own mistakes, and everyone at Angry Robot for helping to make this happen.

Thanks as always to my faithful and long-suffering beta readers, and to Diane for putting up with me when I'm writing.

The most thanks of all are due to you, my readers, for your continued enthusiasm and support. I wouldn't be here without you.

ABOUT THE AUTHOR

Peter McLean was born near London in 1972, the son of a bank manager and an English teacher. He went to school in the shadow of Norwich Cathedral where he spent most of his time making up stories. By the time he left school this was probably the thing he was best at, alongside the Taoist kung fu he had begun studying since the age of 13. He grew up in the Norwich alternative scene, alternating dingy nightclubs with studying martial arts and practical magic. He has since grown up a bit, if not a lot. He is married to Diane and is still making up stories.

talonwraith.com • twitter.com/petemc666

ANGRY ROBOT

We are Angry Robot.

angryrobotbooks.com

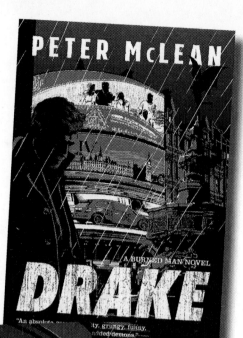

Don't Kiss
Them
Goodbye

Don't Kiss Them Goodbye

Allison DuBois

POCKET
BOOKS

LONDON • SYDNEY • NEW YORK • TORONTO

First published in Great Britain by Simon & Schuster UK Ltd, 2005
This edition published by Pocket Books, 2008
An imprint of Simon & Schuster UK Ltd
A CBS COMPANY

5 7 9 10 8 6 4

Simon & Schuster UK Ltd
1st Floor
222 Gray's Inn Road
London WC1X 8HB

www.simonandschuster.co.uk

Simon & Schuster Australia
Sydney

Published by arrangement with Smarter Than They Think, Inc.

A CIP catalogue record for this book is available
from the British Library.

ISBN 978-1-41651-132-8

Printed and bound by CPI Group (UK) Ltd, Croydon, CR0 4YY